I0525322

EMERALD FIELDS

A MORE PERFECT UNION - BOOK ONE
PEGG THOMAS

SPINNER OF YARNS PUBLISHING, LLC

S PINNER OF YARNS PUBLISHING, LLC
Sault Ste. Marie, Michigan

Copyright @2022 by Pegg Thomas
https://peggthomas.com/
Published in the United States of America
ISBN: 979-8-9850278-6-0
Cover Design by Pegg Thomas – *(Elements of this cover were created using AI technology)*
Cover Art Copyright by Spinner of Yarns Publishing, LLC

All rights reserved. No portion of this book may be transmitted in any form or by any electronic or mechanical means, including photocopying, recording, or by any information retrieval and storage system without permission of the publisher.

This is a work of fiction. Names, characters, and incidents in this book are products of the author's imagination or are used in a fictitious situation with the exception of characters listed in the Author's Notes. Any resemblances to actual events, locations, organizations, incidents, or persons – living or dead – are coincidental and beyond the intent of the author with the exception of those listed in the Author's Notes.

In this series are many actual historical figures. The author has used her imagination to flesh the characters out for the purposes of the series. While using the known facts of the characters, they are not intended to be historically accurate in every detail.

PRAISE FOR EMERALD FIELDS

Pegg Thomas is a gifted storyteller. That gift shines through as Emmie and Russ come to life in this well-researched historical love story. Russ and Emmie's struggles to find their way in a time when men didn't speak of their war nightmares, and women weren't allowed to think for themselves, is beautifully portrayed in *Emerald Fields*. Once I started, I read uninterrupted until the last page. Then I sighed with satisfaction as well as regret that their story was over.

—Cindy Ervin Huff
Award-winning author
of *Angelina's Resolve* and *Rescuing Her Heart*

Be sure to clear your schedule, because once you've started reading *Emerald Fields*, you won't want to stop! Another winner from award-winning author Pegg Thomas! You'll be rooting for Emmie and Russ from beginning until the end.

—Carrie Fancett Pagels
Award-winning author
of *Behind Love's Wall* and *Butterfly Cottage*

A physically scarred hero and a grieving heroine find hope and healing in the letters they write to one another, but can that hope and healing continue when they meet face to face? Fans of Pegg Thomas's Colonial American stories won't want to miss her first post-Civil War offering, *Emerald Fields*. The depth of character and a gripping storyline adds up to one compelling read.

—Jennifer Uhlarik
Award-winning author
of *Love's Fortress* and *Sand Creek Serenade*

MORE BOOKS BY PEGG THOMAS

Native Patriot (May 2026)

Salem Village
The Ragpicker~ prequel novella
The Carpenter
The Midwife
The Brewer (September 2026)

Path to Freedom
Freedom's Price
Freedom's Pride
Freedom's Promise

A More Perfect Union
Emerald Fields
Cobalt Skies
Silver Prairies

Forts of Refuge
Sarah's Choice
Maggie's Strength
Abigail's Peace
Henri's Regret ~ A Prequel Novella

Individual Novellas
Worth Fighting For
Anna's Tower
Her Redcoat
In Sheep's Clothing
Embattled Hearts

Join Pegg's Newsletter
writing updates – sneak peeks – fiber arts updates – personal content
https://www.subscribepage.com/PeggThomas

This book is dedicated to the men who fought and died in the American Civil War, and to those who were wounded as well.

"Descending from these general principles, we find the proposition that, in legal contemplation, the Union is perpetual, confirmed by the history of the Union itself. The Union is much older than the Constitution. It was formed in fact, by the Articles of Association in 1774. It was matured and continued by the Declaration of Independence in 1776. It was further matured and the faith of all the then thirteen States expressly plighted and engaged that it should be perpetual, by the Articles of Confederation in 1778. And finally, in 1787, one of the declared objects for ordaining and establishing the Constitution, was **"to form a more perfect Union."** *But if [the] destruction of the Union, by one, or by a part only, of the States, be lawfully possible, the Union is less perfect than before the Constitution, having lost the vital element of perpetuity."*

Abraham Lincoln—First Inaugural Address, March 4, 1861

Acknowledgments

This book, like so many of my others, started with the root of an idea taken from my own family history. I owe my uncle, Ron Lewis, a huge debt for doing so much research into our family tree. He started back in the 1970s before genealogy was a "thing" and traced both of his parents—my grandparents—lineages back to the mid-1600s when they immigrated from Wales to the British Colonies. There is so much fodder in those stories to fuel my writing for many years to come!

John & Ellen Lewis about 1898

The minor character of John Lewis in *Emerald Fields* is, in fact, my great-great-grandfather. He served in the Michigan Seventh Cavalry at the very end of the Civil War and was then sent to the West to fight in the Plains Indian Wars. He returned home to Michigan at just the right time to ride through *Emerald Fields* and meet with my fictional hero, Russ. Thank you, Great-Great-Granddad!

CHAPTER 1

EMMIE MASON SCURRIED THROUGH the hallway clutching the familiar crisp envelope. She tossed her shawl onto the straight-backed chair outside the door to the music room on her way in. Evans would hang it up and chide her for it later, but that was a small price to pay for ending her anxiety.

Once inside her private haven, she eased the pocket door shut and collapsed into her favorite wing-backed chair next to the piano. The comfort of its burgundy brocade collected her like a mother's hug, releasing the tension that had been building for days.

The letter was more than a week late, nearer two. Emmie had stopped by the post office every day after her shift at the hospital. Her friend had never been this tardy in writing, and Emmie'd feared something terrible had happened. But now, Becky's letter lay on her lap and Emmie's world was back in order. The familiar delicate swirls of her name on the envelope calmed her.

She lifted the carved wooden letter opener, a parting gift from Becky when they'd left school, and sliced through the top. She paused. No whiff of lilacs came from inside. She extracted a single sheet of ivory paper. A bold, jarring script she didn't recognize scrawled across the page.

November 22, 1866

Dear Miss Mason,
 I regret to inform you of my sister's passing this last Thursday, 15 November, 1866.

No! The letter fluttered to the floor. Pain sliced through Emmie's middle even as her mind refused to hold onto the words. It wasn't possible. Not Becky. Lively, musical, cheerful Becky who always knew what to say, what to share, to bring sunshine and light into Emmie's life. It couldn't be true. She picked up the envelope again. Becky's fine script wavered before her eyes.

The page lay on the floor, its black scratchings running together in murky lines. Emmie retrieved it with a trembling hand, her other hand clenching the emerald pendant at her throat.

> *This will come as a shock to you, as it did to me. Becky contracted influenza only eight days before she passed. She implored that I write to you and send her sincerest regrets. Your friendship and letters meant as much to her as if you were family. I found this envelope already addressed, a testament to her devotion to you.*
>
> *It pains me to impart such news in this fashion, but I pray you find comfort in knowing that Becky's final thoughts included you.*
>
> *Your servant,*
> *Russ Fields*

As if she were family. Yes. That was exactly how it'd been between her and Becky from the first day at the Young Ladies Seminary of Pittsburgh. As if they were a part of each other, surely closer than real sisters, which Emmie'd never had. The paper creased in her fingers. She laid it on her lap and smoothed its edges.

Her trembling stopped, and something worse followed—an aching hollowness. She folded the sheet and slid it back into its envelope before rising and moving to the piano bench. The cool ivory met her fingertips and brought them to life. Music poured from her soul and filled the room, its pounding and minor chords expressing what she had no words to say—even if there'd been anyone to listen.

Snow slid from the barn roof in a blinding *whoosh* of icy particles that cascaded onto the shoulders of Russ Fields. He ducked into the building, grateful for the red wool muffler that kept the snow from getting under his coat. His sister had finished knitting it only days before the influenza struck. The ache in his chest, which never quite went away, deepened for a moment.

He wasn't a stranger to loss—no one who had served in the war could be—but to lose Becky to something so senseless and so random ... Most days Russ still struggled to put one foot in front of the other.

Goblin nickered in his stall. The scents of horse, manure, and damp sheep prompted Russ to get moving. If he didn't have the farm chores to do, how would he have kept going? He grabbed the hayfork and pitched enough hay to fill the horse's manger and more for the brown cow in the next stall. The noise drew the attention of those living in the barn's basement. A cacophony of *baa*s and grunts drifted through the seams between wooden floorboards.

"Just a moment." Russ opened a door in the floor that contained a chute, and his black-and-white sheepdog poked his head into the opening.

"Move aside, Jigs." Russ pitched down enough hay to stop the *baa*ing, then he scooped a pail of corn from the bin along the wall and opened another chute door. The kernels pinged into a trough below, and the grunts became squeals of delight.

Sheep and pigs fed, he poured a measure of oats for Song before grabbing the three-legged stool and placing the milk bucket under her. She munched while the *shping-shping* of milk struck the metal bucket. The rhythmic motion allowed Russ's mind to wander.

Had his letter reached Becky's friend in Pittsburgh yet? He winced. What a terrible way to receive such news. Not that there was a good way. He leaned his forehead against Song's shaggy flank. Guilt picked at him. Maybe he shouldn't have read the bundle of letters Becky had saved. His sister wouldn't have minded, he was sure. Her love for Emmie—he should think of her as Miss Mason, but couldn't quite manage it after reading those letters—was obviously returned.

How was it that some people could meet and remain friends for life? He'd met so many men while serving as part of the 7th Michigan Cavalry during the war, yet he wrote to none of them. He might have written to Billy Kline had he lived. Billy and he had mustered in together shortly after the war began.

Russ'd joined the army to get away from the farm, away from the pain and loss. First Ma had succumbed to a cancer, and then his older brother, Frank, had fallen at the first Battle of Manassas. How misguided his thoughts seemed now. How he regretted leaving Pa and Becky by themselves like he had.

Song snorted and stomped her hoof narrowly missing the bucket. Russ gritted his teeth and relaxed his hands until the cow resumed her munching.

Billy had wanted to come home covered in the glory of battle and reunite with his sweetheart. Instead, he lay in the ground outside of Gettysburg. They'd been a team, him and Billy. After that battle, things had gone downhill for Russ.

Song swung her head.

"Sorry, girl." He relaxed his grip again. "Almost done." The doe-like eyes with long lashes winked at him. He finished and pulled the bucket out of the cow's way. He stood and rubbed the scooped hollow between her eyes. "You miss Becky, don't you? So do I, but we have to make the best of things now."

The best of things. He had no idea what that meant. He rubbed the stiff, leathery scars on the left side of his face. If it were spring, he could burn off his sorrows planting corn and shearing the sheep. If it were summer, he'd be hoeing weeds and watering the garden. If it were fall, there'd be the harvest to bring in and wood to put up. But it was winter, and an early one at that. Snow on the ground so early meant a long season ahead.

He patted Goblin's pale rump and pulled open the barn door. Snow blew past, almost obscuring the house only thirty yards away. He stepped into the swirling whiteness with Jigs at his heels.

How did one survive grief at a time like this?

"Emmie, you must eat something. It's been—" Father turned his head and coughed, the deep wracking sound filling the formal dining room.

Emmie rose and came to his side and pressed a clean napkin into his hand, wishing she could breathe for him. "Breathe now, that's it."

Father's wheezing meant the worst of the spasm was over, and Emmie's chest eased along with his. They were getting worse, these spasms. She must be mindful not to vex him. That seemed to bring on the attacks. It was one of the things, anyway.

She'd seen enough men like this, other men who'd worked in the steel factories their entire lives, her friends' fathers, brothers, uncles, and men at the hospital. Her father and brothers may have been safe from the war in their roles at the steel mills, but that didn't mean they weren't scarred by it. They carried their scars inside, deep in their lungs, from working extra shifts to keep the Union's engines of war working.

Father patted her hand. "I'm all right now." His hoarse voice and bluish lips said otherwise. "Eat your dinner, my dear."

Emmie returned to her chair, the only one of the nine empty seats out of formation beside the long table. She lifted her crystal water goblet and took a sip. Then she sliced a piece of pink beef and chewed. It might as well have been coal dust in her mouth. Between her grief over Becky and worry over Father's health, she only went through the motions of eating to please him.

"These things take the wind out of us for a while," Father said, "but then it's time to move on."

If he insisted on talking about Becky's death, without ever mentioning her beloved friend by name, Emmie wouldn't be able to swallow another bite. She'd have to change the subject.

"What about Christmas?" She asked. "Are Archie and Richard coming with their families?"

He sat back in his chair and dabbed his lips with a napkin. "Archie thinks it's time one of them hosted the family gathering." He lifted one shoulder in a half-shrug. "He worries about the hubbub being too much for me."

In that, she might agree with her eldest brother. Father's spasms were draining the life out of him. He loved his grandchildren, but they were a boisterous group on the best of days, and all eight together could be a handful.

If James hadn't died in battle at Cold Harbor, she might have been married by now and have added to Father's passel of grandchildren, maybe even with a second one on the way. She pressed her hand to her stomach. James had been determined to fight. He'd said he'd rather die in battle than have his breath squeezed out of him working the mills.

Father coughed again.

Maybe James had been right. Even though Father had risen through the ranks to become an influential part of the management in the mills, his early years working steel had taken their toll. Not even the cheerful flicking of the candles in their silver holders could liven up his gray face.

Emmie cut another piece of beef and chewed, her mind drifting to where it best liked to wander, over the fields of Becky's farm. Her friend's letters had brought the place to life with its colors and scents and sounds. They were sprinkled with the antics of a gray horse, a brown cow, a flock of wooly white sheep, a sty full of pigs, and a black-and-white dog. Compared to the gray skies and gray streets of Pittsburgh, Becky'd made the farm in Jonesville, Michigan, seem like heaven on earth.

Emmie's dream of seeing it for herself melted like the butter puddled on her untouched mashed potatoes.

Yet, there was someone still there—Becky's brother. Would he welcome a return letter from her? Nothing lengthy, just an acknowledgment that she'd received his. She stopped mid-chew. It truly was the least she could do to express her sympathies to him. Yes. She scooped up a bite of the potatoes. She would write Mr. Fields that very evening.

Why hadn't she thought to do so before?

Before Becky had taken ill, she'd often run the errands in town for Russ, saving him the emotional turmoil those trips to town caused. He pulled his wide-brimmed hat lower on his forehead and tugged his muffler around his chin, then gave the reins a little slap over Goblin's rump.

"Move on. The sooner we get there, the sooner we can get back home."

Goblin tossed his head and picked up his feet, his shoes digging through the snow to grip the frozen lane underneath. The harness jingled, and the wagon's wheels creaked in the cold. He should grease those axles again.

The town was dressed for Christmas with greenery and red bows in almost every window. Even the blacksmith shop had a rope twisted with holly vines strung over its door. Russ dropped off a broken gate hinge for repairs. Then he stopped at the general store, the familiar scents of lye soap and oiled leather greeting him at the door. He gave the clerk his list and was looking at a pair of boots when the bell above the door jingled. Three ladies entered. By reflex, Russ tucked his chin to his left and tilted that side of his face away from them. Not for the first time, he wished his scarred skin would grow whiskers to hide at least the bottom half of his face. Or that he could wear a patch over his missing eye, but the lumpy scar tissue made it too uncomfortable.

The women took a while to choose their purchases, but he waited more or less patiently until they left, then approached the counter.

"That's your wagon out front with the gray hitched to it, isn't it?" the young clerk asked, eyes shifting away from Russ's scarred face.

"It is."

"I'll have you loaded in a jiffy."

Back on the wagon, Russ almost passed the post office. Seemed a waste of time to enter with Becky being gone. Wasn't likely anyone would write to him except for his older sister, Cilla. Even so, he pulled Goblin to a stop and went in.

"Afternoon, Mr. Fields." Mrs. Russell, who worked as postmistress, bobbed her white head at him, "You're here for your mail, I suppose."

Why else did anyone come into the post office? But she asked the same question to everyone, so it was silly to be annoyed. At least she looked at him—without flinching—as she asked. She'd lost her youngest son in the war. When Russ had returned, she'd told him that she'd have given anything to have her boy back, no matter what shape he'd come home in. Maybe that was the real reason he'd stopped today, so that at least one person would look at him for who he was and not how he looked.

"Yes, ma'am. But I don't know if there'll be much mail now that..." He let his words trail off.

"Miss Becky was a letter writer, no doubt about it, but I do believe you have one today." She fished her fingers into a slot behind her. "Yes. I thought I remembered seeing it come in. It looks the same as those envelopes your sister used to get so regular." The old lady beamed up at him, her round eyes, narrow nose, and tilted head bearing an uncanny resemblance to a bird.

"Thank you, ma'am." The envelope was the same type he'd opened and read from Becky's collection. He tucked it in his inside coat pocket, touched his hat brim, and backed out of the building before the old lady could ask the question he couldn't answer.

Why would Becky's friend write to him?

He climbed onto the wagon and chirped to Goblin, who, as usual, was more agreeable to picking up his feet on the return trip home. They rolled past the frozen countryside, up and down the gentle swells of the landscape until they reached the lane to his farm.

His. No longer his and Becky's. He should have swung by the cemetery before he left town, but that meant getting close to the church. He wasn't ready for that.

With the purchases unloaded and Goblin cared for, Russ ran out of reasons to keep moving. He tapped the front of his coat. The envelope crackled against his shirt.

It was time to face what Becky's friend had to say.

CHAPTER 2

December 5, 1866

Dear Mr. Fields,

    As you can imagine, your letter bearing the devastating news of Becky's passing was difficult to receive. I can only blame shock and grief for my tardiness in answering and offering you my sincerest sympathies. Your sister was very dear to me. Her letters, which arrived almost without fail every second week until this month, have been the bright spots of my life.

    I am sure I don't need to tell you what an exceptional person she was. I miss her deeply and fear that I always will. In truth, the last thing I want is for those remembrances to fade. I could not have loved her more had she been my own sister.

    Becky shared so much about your family with me over the years that I feel as if I know you all. Your older sister, Cilla, must be run ragged keeping up with her six boys. I'm sure she misses Becky as much as we do. I hope you get to see her and her children sometime. It must be lonely there on the farm by yourself, especially during the winter months.

    Nothing delighted me more than Becky's descriptions of your farm. Her vivid and poetic words made me quite envy your life there. Pittsburgh is such a gray, dreary place. If not for my work at the hospital and caring for my father, I would find it overall depressing.

Please do not think me forward for I am anything but. However, should you desire to continue a correspondence, I would be honored. Sharing our memories of Becky would keep her alive in our memories and hearts. But should that be too painful for you, disregard the suggestion at once lest it add to your burden of grief.

I would be your friend should it suit you,
Emmie Mason

H IS FRIEND. THE PAPER, with its artfully delicate script, slipped from his fingers. Elbows on the table, Russ clasped his hands and leaned his forehead against them. When was the last time he'd called anyone a friend? Years ago. Before a battle in the Pennsylvania countryside. He glanced at the postmark on the envelope. Could something good come out of that same state?

He rubbed his hands down his face, the scars on the left side rippling under his fingers. There'd been no reference of his disfigurement in the stack of letters he'd read from Emmie—Miss Mason. Could it be that Becky had never made mention of his scars? His missing left eye? The nights he woke Becky with his screams from the nightmares that wouldn't fade? The times the war snuck up on him in broad daylight?

No, it would be just like Becky to not mention any of that. His scars had truly meant nothing to her. Cilla's initial reaction had tempered as she'd reverted to her role as his encouraging—if a bit bossy and pushy—big sister. Of course, she knew of them only by letters. Her husband, Duncan, had moved their family west to Iowa after Russ's enlistment, and Cilla hadn't been back to Michigan since. Not even for Pa's or Becky's funerals. With six children under ten years old, she couldn't have managed it. And Duncan could hardly have kept their boys corralled and run their farm.

He reread the final paragraph of Miss Mason's letter. There was nothing bossy or pushy there. It was only a simple gesture of friendship from a woman who would never see his face.

Something tentative opened a crack deep inside him. Something like... hope? But hope for what? Friendship. That must be it. It was what she'd offered. Maybe he was ready for that again.

Evans strode toward her as Emmie swept her shawl from her shoulders and hung it on the hall tree. The butler's face was pulled into lines more dour than normal. He stopped and inclined his head in her direction.

"Miss Mason, your father has taken to his bed."

"Already?" She glanced at the grandfather clock across the hall. It showed half past three o'clock. "Is he ailing?"

"I'm afraid he is. I've taken the liberty of sending for the doctor."

Emmie's breath left in a slight gasp. "I'm sure you did the right thing. I'll see to him until the doctor arrives." There was no need to ask what had happened, so she dashed up the curved staircase.

Father's wheezing greeted her before she reached his room. At least he wasn't coughing. She tapped on the door and pushed it fully open. Mrs. Coates, their part-time maid, rose from a chair beside his bed. The lines around her eyes relaxed as Emmie approached.

"He's in a bad way, miss. He didn't want us to fuss, but—"

"Evans told me. I'll sit with him until the doctor arrives."

"Very good, miss." The older woman tiptoed out of the room.

"Father?"

Pasty gray against the white sheets, he tipped his head in her direction. His eyelids lifted only enough to let her glimpse the bloodshot surface beneath before they closed again. "Emmie." He produced a feeble cough and then wheezed in a couple of breaths. "Told them not to—"

"Of course you did, but never mind that." She laid the back of her wrist against his cool and clammy forehead. "It doesn't hurt to have the doctor look in from time to time."

"Not much... time left."

Emmie held fast to the impassive nurse's face she'd learned to adopt in the hospital. It was more difficult here, in her own home, with her father. If only she'd learned something that could help. But she could do no more for him than for any of the similar patients she'd assisted. Her chest constricted with the desire to breathe for him, and her eyes burned to contain the tears she would not shed. Not now, anyway.

"Perhaps I should send for Archie or Richard."

"No." His head moved a fraction from side to side, but his eyes never opened. "No need." His mouth relaxed, and he wheezed as his head lolled on the pillow.

Emmie gathered his hand in hers while he slept. Downstairs, Cook would be making a batch of beef tea, Evans would be pacing near the door, Mrs. Coates would be dusting something that didn't need it, and they would wait. They'd played this same scene too many times.

Tomorrow, Archie would arrive and once again insist that Father move in with him. Father would object. The argument that followed, no matter how gently worded, would likely bring on another attack.

She pressed his hand to her cheek. Soon, she'd have to let him go. He wasn't far from heaven now.

Heaven.

In her mind, she pictured rolling green pastures dotted with fluffy white lambs, divided by a creek lined with wispy willows that waved in the breeze. There was a barn on the side of a hill against the evening sky. A white two-story house was skirted by a covered porch. A black-and-white dog lay on its steps.

If Father hadn't been so ill, she'd have visited that place by now. Becky's—no—Mr. Fields' farm. Where the air was clear and sweet and didn't ruin a man's lungs.

That was heaven on earth.

"Father is being unreasonable." Archie pushed his fingers through his hair and swiveled to glower at Emmie. "Again."

She kept her needle steady and poked it through the linen in her embroidery hoop. It wouldn't do any good to try to placate him, but she certainly wouldn't be cowed by him either. "So you've said."

"He almost died last week."

"You can't know that."

"Can't I?"

She laid her needlework on her lap. "How is it that you can know what the rest of us mortals cannot?"

"Don't be flippant."

Why? Because it wasn't becoming of a woman? She folded her arms across her chest. "You can't move him against his will. He's in full possession of his faculties. The law won't allow it."

Her brother issued something between a growl and a snort. "When Richard arrives—"

"It won't change anything."

"You're enjoying this, aren't you?"

Emmie closed her eyes and pressed her hand against the ache in her chest. How could he say that?

He let out a loud breath, and she opened her eyes.

Archie rubbed his hand against his brow. "Please, forgive me. I didn't mean that."

"He's all I have left."

Archie eased himself onto the settee next to her as if afraid it might not hold his weight, or perhaps afraid that she might issue the slap he soundly deserved. "That's not true. Richard and I—"

"Have families of your own. I dare say having a spinster sister living in your attic isn't a thought either of you relishes."

"You're not too old..."

She raised her eyes to his. He had the grace to flush and look across the room. Young men were scarce following the war. And the older men, at least those around Pittsburgh, were far too likely to cough out their lives just as Father was doing. Archie knew how she felt about that.

"Oh, I almost forgot." He pulled an envelope from his coat pocket. "I had to post a letter for Caroline—she's forever writing to her sister, you know—so I picked up your mail while I was there."

Emmie's heart fluttered at the sight of the familiar envelope. For a moment, she could almost smell the lilac fragrance that Becky had always added to her letters. She reached for it and read her name in the bold script of Russ Fields.

Archie didn't release the envelope. He cocked his head at it instead. "I say, isn't that a man's writing?"

She swallowed and tugged the envelope out of his grasp. "It is."

"Well, who would be—"

Richard entered the room. "Sorry I'm late. One of the children awoke with an earache this morning. Fannie needed me to fetch some medicine before I came over." He flicked a glance between the two of them. "Did I interrupt something?"

Emmie drew in a deep breath. "Archie thinks he should move Father to his home, whether Father wants to or not."

"I don't see how you can manage that," Richard said.

"Well, I'll let him try to convince you. I've heard it all before." Emmie rose and set her needlework in the basket beside the settee. With a lift of her chin, she exited the room and headed up the stairs to her bedroom, pausing at Father's door long enough to hear his gentle wheezing.

Once inside her room with the door locked, she sat at her desk and worked her fingernail under the flap of the envelope and extracted three pages. Three! She took a steadying breath.

December 13, 1866

Dear Miss Mason,

Your letter came as a pleasant surprise. Having delivered my message, I had no thought of hearing from you again.

I must confess to an indiscretion that I hope will neither offend nor alarm you. I found three bundles of your letters that Becky had saved. I read them. While Becky mentioned you frequently, I knew very little about you other than that you two had met at finishing school. Having read them and learned more about you, your offer of friendship is most welcome.

You mentioned that Becky often described the farm. Did she tell you of our winters here? Just this morning,

*I had to free one of the sheep who had fallen onto its
back between a snow drift and a fence post. With its
heavy fleece and an obstacle on both sides, it could not
right itself and would surely have perished had Jigs, the
sheepdog, not alerted me.*

Pure bliss filled every crevice of Emmie's heart. As his sister had
done, Mr. Fields transported her to a land so different that it was
like visiting a foreign country. The letter continued with a story about
Goblin—what a name for a poor horse—and an ice-cutting day at a
pond. She could almost see the dazzlingly white snow and the steam
plumes rising from Goblin's nostrils.

*I didn't mean to carry on so. Perhaps my sister's
knack of storytelling is a family trait. I look forward to
hearing more about you and your life in Pittsburgh when
you have the time.*

*Your friend,
Russ Fields*

Emmie sank against the chair back and read the letter again.

Jigs barked, the old dog's rough voice cutting through the cold air.
Russ shielded his eyes as a rider crested the hill on the farm's lane.
An unfamiliar palomino with a wide blaze on its face pranced toward
him. The man on its back bounced around in the saddle like a child's
paddle-and-ball toy.

A stranger.

Russ pulled his hat down and cocked his face to his left. The
work-sled he stood on shifted as Goblin caught sight of the strange

horse. "Easy, boy." He picked up the reins that had been wrapped around the sled's brake bar, and the animal relaxed.

"Good morning, sir." The man waved as if Russ couldn't see him coming. "How are you this glorious morning?"

Russ stabbed his pitchfork into the manure pile on the sled at his feet, then looked at the path of brown-covered snow in the tracks of the sled. Spreading manure was a necessary but far from glorious way to spend a morning. He kept the left side of his face away from the stranger. "I reckon I'm holding my own."

The stranger pulled his horse to a stop, but the animal cut around in a circle, and the man took a moment to straighten it out. "My pardon. I rented this beast at the livery, but we haven't quite gotten on as I'd hoped."

Russ waited.

"Are you Cyrus Fields?"

"I am." But how did this fellow know that?

"Ah. Splendid. I'm Pastor Stanley Anderson. I've newly arrived to shepherd the Jonesville Baptist Church."

The pungent odor of manure rose in the frigid air as Russ continued to wait, hoping the man would talk himself out and leave.

The fellow cleared his throat. "Yes, well, your name is on the church rolls—"

"You can take it off if it bothers you." He had no time for this. He moved Goblin along for several feet and then stopped and tossed off several forkfuls of manure.

"Mr. Fields, I'm afraid you've misunderstood me."

"I doubt it." Russ slung another forkful and moved Goblin again.

"You see, I came out here to—"

Russ turned his face toward the pastor without bothering to hide his damaged side. The pastor blanched, and he tightened the reins in his hand until the horse reared. He clung to the saddle as the animal pivoted and bolted back toward town.

"Another time, Mr. Fields!" he yelled over his shoulder.

Not likely.

That man, no doubt, would turn out like all the others sitting in those dark pews on a Sunday morning. They liked a good sermon but they didn't see fit to live it out in their day-to-day lives. They'd be all about saving the lost until the lost didn't look like them. Until the lost didn't live the way they lived.

Until the lost came home from the war without an eye and scarred from battle.

CHAPTER 3

"**F**ATHER IS TOO ILL to keep Christmas anywhere but home this year." Emmie straightened the red bows decorating the mantel. "And I don't think it wise to have all the children here at once." She turned to Richard.

He looked out the window.

"You're probably right," Archie said. "It bothers me that he's not downstairs yet. It's been days."

"He grows weaker with each major attack." Weaker than her brothers realized, but she saw no benefit to enlightening them. If Father wanted to keep up appearances, that was his choice. They all knew it was just a matter of time.

"I'll bring my family by in the morning tomorrow, and Richard can arrive with his brood in the afternoon. That should be satisfactory." Archie was forever the take-charge older brother, plowing forward and making a way.

"If you stay no more than an hour each, with enough time for Father to nap between, I think that will work. I'll be sure he's dressed and downstairs by half past ten. I'll have Cook prepare a sideboard of delicacies instead of a full meal." The children would love that. Father hadn't eaten a real meal in days, and she suspected sitting at the formal table would be too taxing for him.

Archie stood and straightened his vest. "Very well, I'll just pop up and see him before I leave."

Richard watched him go and then turned to Emmie. "Father hasn't got long, has he." It wasn't a question.

She shook her head. "He'll put a brave face on it, but I don't think he'll see the spring. Men at the hospital in his condition—"

Richard raised his hand and shook his head, sinking onto a chair. He'd no stomach for such talk.

Emmie sat in the chair beside him and took his hand. "We'll muddle through, you'll see."

"But what about you?" His clear gray eyes, so like their father's, clouded with doubt. "What will you do if... when..."

"Much the same as I'm doing now, I suppose. My mornings at the hospital, keeping this house, and charity work as needed."

Richard squeezed her hand. "You can't stay here in this house all alone."

"I won't be alone."

"The servants don't count."

"I think—"

He squeezed her hand again before letting go. "I know times are changing, what with so many widows struggling by on their own after the war, but you're not a widow."

"I'm as good as. If James had lived—"

"But he didn't."

She opened her mouth to argue, then snapped it shut. He was right, as far as society would see it.

"I don't mean to be unkind. You know I always liked James."

She nodded. Richard had stood by her choice, even when Father was less than thrilled with it. In fact, without her brother's support, it was unlikely Father would have ever given his permission for the engagement.

"I believe I would do very well for myself. Father has put money in an account for me."

"He has, but as you know, he has deeded the house to Archie."

Richard was watching her fingers, so she let go of the emerald pendant she always wore and tucked both of her hands into the voluminous folds of her skirt.

"Surely he won't ask me to leave."

He shook his head. "I wouldn't count on it, little sister. The only way he'll allow you to remain here is after he's moved his family in. Archie isn't one to buck tradition or make waves in society."

That was an understatement. Father was the one who had raised their family to its social standing, but it was Archie who guarded it. Zealously. Still, he wouldn't deprive her of her home. Would he?

The bulletin board at the feed store was filled with scraps of paper, but only one caught Russ's eye. Old Jack Keen was selling one of his rams. Nobody had better rams in the county than Old Jack. Russ rubbed the back of his neck. There was no price on the paper. That wasn't surprising. Old Jack was a cagey one, always playing his hand close to the vest. Still, it might be worth a ride out to his place to take a look.

Inside, he placed his order for seed corn, the new kind everyone had talked about last year. His father had grown the same variety of corn his whole life, but Russ figured if the new variety lived up to half its reputation, it'd be worth trying on a couple of acres. If it did well and he had extra to sell, maybe he could purchase one of those sulky plows in the fall. Of course, he'd need to purchase another horse. It'd be too much for Goblin to pull one of those newfangled things on his own.

After paying for the seed corn, he climbed into the wagon. It'd been just a week since he'd mailed his letter to Emmie—Miss Mason—so it was foolish to be expecting anything in return, but he pointed Goblin toward the post office and slapped the reins on the gray's rump anyway.

Russ entered the small post office, ducking under pine boughs that had slipped from their nails above the door.

"Oh, goodness me. Mr. Fields, would you be so kind as to fix those for me?" Mrs. Russell asked. "It would save me having to find a stool to stand on."

"Yes, ma'am." Russ tucked the greenery back in place.

"Thank you. That's much better. We must look festive on Christmas Eve, you know."

Christmas Eve. He'd forgotten all about that.

"You're here for your mail, I suppose."

"Yes, ma'am."

"I don't believe there is any, but let me look." She wiggled her fingers in the slots behind her. "No. Maybe next Monday when you stop by."

He touched the brim of his hat and hoped the irrational disappointment didn't show on his face. Of course there wasn't a letter. He hadn't expected one, after all. So why the disappointment?

He left the wagon tied outside the post office and walked to the general store. It was packed with people, no doubt buying last-minute presents for their loved ones. There would be no nicely wrapped presents at his farm. Nor any festive meal. No tree stood in his parlor draped with the decorations Becky had packed away last year.

Maybe he should have found a way to go to Cilla's this year. He'd never seen the twins, or the two younger boys. They'd had just the two older boys when Russ had enlisted. But who would have done his chores at the farm? Still, part of him wished he'd made the effort to find someone to take care of his animals for a week or so, or at least that he'd thought to buy gifts and send them. To the boys, at least. It was too late now.

He looked over a table laden with gift ideas. What would Emmie appreciate? Not that it mattered. As new as their friendship was, it wouldn't be appropriate.

He handed the boy at the counter his list, then helped pack his purchases on the wagon. Once the town's traffic was behind him and Goblin was trotting for home, Russ planted his feet on the wagon's kickboard, elbows on his knees.

Emmie was used to finer things than the stuff for sale at the general store. Her letters to Becky had told him that. They had servants, for one thing, people who did the cooking and cleaning. What did a woman do all day if someone else did those chores?

Emmie worked at the hospital as a nursing assistant, but surely that didn't take all her time. Or did it?

Unwelcome flashbacks of the army hospital clouded his mind. He closed his eye. Men groaning, some crying, others swearing, nurses with dark circles under their eyes hustling from one cot to the next. The smells of blood, infection, and unwashed bodies crammed into a space far too small. The stench of camphor clinging to the doctor who lifted his bandages.

He dropped his head between his hands and breathed deeply of the frosty, clean air. He was in Michigan. He wasn't in the hospital.

The steady clip-clop of Goblin's hooves sounded nothing like a cavalry charge. He wasn't on the battlefield. He opened his eye and focused on the gray rump in front of him. He was home. It was over.

God, let it be over.

Father hadn't come downstairs yesterday. He'd been too wearied from their Christmas company the day before. She'd taken him a tray for supper, but he'd hardly touched it. She should speak with Cook about that. Perhaps they could concoct something that would appeal to him for tonight. She glanced at the grandfather clock. No time now.

With a peek out the window, she fetched her heavy cloak. She wrapped it around her shoulders and settled the hood over her starched nurse's cap before leaving the house. A fluffy carpet of white muffled her footsteps and turned the gray surroundings into a wonderland every bit as magical as Alice's.

Richard had given her that book for Christmas a year ago. This year, he'd given her a new stationery set. She'd had to tell him of Becky's death then. Both her brothers had met Becky several times during their holidays from the Young Ladies Seminary when Becky would stay with her, the farm in Michigan being too far a journey for the shorter breaks.

She'd use the stationery to write to Mr. Fields, but it was best if her brothers didn't find out about that. They'd never understand, and they'd approve even less.

She picked up her pace and made it to the impressive front doors of West Penn Hospital before the church bell down the street chimed the hour. After stowing her cloak in the nurses' closet, she donned a fresh apron and hurried to the head nurse's office. Her tap on the door brought an order to enter.

"Good morning, Nurse Ballard."

"Ah, Miss Mason. Please, have a seat."

The head nurse turned to file the papers in her hand while Emmie sank onto the edge of a straight-backed wooden chair. She'd never been asked to sit before and resisted the urge to ask why. One didn't ask the head nurse questions. One listened and obeyed.

Nurse Ballard finished her task and took her seat across the tidy desk from Emmie. She folded her hands on top of its dustless surface. Her face softened to an almost compassionate expression.

"Miss Mason, it pains me to be the one to inform you of unpleasant news."

Emmie's heart dropped to her stomach.

"The hospital's board of directors met last evening. The decision was made to cut back the assistant nursing staff."

Emmie straightened in her chair, hand rising to her throat, bare of its usual pendant. Nurses and nursing assistants weren't allowed to wear jewelry while on duty, but she missed its comforting presence.

Nurse Ballard shook her head, stalling anything Emmie might have said. Even if she could have pushed words past the lump in her throat.

"Our census is down, and we have more hands than we can use at this time. It was the board's decision that we retain those women who most need the income, particularly the widows."

Once again, being almost a widow didn't count. The unfairness of that smacked against the common sense that told her she was being selfish. She worked because she wanted to, not because she had mouths to feed at home.

Nurse Ballard sat back and waited.

"I understand. I will miss working here, more than you can imagine, but the board is wise to give the positions to those most in need."

"Well said, Miss Mason. Please note that your work has been exemplary, and, should our staffing needs increase, you will be one of the first I request be recalled."

It brought a hollow sort of comfort, but it was still nice to hear. Emmie nodded, dropping her hands into her lap.

"And now," Nurse Ballard rose, "I must be about my duties. Best of luck to you in your future endeavors."

Just like that, she was dismissed. Set adrift. Left with... nothing.

"Look at his top line why don't you?"

Russ had to admit, the ram's back was as wide and flat as an ironing board, but Old Jack wasn't likely to give him away, either.

"I'd keep him myself, but he's the sire of half the ewes I own and the grandsire of more than a few." Old Jack pushed his battered felt hat back and scraped his gloved fingers across his forehead. "And seeing as you serviced our country, I'll cut you a deal on the price."

"Mr. Keen—"

The old man raised his hand. "I mean it. I may be known as a stingy old coot." He grinned at Russ, showing more gaps than teeth. "I may even be one. But I know you gave up a lot to keep this country together, boy, and I'm proud of you. I know your pa was too."

Russ blinked and shook his head. "I don't think he ever really got over Frank's death."

"No man can lose a son and not be scarred by it. Your pa's scars were on the inside, but he was a good man. Honest. A good farmer. One of the best around these parts." Mr. Keen rubbed his bristly jaw. "I was right sorry to hear about your sister."

Russ swallowed against the tightness in his throat.

They stood like that for a few moments, side by side, with their boots in the snow, staring at the broad back of a ram who was giving them a sheep's equivalent of the evil eye. No doubt about it, that top line would look mighty good on his crop of lambs next year, and he hadn't exposed the yearlings to a ram yet.

"I'll take him."

By the time they'd wrestled the animal into the wagon and secured him, a two-man job considering the ram's size and strenuous objection to the whole ordeal, Russ was sweated through and starting to second-guess his purchase as he handed over the cash.

"You let me know how he works for you, boy."

Russ touched his hat brim and slapped the reins on Goblin's rump. He didn't really need anything in town this week, but since it was Monday, he'd drop by the post office... just in case.

The ram bellowed for the first mile, baaed for the second, and had reduced his displeasure to a series of ominous grunts by the time Russ pulled to a halt. He climbed down and straightened his coat. There was nothing he could do about the odor of sheep that clung to it, however.

He stepped into the building.

"Mr. Fields." Mrs. Russell smiled at him. "You're here for your mail, I suppose."

He returned her smile, amused that she never changed her greeting. Somehow it was easier to hear those same words when there was a chance that a letter awaited from Emmie.

"I know you generally come on Mondays, so I made sure and kept it close." With a wink, she pulled an envelope from one of the slots and waved it at him. "Am I right?"

"You are, ma'am."

She handed it to him and cocked her head at the door. "What's all the fuss out there?"

Russ glanced out the window. The ram was back to bellowing, and a crowd had gathered around the wagon.

"I bought a ram off Mr. Keen."

Her face shriveled into a good impersonation of a raisin. "I hope that old tightwad didn't take your last dollar."

He chuckled. "No, ma'am. I can assure you he didn't."

She gave a satisfied nod, and Russ hurried back to his wagon. The crowd was kids, school being out until after New Year's Day. A couple of the older ones took a look at him, cried out, grabbed the younger kids, and they all took off running.

Any other day that would have saddened him, but today, he had an envelope in his pocket with his name written in a lovely hand. Today, he wouldn't let it bother him.

Once he had Goblin pointed toward home and the ram once again reduced to grunts, he tore the envelope open and pulled out four sheets.

December 27, 1866

Dear Mr. Fields,

If ever there was a week I needed a friend, this is the one. You'll know from my letters to Becky that my father has a lung disease that takes so many of our mill workers. He's been weakened by a particularly nasty attack. We kept Christmas very quietly this year because of this, although both my brothers and their families came to call. I guess it wasn't all that quiet with the children running about.

He could almost envision it. Surely Cilla's family's day had been just as boisterous. Nothing like the silence and cold pork sandwich he'd eaten.

Then, just yesterday, I was let go from West Penn Hospital due to a reduced need for staff. I confess that this causes me great distress. With Father's health failing and knowing that I will at some point be on my own, I had planned to dedicate my life to my hospital work. There are other hospitals in Pittsburgh, of course, but not close to our home.

Russ suppressed a shudder. How could anyone desire to spend their days at a hospital?

As you might remember, again from my letters, my fiancé was killed in the war. Had I been a war widow, the hospital would have kept me on. But James was taken before we married. I lost the man I loved, and now I've lost my life's work as well.

The wagon jolted over a frozen rut, and the ram thrashed around behind Russ. A gust of wind tore the top sheet of paper from his grasp. He pulled Goblin to a stop, crammed the remaining pages into his pocket, and jumped off the wagon, chasing the fluttering sheet across the snowy field. He'd just gotten his hand on it when Goblin snorted. Before he could do more than turn around, the gray horse had broken into a trot, heading home. Russ hadn't set the brake. With a shout, he took off in pursuit.

Had he lost his mind? What was he doing trying to read a letter while driving anyway? He slowed and gritted his teeth as Goblin kept trotting toward home. He'd be waiting at the hitching rail when Russ got there.

Well, the long walk would give Russ time to consider how ill-advised it was to continue his correspondence with Emmie. It had obviously addled his brain.

CHAPTER 4

I am having second thoughts about sending this letter at all, so gloomy are my writings. If I manage to post this, and if it is indeed too much for you to respond to, I will perfectly understand. I so enjoyed your letter telling me of the farm and your animals. It brightened my day, my whole week. I'm sure my letter will do nothing of the sort. And for that, I am sorry.

Your friend,
Emmie Mason

RUSS FINISHED HIS THIRD reading of the entire letter in three days. He'd brightened her day. Her whole week. When was the last time he'd brightened anyone's day? Maybe his too infrequent letters to Cilla brightened her days. They were family, after all. But Emmie... Emmie wasn't. There was nothing he could do about her father or her work at the hospital, but he could keep writing to her. He could share her burdens albeit long distance. And be her friend.

Even if it led him to do more daft things like reading while driving. He fetched pen and ink.

January 2, 1867

Dear Miss Mason,
I received your letter and felt the pain in which you wrote it. Having lost Pa barely a year ago, and Becky

only six weeks ago, I understand. Your writing caused me no hardship, in fact, if writing me eases your burden, please feel free to write more about such matters.

As to your hospital work, I confess I do not understand how anyone could wish to be in a hospital. Having spent some considerable time in one during the war, I will never enter the door of another. The memories are not at all pleasant.

Let me write of more happy things. Two days ago, I purchased a new ram to improve my flock of sheep. The man I purchased him from sold him to me at a steep discount, and I must say, I was at first inclined to turn him down. Charity is a hard thing to accept, but he said that he respected my efforts in the war and wanted to show his regard in this way. I was most humbled by his thoughts and by his willingness to look me in the eye and say it.

Russ pulled his hand away from the paper. What had he almost written? Perhaps he should start over again. He reread the words. No. She wouldn't be able to read between the lines. There was nothing to suggest that he was grossly disfigured.

He bent back over the sheet and wrote more about the farm and his plans for improvement. As tongue-tied as he normally was with people face-to-face, his words on the paper flowed almost faster than he could scratch them out.

Was this what Becky had felt as she'd written Emmie so faithfully for the past several years? He stared into the lamp's glow, a whiff of kerosene lingering in the air. He'd often teased his sister about having nothing to write about more pressing than how high her bread dough had risen that morning. She'd usually swatted him with a towel or a broom, whichever was closest to hand.

He shouldn't have teased her. What would he have done without Becky's regular letters while he was at war? Sometimes they'd arrived by the handful when no mail had reached the troops for weeks on end. They had been, without doubt, his bright spots of the war. His own letters back to her, which he'd found tied in a small bundle next to

Emmie's, had been short, sparse affairs. There'd been little of the war he'd wanted to share with his sister.

Jigs pushed his cold nose against Russ's hand. He ruffled the long hair around the dog's ears. "You miss her too, don't you?" The dog gave a soft sigh.

Now it was Russ's turn to offer someone support through letters. He rested the end of the pen against his chin and smiled. What was that feeling welling inside him?

Was it something akin to… joy?

Emmie sank onto the settee, her fingers tangling in the fringe trim on its edge. Father and Archie were closeted in the study with the door closed. Why had they excused themselves from her presence? A worried knot formed in her middle. Father had never kept his business affairs secret from her, at least, not since she'd finished school. That could only mean they were discussing her and her future. Or what they wished her future to be.

It had been two weeks since her termination by the hospital. Father had seemed almost relieved when she'd told him. He'd never really approved of her working there, but while the war raged on and their brave soldiers needed care, he'd been tolerant of it. By the close of the war, his own health was such that he didn't kick up a fuss over her continuing. She'd made it her mission to learn all she could about the lung diseases that were far too common in Pittsburgh and applied that knowledge to keeping Father comfortable.

And now this.

This what? She didn't even know what they were talking about. She stood and paced across to the tall sitting room windows. Snow still covered the ground, but it was dirty and worn-looking. This year wasn't starting out at all as she'd planned.

She closed her eyes and leaned her forehead against the cool glass. What did it look like at Russ's farm? Was the snow still pristine white?

Did the sheep huddle in woolly groups to keep warm? Did mist rise from the warm back of his horse as it jogged down the lane? How simple and clean that all seemed compared to here.

She drew in a long breath. Beeswax and orange oil almost masked the ever-present stench created by the steel mills. Becky's letters had been scented with lilacs. She missed that. She missed her best friend. Would Russ write her again, or had her last letter effectively sealed the end of their correspondence? What had she been thinking to write such personal hurts to a virtual stranger?

The study door creaked open, and footsteps struck in the hall. Too firm and too fast for Father. Emmie turned from the window as Archie entered. He stopped when he saw her, his brows drawing together. He ran his hand through his hair, mussing it so it glinted under the flickering light of the oil lamp. When had it started to turn gray?

"Father and I have been speaking."

She resisted the urge to roll her eyes. "So I gathered."

"Well." He cleared his throat. "Father wishes you and me to come to an agreement for when..."

Emmie straightened and crossed her arms. "I am of age. I don't need anyone's permission—"

"Legally, you are correct." He paced a few steps and swung back to face her. "Hang it all, Emmie. I'm your brother."

"As if I didn't know that?"

"Some days it doesn't appear that you do. I'm responsible for—"

"I'm of age."

"Emmie." He wore that *if you'll only be reasonable* look she hated. "You are of age, and past the age to settle on a suitor." He arched his brows. "How old are you now?"

She did her best to keep her features smooth and impassive. "I'll be twenty-three come May."

"Yes, that's what I thought."

She couldn't refrain from the very unladylike snort that followed. Archie had been married and out of the house before Emmie was born, so they'd never been close, but that he couldn't remember he was twenty-one years her senior still hurt.

"I'm sorry, Emmie." He studied the carpet and tugged at the hem of his vest. "Yvonne chides me for not remembering her age as well. She came along so many years after David and Belinda..."

As if being a late-in-life child made one easy to forget. Emmie sighed.

"Father and I just want to see you settled. See you make a good match."

"A good match?"

"Yes, and to that point, Caroline and I would like you to come to dinner a week from Sunday. We'll be having a special guest."

He certainly couldn't mean—

A knock interrupted before she could form a scathing reply. They waited until Evans appeared in the doorway.

"Miss Helen Edwards to see you, miss."

Emmie's closest friend among the nursing staff. "I'll meet her in the music room."

She turned to Archie. "I can't see why we have to discuss this now."

"Because Father wishes it and he's dying."

Her heart pulsed at the base of her throat, but she raised her chin. "I have a guest. Please excuse me."

"We'll talk later then."

Not if she could help it. Emmie marched past him, ignoring the hand he held out to her. She continued down the hall and into the music room.

Helen stood near the piano, her riotous blond curls swept back in a becoming fall across her shoulders.

"Emmie." Her friend rushed to her for a much-needed embrace. "I only returned last night and heard the news. How could they have let you go?"

The sympathy in her friend's voice was just the calming balm Emmie needed. Tears welled and wouldn't be denied.

"Emmie, if there is anything I can—"

She straightened and sniffed, meeting Helen's troubled blue eyes. "It's Father."

"He's taken a turn?"

Emmie nodded and then sank back into the embrace and comfort of the one friend who understood her and what she was going through.

The Masons' Sunday dinner had always been a family affair when Emmie was younger. Archie and Caroline, Richard and Fannie, plus their children as they'd come along, had come to Father's house for the meal. She had no real memories of her mother, who had passed while she was a toddler, but the table had been surrounded by the rest of the family. Dinners had been relaxing even as they observed all the proper manners.

Nothing at all like today.

Sitting across from Mr. Shook in Archie's dining room, nothing sounded better to Emmie than to run home and dive under her covers until Monday morning. Everyone, even Yvonne, Emmie's nine-year-old niece, knew full well why Mr. Shook was there. And why Emmie was seated directly across from him.

She'd much rather be seated across from Mr. Fields. His letter, which she'd already read a half-dozen times, had been full of the most marvelously non-Pittsburgh things. Was he eating dinner alone tonight? She sighed. One thing was for certain. He wasn't sitting across from Mr. Shook.

That gentleman was an up-and-coming lawyer about Emmie's age. The son of a prominent lawyer whom folks said would soon be appointed a judgeship. Exactly the type of man Father would love to see her shackled to. As uncomfortable as she was, a lifetime of training in proper manners forced Emmie to engage in small talk. They talked about the weather during the soup, the town's need for more schools during the salad, the high price of coal during the rack of lamb, and they saved the best for last—dissection of that morning's sermon during dessert.

By the time the men adjourned to the study for a pipe or cigar, Emmie's temples throbbed.

"He is nice-looking, don't you think?" asked her niece, Belinda, her ginger-colored eyes wide and innocent. She was what? Seventeen? The same age as Emmie when she'd met James. Had she worn that same look? Probably.

Oh. She patted Belinda's arm.

"Caroline." Emmie caught up with her sister-in-law, and they entered the parlor together. "It would seem that Belinda is much taken with Mr. Shook."

"She's much too young to think of..." Caroline's voice trailed off, and she turned to watch her two daughters enter the room, the youngest giggling at the blushing elder.

"I don't believe she is any younger than you were when you met my brother," Emmie said.

"Of course, but Archie and I met young because we lived in the same neighborhood. It's really not the same thing." Caroline's voice lost all conviction when a gleam entered her blue eyes.

With any luck, Emmie had gotten herself off the hook. Archie would no doubt suggest that Mr. Shook escort her home. Maybe during the ride, Emmie could point out some of Belinda's endearing qualities. The girl had many, to be sure. Once home, Emmie could write about this dinner to Mr. Fields.

A smile tugged at her lips.

January 14, 1867

Dear Mr. Fields,

Your last letter was such an encouragement to me, and I confess I sorely need that now. Your words of a simple life sound like heaven on earth. Things here are not so simple. Father is no worse, but, of course, no better either. The days are long and time heavy on my idle hands. Other than reading to Father, which he seems to enjoy, and needlework which I have no use for, my days are filled with very little except for playing the

piano. Or when my nursing friend Helen can visit.
I miss my work at the hospital.

Russ rubbed the bridge of his nose. Emmie was lonely. Raised as an only child due to the distance in age from her brothers, and without a mother in her life... He couldn't imagine. Cilla, Frank, he, and Becky had been separated by only seven years total. Growing up, their home had been a whirlwind of noise and activity.

Russ had never known loneliness until after Gettysburg. A loneliness not from a lack of people, but from a lack of humanity. That was a different thing. Emmie was lonely from a lack of people in her life. Yes. It started to make sense now.

Yet there were other people whom she never mentioned, the servants Becky had told him about. Did she not spend time with them? Memories of Cilla and Becky in the kitchen, elbow-deep in bread dough and laughter, teased a smile. He shook his head. Maybe he didn't understand anything.

She wrote more about the work she missed and then:

Archie and Caroline had me to Sunday dinner yes-
terday. I would have written you as soon as I returned
home, but the whole event exhausted me. They'd invited
Mr. Shook, a man they obviously fancy as my potential
suitor.

His heartbeat slowed. A suitor? Of course it only made sense, with her father ailing and the need for someone to... Why didn't one of her brothers take her in? The paper crackled between his fingers. He'd never once thought to foist Becky off on someone else. What was wrong with her brothers?

If only James had lived. We were engaged, as
I'm sure you know. But you may not know the whole
story. He joined the Union Army to prove himself to me,
I fear. It's a guilt I live with, thinking that had I accepted
him on his first proposal, he may have never gone. But I

didn't. He proposed again after he'd enlisted. Although Father had reservations, he allowed the engagement. Then James left, and I received the most endearing letters until the last one. That was from his superior officer. It told me that James had died a hero on the battlefield at a place called Cold Harbor on June 3, 1864.

The smell of gunpowder flooded the kitchen. The cries of wounded, the shriek of shells, the roar of cannons, all pressed into the room with him. Russ dropped his head between his hands, palms tight to his ears, eye shut against the flashes of muskets. He jumped to his feet, the chair crashing behind him. Staggering a few steps, he reached the window and pressed his face to the pane.

How long he stood there, he didn't know.

He opened his eye, his breath frosting the glass. His barn, fuzzy through the clouded window, stood strong and tall against the purple and orange of sunset. Solid. Real. He pulled his hands from his ears to the quiet of a Monday evening outside of Jonesville, where the only battles raged not on the ground... but in his mind.

CHAPTER 5

T HE MUSIC SURROUNDED EMMIE. Cool and smooth, the piano keys slid beneath her fingers. She'd long ago stopped looking at the music. It was "Grand March of Cinderella," one of her favorite pieces, and she knew it by heart. Its flowing notes usually soothed her inner turmoil.

If she were good enough—no—if she'd been born into a family of different social standing, she might have made music her profession. There was no way a young woman of her class would ever perform on a stage. Her family and friends would have turned their backs on her if she'd tried. Although, most of her friends had melted away over the past three or four years. Not melted away, exactly, but moved on. They'd married and set up their own homes, tended their own children, met with other married women and their families.

The notes flew from her fingertips. She was destined to be an old maid unless Archie managed to find someone who looked at her the way James had. Or someone who wrote letters that touched her heart like Mr. Fields. She ended the song with a strong chord, her shoulders dropping.

"Miss Edwards to see you, miss." Evans stood in the doorway to the music room.

Emmie straightened and a smile pulled her from her doldrums. If any friend could understand, it was Helen. "Send her in and have Cook prepare some coffee and whatever light lunch she has to go with it." Her friend's preference for coffee over tea was one of the things that had brought them together at the hospital, around the nurses' coffeepot.

Helen breezed into the room.

Emmie met her friend halfway and took her hands, squeezing them. "I'm so glad you're here. Come, sit, and tell me everything I'm missing at the hospital."

Helen perched on the edge of the chair across from Emmie's favorite. "I have exciting news."

Emmie sucked in her breath. It couldn't be a recall for her. That would have come from Nurse Ballard herself. But she couldn't squelch the tiny flicker of hope.

"There's a new doctor who's come on staff."

The hopeful flicker guttered out.

"His name is Timothy Lawson and his specialty"—Helen leaned closer—"is reconstructive surgery. What they are calling plastic surgery now."

"What a fortunate addition for the hospital." How many of their Civil War patients could have been helped by such a doctor? Men who'd been mangled by bullets, shells, and shrapnel, which left gruesome scars.

"You'll never guess who he studied under."

Emmie shook her head, her mind reeling with all the possibilities this would afford the hospital.

"Surgeon J. Cooper McKee."

"Dr. McKee?" The medical journals had lauded that man's success rate with reconstructive surgeries. "He's a pioneer in that specialty."

"Just think," Helen said, "if Dr. Lawson can do half of what Dr. McKee has written about—"

"He could change so many lives." Emmie's heart lightened at the thought.

"My thoughts exactly."

"But, those who needed that type of work have been scarred for so long now."

"I know, but Dr. Lawson says it's not too late to help them."

"You've spoken with him, then?" Not many doctors spent time speaking with the nurses. They generally barked orders and expected them to be carried out without delay or comment.

Helen's cheeks pinkened. "I have."

Emmie scooted to the edge of her seat. "Helen?"

"Dr. Lawson is tall, very good-looking, and very single." A gleam twinkled in Helen's blue eyes.

"And he's caught your interest?"

"Let's just say, I wouldn't turn a corner to avoid him in the hallway." Helen's laughter was refreshing and relaxing. Their coffee and sandwiches arrived, then Helen went on to share the doings and the gossip of the hospital while Emmie soaked it in.

How she missed the interaction with someone outside of her family. Then a sober thought intruded. If Helen and her doctor were to marry, then she, too, would move on and leave Emmie behind.

The bite of turkey sandwich she'd taken landed in her middle like a hunk of stone.

January 27, 1867

My Dear Miss Mason,

My dear? Why had he written that? Russ stared at the paper on his kitchen table. What was he thinking? He was thinking of Emmie Mason. Thinking of her far too often. He'd no right to do that. He should scrap this sheet of paper and start again. She was a lonely young woman facing emotional distress who might read more into that greeting than he intended.

Who was he kidding? It was exactly what he'd intended—in his heart.

What harm could come of his thinking about Emmie in such an intimate manner? She was hundreds of miles away in Pittsburgh. She was far above him in social standing. He'd never seen her image, but he knew she was beautiful. She couldn't be otherwise.

He shook his head. They'd never meet in person. Someday, one of her brothers would introduce her to a suitable man. Someone of equal social standing of whom they approved. Someone much more important than a simple farmer. And someone with a handsome face she could fall in love with.

He forced his fingers to loosen on his pen before the wood barrel snapped.

> *I am sorry to hear of your loss and regrets regarding your fiancé. The war took so many good men from us. I suspect that's true on both sides. Other men, it left forever changed.*

He ran his hand across the ridges and valleys on the left side of his face. The skin puckered and pulled beneath his fingertips. Shadows of remembered pain darkened his thoughts. He stared at the letter's greeting until his breathing steadied, then dipped his pen into the ink.

> *Let me tell you what has kept me busy this past week. We've had two snowstorms come through and bury the pastures. The horse and cow do fine, but the poor sheep can barely move through its depth. The new ram, who appears to have taken a fast dislike to me, charged me when I approached the water trough. The deep snow slowed him considerably, and I was able to avoid being hit. He'll bear watching from now on.*

Russ rambled on about the farm for another page and a half before blowing on the sheets to dry the ink and folding them for the envelope. He scratched her address on the front and then sat back in his chair. Jigs laid his head on Russ's thigh, and he rubbed the dog's silky ears.

A refined young woman from Pittsburgh, and he was writing her about snowstorms and farm animals. She had professed to enjoy it. She seemed to relish their correspondence as much as he did. Or maybe he was simply fooling himself. Still, it was harmless enough, and it gave him a reason to stop by the post office. One Monday to mail a letter, the next Monday to pick one up. That was little enough to look forward to each week.

Once her brothers found her a suitable husband...he'd lose even that.

Emmie sat curled in the wide chair by her bedroom window. The thick clouds threatened snow, which would cover the gray layers on the ground. An open book lay forgotten on her lap. A tapping sounded on the door. "Mr. Richard awaits you in the parlor when it's convenient, miss." The butler's voice was muffled through the heavy wooden door.

She hurried to open it. "Tell him I'll be down directly."

Before going down, she checked her hair in the mirror and brushed a couple of wrinkles from her skirt. Not that Richard would critique her appearance. Nor was he likely to push a suitor at her. He was probably just there to visit Father.

Yet, he'd asked for her.

Emmie's slippers whispered on the polished oak stairs and down the hallway to the parlor. Richard paced in front of the fireplace, and Fannie sat on the settee with the baby in her arms.

"Emmie." Richard paused with his hand on the mantel.

"Hello, Richard, Fannie. How is our little Ned?" The baby turned a toothless grin in her direction. He had the most adorable blond curls, inherited from his mother.

"We're fine. Just fine." Richard looked at Fannie.

"How is Father Mason?" Fannie asked.

"He came down for breakfast, but he's returned to his room to rest. He's much the same and prefers his quiet solitude. Talking steals the breath from him and fatigues him so." Emmie clasped her hands in front of her. "Of course, Evans is stationed outside Father's door, should he need anything."

Richard rubbed the back of his neck. "Fannie and I came to talk to you, but I'll pop up and see him before we leave."

"To talk to me?" Suspicion crept along her backbone and caused a slight pounding at the base of her skull. Why did her brothers—or at least their actions—have this effect on her?

Fannie smiled and jostled Ned on her shoulder. "We understand that Archie had you over for dinner on Sunday."

"Yes." Emmie sank onto the chair near the settee, and Richard sat next to his wife. "It was his ham-handed way of trying to foist me off on a husband."

"He means well—" Richard started, but Fannie's hand on his arm cut him off.

"You have a home with us, always," Fannie said. "In fact, your help would be much appreciated." She smoothed the baby's fair curls.

Emmie reached out, and Fannie passed Ned over, his little hands grasping at the front of her dress. Who cared about silly old wrinkles anyway? "You know I'm happy to help any time you ask."

Richard cleared his throat. "What we're trying to say, in a somewhat less ham-handed way than Archie, is that you needn't worry about where you'll live. Our home is always open to you."

In that moment, a love never outrightly spoken shone in her brother's eyes. Swallowing against the burn of emotions, she nodded. She might be a help to them with the children, but their house was hardly large enough for them and their brood of five. While deeply touched, she'd no desire to be cramped into her brother's attic. She'd rather be somewhere with open spaces and acres of grassy hills. Maybe even a few sheep.

"Oh, lest I forget." Richard reached into his inner coat pocket. "We heard the train leaving the station on our way over, so I picked up the mail for you." He glanced at two letters in his hand. "One is for Father and one for you. The postmark says Michigan—"

"Thank you." Emmie balanced Ned against her shoulder and snatched the envelopes from Richard. She turned her face against her nephew's hair, hoping to hide behind his bright curls the heat gathering in her cheeks.

"Who do you know from Michigan?" Fannie asked.

"My friend from The Young Ladies Seminary."

Richard's brow puckered. "Didn't you mention recently that she'd passed away?"

She shouldn't have divulged that information. "She did, but I've stayed in contact with her family." That was all her brother needed to know, but Fannie's lips twitched before she schooled them back into a sedate line.

"Do you think Father Mason would be up to a visit from Ned and me this morning?"

Bless her sister-in-law for changing the subject.

"I'm sure he would if you don't stay too long."

Fannie stood and waited for her husband to join her, then she scooped Ned from Emmie's arms. "We won't tire him, and then we'll see ourselves out."

Emmie wanted to hug her, but she merely smiled and inclined her head.

"Do you not think we should press our case about Emmie moving in with us?" Richard asked as his wife shooed him from the parlor.

Emmie didn't hear Fannie's response because she couldn't tear her eyes away from her name on the envelope in bold, angular strokes. She scurried to the music room and her favorite chair. With infinite care, she broke the seal and extracted the letter.

January 27, 1867

My Dear Miss Mason,

My dear. A sigh slipped from her lips, and she snuggled deeper into the plush upholstery. Her throat tightened as she read on through his brief expression of sympathy. Russ had lost his brother to the war. No doubt he'd also lost countless friends. He didn't delve into any of that in his remarks, but men rarely did.

She devoured the rest of his letter, giving a little gasp at his near-miss with the angry ram and laughing aloud at the antics of a half-grown piglet that found more ways out of its pen than any other Russ could remember.

Emmie wasn't empty-headed enough not to realize the work involved in running a farm, especially by himself. Still, the idea of living as Russ did appealed to her beyond her ability to express. Unless...

With the letter carefully returned to its envelope until she would read it again—probably several times—this evening, Emmie moved to her piano bench and let her fingers hover above the keys for a few breaths before plunging into "Sonatina in C Major" by Johann Anton André, a lighthearted piece that filled the music room with hope and... something sweeter.

My Dear Miss Mason...

CHAPTER 6

January 31, 1867

Dear Mr. Fields,

I F ONLY SHE WERE bold enough to write *My Dear Mr. Fields*. Emmie's hand trembled above the letters on the page. His use of the endearment still thrilled through her veins, even though she'd read it numerous times since Richard had delivered the envelope yesterday. But to be so forward... no, she dare not.

Not yet.

> *Your letter arrived yesterday at a most opportune time. My brother Richard was visiting here with Fannie and their youngest child, little Ned. Richard is nothing like Archie, thank goodness. One Archie per family is more than enough. Not that he's intolerable, you understand, but he does tend to want to have his way more often than not. Perhaps that's the lot of a firstborn.*

Russ should understand that, being the third oldest in a family of four. Russ. When had she started to think of him in the familiar? They'd corresponded for no more than two months, but somehow it seemed longer, as if they'd known each other for... what? Years? Now she was being silly. But Becky had written about her brother frequently. Maybe it wasn't silly that Emmie felt this type of connection so strongly.

How many times over the past three years had she longed to go and visit Becky? If Father hadn't been so ill. If she'd had someone to travel with. She'd have met Russ in person then. If... if she could do it over again, she'd have found a way to make it happen. She swallowed against the lump that rose in her throat at such a lost opportunity. And at the loss of Becky, which was ever close to her heart.

> *We're all spending more time with Father. As much as he'll allow. Father has never been the type of person to want others hanging about unnecessarily. He quite cherishes his solitude with just the newspaper for company. In truth, it tires him to have to make conversation when each breath is difficult enough for him to accomplish. Even while I worry that he might slip away from us while alone in his room, sometimes I think he would prefer it that way.*

She stopped writing and listened, not that she could hear Father's breathing from the desk in her room, but... She sighed and stared out the window. Cold rain washed the glass and blurred the world beyond. Father had shooed her from his bedside again that morning. His breathing had been too labored to join her downstairs. He'd sipped a bit of tea Cook had sent up on a tray but had refused a bite of egg or toast.

She blinked and returned her attention to the page.

> *The idea of losing Father so soon after Becky pains me beyond words. But I expect you understand more than most, having come through the war only to lose your father almost upon your arrival home and then your beloved sister.*
>
> *There isn't a day I don't think of Becky, think that I should write her about this or that. She was my confidant, my best friend. If not for you, I don't know what I'd do, who I would express myself to.*

That was a bit forward, but she refused to start over. It was how she felt, and he should know it. Who better to share Becky's loss with? Who better to understand her feelings about Father?

She filled the rest of the letter with Helen's recent visit and the buzz about a new doctor in town. She stopped with her pen poised at the end. Dare she? She straightened her back and flexed her fingers against the pen. Her other hand closed around the emerald pendant. Why not?

> *I pray that you remain well and happy while I eagerly await your next letter.*
>
> *Your very dear friend,*
> *Emmie Mason*

Russ dumped the wheelbarrow load of hay into the sheep pen. Although the sun was tepid at best, it was too nice a day to keep the animals inside. He righted the wheelbarrow when movement caught his eye. A man on horseback, arms flopping with every step the animal took.

The preacher, on a different horse this time, brought the animal's bone-jarring trot to a halt beside the sheep fence.

"Good morning, sir." The man looked around at the muddy fields, bared by the recent thaw. "It's a glorious day, isn't it?"

Did a preacher have to talk like that?

"It'll do." Russ stabbed the hayfork into the mud and angled his stance to keep his eye on both the preacher and the ram.

The preacher dismounted and straightened his coat. "We didn't get a chance for a proper visit my last time here. As you may have noticed,"—the man grimaced— "I'm not much of a horseman."

Russ nodded. "You're from the city then."

"Well, yes. Chicago. But I'm a quick learner, and the first thing I learned was to be specific with the stable owner as to the type of horse I require." He smiled, the action livening his thin face. "I'm Pastor Stanley Anderson." He bowed his head slightly.

Russ fingered his scars. "Russ Fields."

"Russ? I was told—"

"Nobody calls me Cyrus unless they don't know me." He'd been named after a great-uncle he'd never met. His family had always called him Russ.

"I'm pleased to meet you." The preacher tied his horse to the fence and made as if to climb over.

"I wouldn't do that—"

"Oh, it's no bother. I'm not so city-bred that I can't get my boots dirty." As Pastor Anderson's feet hit the ground, the ram's head jerked up, and twin plumes of white shot from its nostrils.

"Preacher, you'd best—"

The ram's head dropped, and it backed up, its front hoof stomping the ground.

The preacher, ignoring the beast's warning or ignorant of its meaning, approached Russ with his hand out. "I want to issue you an invitation to—"

Russ grabbed the outstretched hand and pulled the man behind him just as the ram charged. The preacher hit the ground with a sodden thump while Russ grabbed his hayfork and wielded it like a bayonet in front of the ram's face.

"Back off, you bugger, you."

The ram snorted again, backed up, and stomped its foot, its head still lowered. Jigs came tearing from around the barn, barking up a storm. That took the ram's attention from Russ and the preacher for a moment.

"You okay, preacher?"

The man rustled behind him, but Russ never took his eye off the one-hundred-eighty-pound woolly beast in front of him.

"I'm fine." The shaky voice was less than convincing. "Is that animal really so dangerous?"

"He's not much different than a bull, just shorter and woollier. Stay behind me and we'll work our way over to the fence. If I say to run, you hightail it and vault over." Sensing the man's compliance, Russ side-stepped through the mud, keeping the wheelbarrow between them and the ram.

Once the preacher was over the fence, Russ used the hayfork as a pole and vaulted over. Jigs's barking took on an urgent sharpness just before the ram hit the sturdy oak fence with a resounding crash. That was close.

The preacher's face paled under a thin coating of mud. "Yes, well. I see what you mean."

"Your next lesson, preacher, is that when a farmer tells you to stay put, you should stay put."

"Lesson learned, I assure you." The man looked at his muddied clothes. "And it appears this visit will end no better than the last, but before I return to town, please let me issue that invitation for you to join us for church next Sunday."

"I don't think so."

"If it's because of..." The preacher glanced at Russ's scars. He didn't flinch, but neither did his look linger.

"My face that frightens children?"

"I wouldn't put it that way—"

"Others have. Some that sit in your pews."

"Surely we can—"

"Good day, preacher. Save your visits for others. I won't be joining you for church. Not this Sunday. Not any Sunday."

Russ pivoted and headed for the barn. He'd been rude and he knew it. Knew his ma would have been very disappointed in him. So would Becky. His stride slowed. So would Emmie, probably. He turned to the preacher who had already mounted his horse.

"It's not your fault," Russ said. "I'd no call to be rude. But that's just the way things are."

The preacher walked his horse toward Russ. "Things can change, Mr. Fields."

"Maybe. But I wouldn't bank on it. Good day, Pastor Anderson."

His rudeness addressed, he touched the brim of his hat and entered the barn. Some things could be changed, and some things couldn't. He pulled the harness from its peg on the wall and tossed it over Goblin's back.

"Let's go to town." It was the Monday for a letter to arrive from Emmie. He hoped that hadn't changed.

"Father, it's so good to see you downstairs." Emmie rose from her chair and walked to his side. He coughed and nodded, accepting her arm of support as he wobbled. She directed him toward the chair she'd just left. He sank onto the cushion, barely causing a dent.

She blinked several times before kneeling beside him and pasting on a smile. "What can I do for you? What would you like?"

"Sunshine." He wheezed in a breath. "Would be nice."

She patted his arm. "I'll do my best, but you know sunshine is scarce in February."

He smiled, more with his eyes than his lips, and she swallowed against the pressure in her throat.

"Archie coming," he said. Full sentences had gotten more difficult for him over the past week.

"I'll leave you men to talk when he arrives. Until then, can I get you a cup of tea? Maybe one of Cook's cranberry scones?"

He nodded and patted her hand. "Tea and music."

She rose and strode from the room, fighting the urge to give in to the pressure behind her eyes. With Cook scurrying to prepare the tea, and doubtless something to tempt Father even though he wouldn't touch it, Emmie returned to the music room and settled onto her piano bench.

"What would you enjoy hearing this morning?"

He rested his head against the chair with his eyes closed and waved his hand vaguely in her direction. "You choose."

Something hopeful then. Uplifting. Perhaps a hymn.

Fingers lingering only a moment against the cool ivory, Emmie began "What a Friend We Have in Jesus." Father's eyes remained shut, but a smile tugged at the corners of his mouth.

She loved playing the hymns and had many of them committed to memory. If only their church would allow a woman to play, she'd have learned the organ as well. Becky had written of their church pianist—a young woman—who played each Sunday. She'd said her church didn't even own an organ. To be able to play such stirring music in any church would be an honor. If only.

Cook entered on the second time through the piece. Emmie nodded toward a small table, and Cook moved it next to Father before setting the tray on it. If he heard her, he showed no sign. Had he fallen asleep? Emmie let her fingers trail off on the final chord.

"Another."

So he wasn't sleeping, the old fraud. She grinned. "Only if you take a sip of tea and a pinch of whatever that is Cook left on the tray." The aroma of cinnamon added to the comfort of her favorite room.

He opened his eyes and sat up straight, raising an eyebrow at her bribery, but he took the sip and popped a bite into his mouth. Then he nodded to her and rested back against the chair while he chewed.

"Come Thou Fount of Every Blessing" spilled from her fingers to the keys. She wished—not for the first time—that she had a voice to go with her music. But she lacked any illusions on that part. Beauty came from her fingers, and never from her vocal cords or her looking glass.

"Have I walked in on church today?" Archie's voice cut through the final notes of the hymn.

Father roused a bit and dusted non-existent crumbs from his vest. "Come in." He wheezed, and Emmie shot her brother a warning look.

Archie cocked his head as if he hadn't a clue what Emmie meant. And he probably didn't. Archie had the gift of subtlety about as much as she had the gift of voice.

"I'll leave you gentlemen to your visit." She slid from the piano bench and brushed by Archie with a whispered, "Don't overtire him."

Archie's grunt was his only response. With any luck, he'd take her point to heart.

Emmie climbed the stairs to her room and removed Russ's most recent letter to read again.

This was getting out of hand. Russ leaned his elbows on the table, his forehead resting on his palms. The lingering odor of scorched bacon clung to the kitchen, a perfect match for his mood. He'd botched his dinner—again—and he'd botched this whole thing with Emmie. He was tempted to toss the blank sheet in front of him into the kitchen stove. It would burn even better than the bacon.

I pray that you remain well and happy while I eagerly await your next letter.

Your very dear friend,
Emmie Mason

His very dear friend. She had no idea what this was doing to him. Thoughts of Emmie were taking over his days. He'd even dreamed about her a few times. Every sane fiber in his body demanded that he stop writing her. He glanced at the calendar with the feed store logo at the top. Sunday. If he didn't write tonight, there'd be nothing for him to mail in the morning. He just couldn't... what?

Disappoint her?

Deprive himself?

He should. He was becoming too attached to a faceless, voiceless, distant woman who had no idea who he was. She knew he was Becky's brother, but she didn't know *him*. He wrote to her about the farm, the weather, his animals, and other things, but he avoided telling her about himself. He couldn't mention his scars, the way the distant shot of a hunter would have him diving for cover, the nights he awoke screaming names of men he could barely remember when he was awake. Names of soldiers who had died next to him on the battlefield or in the hospital.

Emmie Mason had no idea who he was... and he couldn't tell her.

The windows were dark. Russ lit the kerosene lamp on the kitchen table. The blank page still stared at him. He reached for his pen.

February 10, 1867

My Dear Miss Mason...

CHAPTER 7

February 10, 1867

My Dear Miss Mason,
   It grieves me to hear of your father's failing health. Having known this loss, you have my deepest and most sincere sympathies. There is nothing I can offer you but one piece of advice, to spend each moment that you can beside him. I know you have written of his detachment, but consider that he may be trying to save you from heartache by his actions. In truth, you will regret each moment you missed with him far more than you'll suffer from witnessing his decline.

EMMIE STOPPED READING. How perfectly Russ had summed up the situation in her home. She had longed to be by Father's side, had chafed at his preference to spend his days alone. She'd thought she was meekly submitting to his desires. What if that hadn't been his true desire at all? What if Russ was correct? What if Father was only trying to spare her emotions?

She pressed the back of her hand to her mouth. Why had she not seen his actions for what they might have been?

Please don't berate yourself for not thinking of this.

How well he knew her already.

Men rarely wish to burden their families with situations that cannot be changed. Fathers want to protect those they love, and I suspect that applies even more to a daughter. I saw my father shield both Cilla and Becky from unpleasantness on more than one occasion while not sparing either Frank or me.

Of course. Father's talk with Archie last week. Doubtless he'd spoken of things pertaining to his illness, the house, and his assets. Things he'd not mentioned to Emmie. Oh, why hadn't she thought of this?

She sighed. Because she'd been sheltered, just as Russ surmised.

On a different note, another of Becky's friends got married and moved away. She'd been the pianist at the church for the past few years. It seems impossible that Becky's friends hereabout are all married now. Time marches on, as they say.

Then it marched on without Emmie. Around her, it seemed to stand still and stagnate—she snapped her attention back to the letter in her hands.

She'd been the pianist at the church...

Did this mean that the church needed another pianist? Emmie let the letter drift onto her lap as she stared out the window, seeing nothing other than her reflection against the gray sky. Could she summon the courage to write the church and ask? No. Certainly not now. Even if she wanted to—and she did—she couldn't leave Pittsburgh. The timing was all wrong.

After Father was...

In the future, she might work up the nerve to inquire about a position somewhere else. Somewhere far from Pittsburgh's dirty streets and toxic air. The vision of rolling hills and a sky so blue it almost hurt the eyes came as her lids drifted closed.

It would never happen. How could she leave? Her brothers wouldn't allow it.

But for now, she could finish the rest of her letter and dream about better things.

The change in Father was subtle, but Emmie could see it after only two days. Russ had been correct, she was sure of it. Father had been hiding in his room to avoid her seeing his decline. He'd been surprised—not irritated—by her continued presence in his room these past two days, and he'd consented to come downstairs again. Perhaps he was done avoiding her now that she'd made a pest of herself.

Emmie walked to the bookcase in the parlor where the novels were stored. "Shall I read out something to you, Father?"

He turned his head toward her without lifting it from the high back of the chair. "Yes." A smile curved his colorless lips, but even more, a sparkle shown from his eyes.

She would be forever grateful to Russ.

"How about *Alice in Wonderland*?" She smothered a giggle at the expressive squint of his eyes. "I know, *Silas Marner*. That's much more to your liking."

He nodded. Speech took precious air from him. Emmie didn't mind his silence. It was enough to have him near. She settled on the settee and opened the book.

"'In the days when the spinning-wheels hummed busily in the farmhouses—and even great ladies, clothed in silk and thread-lace, had their toy spinning-wheels of polished oak—there might be seen, in districts far away among the lanes, or deep in the bosom of the hills, certain pallid undersized men, who, by the side of the brawny country-folk, looked like the remnants of a disinherited race.'" Even her reading directed her thoughts to the countryside.

She read until Father's breathing altered, assuring her that he slept. Then she put the book aside and slipped from the room. She entered the music room to fetch her needlework. The urge to sit and play a while rose within her, followed by wayward thoughts of being a church pianist someday. Her fingers lingered on the polished wood of her piano, but she shouldn't leave Father unattended in the parlor. He might wake and try to rise by himself. With her needlework basket over her arm, she entered the hall and heard a muffled thump.

She dashed down the hall to the parlor door. Father lay in a heap in front of his chair.

"Evans!" she yelled toward the back of the house. "Evans, come quickly!"

She rushed to Father's side. He didn't appear to be breathing. "Father." A lump in her throat the size of an egg made the word difficult to say. She pulled him into a seated position and then laid him flat on the floor as Evans arrived.

"Help me. He's not breathing."

Evans knelt and raised his master's shoulders off the floor, then gently slapped the pallid cheeks. Father gave a little gasp.

Emmie gasped as well. "Has this happened before?"

"A few times, miss."

And she hadn't known. What a useless daughter she'd been. And then when Father had needed her most, she'd panicked and called on Evans. But in the back of her mind, Russ's words about sheltering steadied her. Doubtless, Father'd never wanted her to see him this way. But she had, and she would from now on, for however long they had left together.

"Help me move him to the settee and send a message to Archie—no, to Richard." Evans gathered Father's upper body while she slipped her arms underneath his legs. He weighed almost nothing as they lifted him.

Emmie ignored the hot pressure behind her eyes. There would be time for that later.

"Father." She knelt beside the settee as Evans hurried off. "Can you hear me?" She took his hand in hers. "Give a little squeeze if you do."

The pressure on her fingers was slight, but it was there. She drew in a deep breath and held it for a moment, then let it out as her chin sank to her chest, thankful they had a little more time.

She shouldn't have left him alone, not even for a moment. Archie would be furious and call her all kinds of a fool for not insisting that Evans remain on hand. He'd be right. But she wouldn't let it happen again. Never again. She straightened and pressed Father's dry hand to her lips.

Goblin limped into town with Russ walking beside him, the empty wagon rolling behind. An early thaw's sucking mud had done its worst and partially wrenched a shoe from Goblin's back hoof. The offending shoe hung sideways, having resisted every effort of Russ's to pull it the rest of the way off. At least it hadn't cut Goblin's sole, the exposed nail ends having been pushed off to the side.

Russ led the horse straight to the farrier's shop, which sat beside the blacksmith's. Both men, brothers, stood talking outside between their shop doors. The shorter brother pushed away from the wall and approached Russ.

"What can I do for you?"

"He's half-dislodged a shoe." Russ pointed to the hoof. "I couldn't pull it free and didn't want to make it worse for the old boy." He patted Goblin's shoulder.

The farrier bent over and lifted the hoof. "Ah, that's an easy fix. No real damage done except to the shoe." He shot a glance at his brother. "I'm going to try one of those newfangled shoes on this one. What do you think?"

The blacksmith grunted and stepped into his smithy.

"Go ahead and unhitch, I'll get my tools." The farrier let the hoof down and faced Russ, averting his eyes from the left side of Russ's face to a point somewhere over his right shoulder as he walked into his shop.

Russ was used to it, but he dropped his chin and angled the damaged side of his face away. He unhooked the harness and led Goblin from the wagon.

The farrier reappeared with his hands full of tools. He picked up Goblin's hoof and secured it in the crook of his leg. "My brother can't get used to these pre-made horseshoes, but I think they are the way of the future."

"Seems like more and more things are made in the city and shipped out here to us." Russ kept his face turned away, even though the man was bent almost double as he worked to remove the damaged shoe and set the new one.

It felt strange to make small talk again. Strange and... almost normal. Like before-the-war normal. Other than speaking to Mrs. Russell at the post office once a week, and the two short visits by the preacher, it had been a long, lonely winter without Becky.

Jigs was good company, but the old dog was so hard of hearing that talking to him was a waste of time. Goblin and Song weren't much for conversation, and what Russ had to say to that nasty ram wasn't fit for anyone to hear.

The farrier crimped down the last nail tip and let go of Goblin's hoof. The horse placed it on the ground gingerly, then gave a bit of a stomp before tossing his head.

"Feel better, boy?" Russ ran his gloved hand over the animal's forehead.

"He should be fine," said the farrier. "There was no bruising to the foot."

Russ reached into his pocket and drew out a handful of coins. He paid the farrier and then hitched Goblin. Once on the wagon seat, he flicked the reins and drove to the general store. He pulled out his list and handed it to the clerk.

"We'll have your order ready in a half hour or less." The clerk said the same thing every time, but Russ knew it'd be ready in more like ten minutes. On such a nice day, he'd walk to the post office and back.

The bell jingled over the door as Russ opened it.

"Good morning, Mr. Fields. I know it's a Monday when I see you step through that door. You're here for your mail, I suppose."

"Yes, ma'am."

Mrs. Russell reached into a slot and pulled out an envelope. "And you see? I've got it right here for you."

"Thank you, ma'am." Russ took the envelope, glancing at the familiar writing.

"Faithful, she is." Mrs. Russell cocked her head in that birdlike way she had. "I dare say, maybe something wonderful will come of this."

Russ crammed the envelope into his inside coat pocket. "No, ma'am. Nothing like that."

"I don't see why not. A girl could do a lot worse, you know."

Mrs. Russell's eyesight must be failing, poor woman, and maybe her memory too. Emmie could do—would do—much better than a scarred and broken farmer. Her brothers would see to that. As they should.

"Good day, ma'am." He tipped his hat and left.

A group of five half-grown boys was hanging around Russ's wagon as he approached.

One snatched a cloth cap from his head and pointed at Russ. "Would you look at that?"

Russ stopped and dropped his chin.

"I ain't never seen anythin' as ugly as that." The largest boy, his chest puffed out, took a step toward Russ. "Looks like someone messed you up real bad."

One of the boys took a step back, a scrawny fellow not more than a dozen years old. "I seen scars like that before. He were in the war."

"A soldier, you say?" The puffed-up boy took another step closer. "He weren't very good by the looks of it."

"What are you boys doing?" The owner of the general store came out with Pastor Anderson on his heels. "Go on. Get out of here. I won't tolerate you harassing my customers." He crossed meaty arms over his broad belly.

"We ain't harassin' nobody, old man." The boy with the cap slapped it back on his head. "We're just lookin' at a side-show freak."

Some of the boys took off running, others laughed and backed away.

Pastor Anderson moved to Russ's side. "I'm sorry about this, Mr. Fields. I'm afraid we're having an issue with the youth being shipped west from the cities. I'll speak to the marshal—"

"Don't bother."

"But—"

"It's not the first time I've heard it. It won't be the last."

"But these gangs—"

"Are ignorant kids trying to make a place for themselves in the world." Russ shrugged. "I've heard similar from folks who are older and more settled. Folks who sit in your pews."

He walked past the speechless preacher and into the store to settle his bill, thankful he didn't have any more places to stop that morning.

He climbed onto his wagon and chirped to Goblin, who was more than willing to pick up the pace on the way home.

Russ patted his chest, the reassuring crinkle of the envelope a welcome sound. His only friend might be hundreds of miles away, but Mrs. Russell was right.

Emmie was faithful.

After the midday chores and a lunch of smoked ham with a wizened apple from the cellar, Russ retrieved the envelope. He slit the top open. The faint scent of something flowery emerged with the pages. He brought it to his nose and sniffed. Roses maybe. Or maybe not. He wasn't much good at telling the smell of flowers apart. But whatever it was, he liked it. He unfolded the sheets.

February 15, 1867

My Dear Mr. Fields,

His heart knocked against his ribs. Placing the letter on the table, he smoothed out the creases. Had she really written that? He rubbed his eye and looked again. The words were still there. He touched the scarred side of his face. She'd written it, but only because he hadn't told her the truth. He pushed the twinge of guilt aside and read on.

I cannot thank you enough for your last letter. You were correct about my father. Last evening when he suggested that I leave and find something else to do, I assured him that I truly wanted to stay by his side. He seemed a bit surprised, but not the least disappointed. Talking is very difficult for him, so I read to him. He

*closed his eyes, but I know he didn't sleep. It's a memory
I'll keep with me always. I cannot thank you enough.*

Warmth spread through him, the first real warmth he'd felt since the gang of young men had faced him in the muddy street that morning. Mrs. Russell's words came back to him. Maybe something wonderful could come of this, even if it wasn't the way the old postmistress thought.

Maybe it would be that he'd help his sister's dear friend through a very difficult time before she accepted a man her brothers would choose for her and move on with her life. That would be something wonderful.

But it left a hollowness in his middle.

CHAPTER 8

E MMIE PACED IN FRONT of the parlor windows, fingers worrying the
emerald pendant at her throat. She cast a glance at Father, still
napping on the chaise lounge Archie had delivered a few days ago. Not
only was it safer than the chair for Father to nap in, but the raised head
seemed to ease his breathing much more than the flat settee.

Outside, the natural gray of late February blended with Pittsburgh's
constant smoky hue. It was a wonder anyone could breathe out there.
Doctors at the hospital often had complained that air from the mills
and foundries was killing their populace.

Father had pulled their family up to the point where neither Archie
nor Richard had needed to work in the mills very long. Their jobs were
connected to the mills—as were so many in the city—but they served
in the offices and had some distance from the worst of the foul air.
Whether he realized it or not, he'd probably saved his sons from his
own fate.

How many of the mill's men had she helped nurse at the hospital?
How many times had this same fate played out before her eyes? As
much as she wanted to be here for Father, it would be so much easier
to go back to the hospital and bury herself in the work there.

Did that make her a coward or a bad daughter? What would Russ
think if he knew her feelings right now? She stopped pacing and leaned
against the window frame. He'd already told her to spend every moment she could with Father. But it was getting more difficult than she'd
thought. If only she had someone to share the burden with. Richard
and Archie came by daily now, but it wasn't the same. Watching a loved
one die—

Father's wheezing changed pitch, and she hurried to his side. He
struggled to sit up.

"Let me help you." She steadied him by his shoulders, as frail as a baby bird's.

"Drink."

She reached for a glass of water on the nearby table. "Here."

His hands shook, so she steadied the glass against his lips, their bluish tinge darker than normal. He swallowed twice, and then shook his head. His hand squeezed hers as gently as a butterfly landing on a dandelion.

"Love you, Emmie." Moisture pooled in his dark eyes.

She tried for a smile, but it wobbled, and tears weighted her lashes. "I love you too."

"Won't be long." He gasped for breath. "You'll be fine. Archie—" A wracking cough cut short his words. She watched helplessly, the weight gone from her lashes as dampness washed her cheeks. It took several moments until they both could breathe again.

"Don't speak. There's no need." She pulled her handkerchief from her sleeve and dried his tears before wiping her own.

"Archie will—" He couldn't finish.

"I know he will. I'm not worried." She was, but she'd never admit that to Father. Not when her words erased the lines across his forehead. His lids sagged. She settled him back in the chaise lounge. His fingers curled around hers.

"Love you."

His wheezing had dropped into the rhythm of sleep before she could push the words past the tangle of emotions in her throat. "I love you too."

The sharp crack of splintering wood shot across the barnyard. Russ dove behind the corner of the barn, the milk pail clattering at his feet. He pulled his legs in close to his body and slowed his breathing until he could hear the trickle of water melting off the snow on the barn's roof.

Heart galloping in his chest, he peeked around the corner. Another sharp crack, and he clapped his hands over his ears.

The acrid sting of gun smoke filled the air. Bullets whizzed overhead and slammed into the trees around him. The snap of small limbs breaking, crashing onto the forest floor. Shells exploded in the distance. Men moaning, swearing, officers yelling, the fatal scream of a horse before it went down. The sounds surrounded him. Bit into him.

Time stood still...

The cow lowed in her stall. Russ uncurled his body, each joint stiff from their time locked in that position. The air was clean and cold in his lungs. A jay scolded him from the oak tree in the yard. The ghostly pallor of a winter sun shone through a haze of high clouds. It must be mid-morning.

No war. No death. No destruction.

On shaky legs, Russ entered the barn. Song lowed again, anxious for relief from her burden of milk. A fractured stall board hung haphazardly into the center aisle of the barn. The ram stood back against the wall, a bloody smear on its forehead. The fool animal.

Russ wiped his hand across his brow. He was going to have to do something about that ram. The ewes should all be bred by now. As nasty as the animal was, Russ should do himself a favor and put a bullet between its eyes. But even the thought of picking up a gun turned his stomach. Maybe later, after this spell wore off.

Maybe.

He made sure the bucket was still clean, then poured Song's oats in the manger of the stanchion. The cow was as tame as that ram was crazy, but he still secured her before setting the bucket underneath and sliding the three-legged stool under him. He really ought to sell her. He mostly fed the milk to the pigs anyway. But Becky had loved this cow, had named her Song because of her mellow lowing.

Without anyone to turn the milk into cheese or the cream into butter, it didn't seem worth the time to milk her. He could just let her dry up and not have her bred this year. He leaned his head against her warm flank, the scent of warm milk rising from the pail. If Cilla lived closer, he'd take her the milk. They kept two cows on their farm in Iowa to feed their ever-growing brood of children.

There'd be no children here on his farm. Not unless he found someone—

He snorted. That was never going to happen. But if it could, if there were even the smallest chance, he knew who he'd want it to be. Even if a woman like her didn't know a thing about working on a farm.

February 22, 1867

My Dear Miss Mason,
I rejoice with you that your time with your father is improving. It seems our loved ones are here for only a short time. Make every memory possible to comfort you in the years ahead. Memories to share with your children and your children's children.

The wisdom of Russ's words washed over Emmie all the more in light of the afternoon's events. Archie had arrived, full of himself as always, and in his attempts to cheer Father, had instead sent the poor man into a fit of coughing from which she'd feared he would not recover. Richard was summoned and sat by Father's side now. That was the only reason she'd shut herself in her room to read Russ's letter.

She smiled at his assumption that she'd have children someday, let alone grandchildren. The list of eligible men had shrunk drastically after the war. Those who'd returned had found wives quickly and gotten on with their lives. A couple had cast glances her way, but she'd needed more time to mourn James. Or at least she'd thought so.

Maybe she just wasn't cut out for marriage.

Speaking of children, our town has been overrun by a gang of older boys. Shipped west from the cities to better themselves, they've been let loose without any real direction. They were supposed to be adopted, and maybe

*some of them were, but now they roam the streets and
back roads and are becoming a problem. Seems like the
church ought to step in and do something. Better them
than the marshal.*

The Orphan Trains were controversial, but surely the children were better off in the fresh air and open spaces of the Midwest than they were in the disease-ridden city slums. Given her choice, she knew which one she'd take.

One she still might take. The idea of being a piano player for a church somewhere had taken root. When the time was right, before Archie could foist her off on some potential husband, or before she was stuck away in Richard's attic, she'd need to explore that option more fully.

What were the chances that the church in Jonesville would still need someone? No. That was too much to hope for. Uprooting her life and moving to a new town—perhaps a whole new state—would be easier if she knew someone in that area. Russ was the only person she knew outside of Pittsburgh, other than Father's sister in Boston. Moving in with Aunt Dorcas was a less appealing option than Richard's attic. All she remembered of her aunt's two visits, the last one at least ten years ago, was that the woman looked down her nose at everything and smelled strongly of pine oil.

*The land seems on the cusp of an early spring.
The snowbanks are shrinking, and just yesterday I saw
a pair of Canada geese returning. They'll no doubt regret
their eagerness to return north when March roars in like
a lion, as it usually does around here.*

It still must look better with the rolling hills and open skies than it would here in Pittsburgh with ankle-deep slush in six shades of gray. She closed her eyes and leaned back in her chair. What might it be like?

What were the chances that she'd ever see it?

Evans had awakened Emmie shortly after dawn. Still in her nightgown and wrapper, her bare feet tucked into the chair for warmth, she ignored the open book on her lap. Father lay against his pillow, a dry husk of the vibrant man she remembered. Each breath wheezed into the otherwise silent room. She'd read aloud while Father was awake but hadn't finished the first page before he'd drifted off. The bluish tinge to his lips was more pronounced, bordering on purple. His face held no more color than the bleached linen of his nightshirt.

A commotion downstairs announced the arrival of her brothers. She'd asked Evans to hire a carriage to fetch them. Their murmured voices preceded Richard into the room. Two strides in he stopped, and Archie bumped into him from behind.

"He's worse," Richard said. It wasn't a question.

She nodded.

Archie rubbed his hand down his face then stepped around Richard, who hadn't moved. "How bad?"

"He's stopped breathing a couple of times," she said. "Then he gasps and starts again."

Richard blanched almost as white as Father. She rose and went to him, twining her fingers with his and giving a little squeeze.

"He won't rally this time, will he?" Richard whispered, which was unnecessary since Father was asleep, and even if he were awake, he knew the truth as well as they.

Her heart, already full of her own emotions, almost buckled under the added pressure of her brother's grief.

"I don't believe he will," she whispered.

Archie sank into the chair she'd left, looking years older than he had yesterday. He and Father had always been particularly close, as she imagined most fathers were with their firstborn sons.

None of them spoke for what seemed an age. Archie stayed in the chair, his head in his hands, thick tufts of hair poking between his fingers. Richard kept his grip on Emmie's hand as they stood at the foot of Father's bed.

Emmie's feet freezing, she gave Richard's hand one last squeeze. "I'll be back directly. I need to dress and put something on my feet."

"Of course."

She padded from the room and almost collided with Evans. The man closed the door and caught her arm to steady her.

"I'm sorry. I wasn't watching..." The tears she'd held onto as tightly as she could broke loose and washed her cheeks. A half-sob, half-gasp wrenched from her throat.

Evans pulled a handkerchief from his pocket and offered it to her. She buried her face in the crisp linen. He touched her shoulder, and another sob escaped into the handkerchief. Then his arm came behind her, and she was pulled against his chest, the hard vest buttons pressed against her cheek.

"There, miss. You have a good cry out here." Evans' voice pulsed against her ear. "Get it all out, now."

Words so similar to what Father might have said undid her completely. Not until both the handkerchief and his vest were damp through did she finally gain control of herself. She sniffed, coughed, and then straightened.

"Thank you—"

"No, miss. No need to thank me."

She raised her eyes to see the answering wetness in his. Father had earned more than just loyalty with Evans. Underneath the social ranks they both maintained, they were friends. Father wasn't so far removed from the working class that he ever looked down on their servants. She swiped her fingers over her cheeks and offered a wobbly smile before heading for her own room.

She washed the tears from her face and pulled on a plain dress before taming her hair into submission. Properly clad, her feet warmed by stockings and slippers, she returned to Father's room, patting Evans's arm before slipping around the door and pulling it almost shut behind her. She left it cracked open enough for Evans to listen.

Archie still sat in the chair, but Richard knelt beside the bed. The bed coverings didn't rise or fall, but the slight wheeze said Father still breathed.

Emmie crossed the room and laid a hand on each of her brothers' shoulders.

February 28, 1867

My Dear Mr. Fields,

I'm sorry this letter is so short. My father passed on to Glory this morning. Archie, Richard, and I were with him to the end. I shall be forever in your debt for your wise counsel through this most trying time. Even as my heart breaks, I know that my father loved me and am confident he knew how much I loved him. For the first time, I'm grateful for the loss of my work at the hospital. Otherwise, I might have missed out on so much. You have my undying gratitude.

Ever your friend,
Emmie Mason

Russ leaned back in his chair at the kitchen table. Their correspondence started just three months ago with the news of Becky's death. Now it was Emmie's father. Were their letters always to be filled with sadness? What was it Mrs. Russell had said about something wonderful coming from their correspondence? Not likely for the obvious reason, but what if Emmie quit writing when her situation in Pittsburgh changed? He rubbed the heel of his hand on the aching spot over his heart.

CHAPTER 9

M UD SUCKED AT HIS boots as Russ walked across the stubble-filled cornfield. He stopped and shielded his eyes from the glare of the morning sun. Sunday morning. The five miles of rolling hills between him and town blocked any chance of hearing the church bells ring. Not that he'd attend anyway, but the sound would've been nice.

It would remind him of better days. Of Ma fussing to get them all dressed in their Sunday best. Of Cilla scolding him for dragging his good shoes through the mud. Of Frank challenging him to a race for the church steps as soon as Pa parked the wagon. Of Becky perched on Pa's lap, stick-like legs poking from under her frilly Sunday dress.

Life before the war.

Did he even believe in God anymore? He squinted into the glare again. Yes. He did. Someone had set that glowing orb in the sky. Someone told the earth when to change its seasons. Three large-bellied ewes emerged from the barn and stretched after a long night's sleep. Someone prompted the animals to reproduce at the right time for maximum survival.

But did God care about humans anymore? Flashes of memories, vivid in detail and devoid of anything godly, assailed him. Men flying through the air following ear-splitting explosions. Horses plunging to the ground and pinning riders beneath. Smoke so thick he couldn't see the soldier in front of him, only the tail of the horse.

He tried to move his feet, the mud grabbing at his boots. Murky odors of decaying cornstalks dredged up more memories. Dead men laid out like logs behind tents on a muddy field. A cornfield ripped to shreds by bullets, shrapnel, and bayonets.

Heartbeat pounding in his ears, Russ pulled his feet free of the mud and stumbled toward the house. He kept his eyes fixed on the back door. Solid. Real. When his gloved hand finally grasped the metal knob, he closed his eye.

How could God still care about human beings and let all that happen?

His breathing eased and still he stood outside the door, hand gripping the doorknob. He needed to write to Emmie today or he'd miss tomorrow's post. What could he say to her? How could he offer her any comfort when he had none to give?

With her hands clenched at her waist, Emmie waited while Richard settled Fannie and the children into a hired carriage. Archie joined them at the foot of the church steps as the carriage pulled away, then the three siblings walked in silence the four blocks to her home.

Only it wasn't her home anymore.

Father had deeded the house to Archie. As hard as she tried, she couldn't keep the claws of disappointment from scratching at her. At the funeral last Monday, Archie had deemed it right and proper for them to meet and discuss their situation after church. She'd had almost a full week to trim those claws, but they had resisted.

Evans opened the door before they reached it. His normally solemn face carried deeper creases than usual. As well it should since his employment was as tenuous as her place of residence. No, that wasn't fair. Evans had been sincerely attached to Father. He grieved as much as the rest of them. She was being petty, and she hated being that way.

"Thank you, Evans." Archie handed over his overcoat and hat. "Have Cook send a tray with tea and something light to the parlor."

"Very good, sir."

Emmie slipped off her shawl and Richard his coat before they followed Archie down the hall. He led as if he had the right to... which, of course, he did.

Archie waved at them to have a seat, and Emmie's disappointment morphed into irritation. Who was he to invite her to sit in the only home she'd ever known? She clenched her teeth and dropped to the settee, earning a raised eyebrow from Richard.

She scrunched her nose at him.

He shook his head and sank gracefully onto a chair. And why not? He knew where he'd lay his head this evening. A comfort she didn't have. The irritation was turning her stomach sour.

Archie stopped in front of the fireplace, one hand on the mantel, and half-turned toward them. For someone who hadn't fought in the war, he did a fine job of playing the general.

"While we wait for some refreshment—"

Before Archie could get started, Cook pushed through the door with the tray she must have had prepared and waiting for them. They paused while she set out the tea and scones.

"Thank you. Emmie will pour for us."

Would she? She was being petty again.

At Richard's warning glance, Emmie did as Archie had decreed. She made the tea the way each one liked it. Did either even know that she preferred coffee? Probably not. Pasting on the most sugary-sweet smile she could muster, she handed both brothers their cups, then returned to her place on the settee.

Archie said, "Didn't you want—"

"No. Thank you." Emmie smoothed her dress over her knees. "I prefer coffee, actually."

Archie opened his mouth, shut it, and then took a sip of his tea before he cleared his throat. "We need to make some decisions today."

"Why?" Emmie asked.

Her brothers exchanged perplexed looks.

"We need to settle your future." Archie held up a hand when she opened her mouth. "At least, your immediate future."

"Why can't I stay here? It will take you weeks to prepare your household to move in, if that's what you intend."

Archie rocked back and forth from heels to toes. "It is."

"Then let's assume I stay here for the time being, shall we?"

"But, Emmie, you'd be here all alone." Richard's mellow voice was filled with genuine concern for his little sister.

Her heart squeezed a bit, but she pushed on. "You both know I've run the household for Father these past few years, even while working at the hospital."

"Run the household?" Archie snorted. "There's only Evans and Cook. The maid lives out and comes in three days—"

"Mrs. Coates," Emmie said.

"What?" Archie's brows rose with his voice.

"Her name is Mrs. Coates, not 'the maid.'" Honestly, how could her brother be so different from their father in this? Father always knew the names of the people who worked under his roof.

"That's neither here nor there. The fact is, there are only three servants—"

"Then I'll certainly have no trouble carrying on, will I." It wasn't a question, and she did her best to pierce Archie's skin with her stare.

Richard raised his hands. "She's right, Archie. You've weeks before you'll be ready to move your family. I trust you'd rather do that in finer weather, and I'm certain Caroline would appreciate it."

"We're just putting off the inevitable." Archie walked to the window and then swung around to face her. "I'd as soon see things settled now."

Emmie stood, raising her chin. "So would I, but as I didn't inherit the house, the least you could do is give me time to grieve and adjust."

Richard moved to her side, and together they faced their older brother, who bowed his head and plowed his fingers through his hair.

A tiny light of triumph flickered within her.

Archie drew himself up to his full height. "We both know she'd be better off married and settled in her own home."

The light sputtered and died.

Richard said, "She's welcome in my—"

"We've talked this through before," Archie said.

They had? When? Emmie's fingernails bit into her palms.

Archie folded his arms and stared at her. "I'll agree to your staying here on one condition."

"And what would that be?"

"That you consent to have dinner at my house at least once a week."

"Dinner with a side of possible husband, I presume." Her nostrils flared but she couldn't stop them. "Am I to be auctioned off to the highest bidder? Or to the one with the longest pedigree? Or will you pawn me off on the first man who agrees to take me off your hands?"

Archie's face mottled several interesting shades of red while Richard's fingers wrapped around her arm.

"You've gone too far," Richard said. "We've only your best interest at heart."

"Not every woman needs a husband."

"Respectable young women do." Archie leaned against the mantel, his head bowed. "I wish Father had taken care of this before he... But he always did indulge you."

If Father had married her off, she wouldn't be a burden to them now. She swallowed and pulled away from Richard's grasp. "How long do I have?"

"I'll tell Caroline we're moving the first week of May."

Less than two months for Emmie to build a whole new life for herself.

The smack of iron against nail echoed off the hillside as Russ stopped his hammering. Then another sound reached him. He swung his head until his eye focused on the lane behind him. A rider approaching. He snorted and tossed the hammer into the wooden toolbox at his feet. The preacher again, the only man in the area who sat a horse that poorly. Apparently, Russ hadn't made himself clear enough on their last visit. He'd do better this time.

The preacher pulled his horse to a stop near the fence where Russ stood. "Good day to you, Mr. Fields. Doing repairs, I see."

"Winter takes its toll on the fences."

"Yes, I see that. Could you use a hand?"

A second pair of hands would be welcome, but Russ doubted the preacher had ever raised a blister in his life. He'd likely be more hindrance than help.

"I'm fine. What brings you out this way?" As if he didn't know.

"Do you mind if I dismount?"

Resisting the urge to say he did, Russ nodded instead. The preacher dismounted as ungracefully as he rode, and then straightened his coat.

"Thank you. I'm making the rounds to see who in the outlying area has had trouble with the gang of boys who have been hanging around Jonesville."

"Those left by the Orphan Train?"

"The very ones."

Russ rubbed the scarred side of his face. "Not since that day in town."

"Yes, well. It appears they are starting to roam the countryside. Several women have complained of thefts of food, including eggs, meat from smokehouses, and milk taken from spring houses."

"Sounds like the boys are hungry."

The preacher smiled. "Exactly my thought. What we need is employment for these boys. A place to work for what they need." He glanced around the farm. "Perhaps—"

"I don't need any help. I'm sure you can find others who will take in a boy or two."

"Yes, well. I had hoped—"

"I suppose you had, but you're barking up the wrong tree. I keep to myself and do fine that way."

The preacher frowned and slapped the ends of the reins against his palm. "It's not good for man to be alone, to forsake meeting with others."

"Suits me fine." And he wasn't about to be pushed into doing otherwise. "I've plenty to keep me busy, so if you'll excuse me, I best get back to work."

At least the man knew when he was dismissed. He clambered onto the horse. "You're always welcome on Sunday mornings, Mr. Fields. We'd be happy to see you join us."

Russ gave a short nod and turned away. Happy to see him? Half the town crossed the street to avoid him. Most of the other half avoided making eye contact. The only one happy to see him was Mrs. Russell at the post office. He sighed.

At least Emmie was happy to receive his letters.

Cook bustled into the kitchen as Emmie pulled a bottle of milk from the icebox.

"Dear me, Miss Emmie, I'm sorry I'm so late. Let me fetch you a cup."

"I'm perfectly capable of pouring my own cup of milk." Emmie crossed to the cupboard as Cook set two full baskets on the work table near the stove. "Looks like shopping was good today."

"Yes, and I purchased something special for tonight." The old woman's eyes twinkled. "One of the farmers brought in fresh parsnips. Won't that be a treat?"

Fresh anything was a treat in the middle of March. Emmie licked her lips as she poured the milk. "I'll look forward to supper then."

The smile slipped from Cook's face, and she twisted her hands in her apron. "It's so difficult to eat when you've nobody to share the meal with."

Emmie swallowed a sip of milk before nodding. "Speaking of which, I'm to dine with Archie and Caroline tomorrow. Why don't you take the night off and visit your daughter?"

"Bless me, and wouldn't that be welcome? Thank you, miss."

Emmie nodded and turned to leave.

"I almost forgot." Cook hurried to her side. "I posted the letters you'd left in the hall and picked up the mail on my way back. You've a letter."

Careful not to snatch it out of Cook's hand, Emmie smiled and took the envelope. "Thank you, I was planning to pick it up this afternoon. You've saved me a walk."

Cook beamed at her.

Emmie left the kitchen and hurried down the hallway to the music room. She sank into her chair and pressed the envelope to her chest for a moment. The only bright spots in her life anymore were Russ's letters.

She slit the top and pulled out a single sheet.

March 10 1867

My dear Miss Mason,
I read your letter with much sorrow. The loss of a father is something we all expect to endure, and yet

knowing that doesn't make it any easier. I wish I had some pretty words or comforting thoughts to share with you, but I confess that I don't. In fact, I feel particularly inadequate while writing this letter. Forgive me for not having more to offer you.

The farm is a dreary place now as it hovers between winter and spring. I find that I can't even write about much here to cheer you. Perhaps by my next letter.

I must post this tomorrow, and I hope you are not offended by my abruptness. You are always in my thoughts, and your sorrow is my sorrow throughout the day. Just this morning I told Song how much I wished I could write you the kind of letter you no doubt need. The kind you deserve.

Your friend always,
Russ Fields

Reading through the letter again, a lump formed in her throat. This letter, so short and so devoid of joy, was nothing like the others she'd received. Perhaps Russ was too busy to pen anything longer, but it didn't seem that way. It seemed as if... as if he were melancholy.

Her sorrows were his, he said. Were her letters so lacking in joy that they were pulling him into a melancholy spirit? Her hand closed around the emerald at her throat. That wouldn't do. That wouldn't do at all. Before she wrote him in response, she must find some joy to share.

The piano beckoned her, and she moved onto its bench. Her fingers caressed the ivory as she searched her mind for the right song. The type of song to pull her out of her grief. Something fun and lively.

Her fingers pressed the opening notes of "Camptown Races." Her heart might not be into the jolly song, but her fingers were, and perhaps that would help her heart to follow.

CHAPTER 10

E MMIE STORMED THROUGH THE front door and past a round-eyed Evans. She whipped her shawl from her shoulders and pitched it at the hook on the coat tree, little caring if it made its mark or not. Only well-ingrained manners kept her from charging up the stairs in her muddy overshoes. She stopped and rested one hand against the paneled wall while tugging at her overshoe with the other.

"Is there anything I can do for you before I retire, miss?"

Since he probably wasn't willing to shoot Archie for her, she shook her head. "No. Thank you. I'm heading straight up to my room." She tossed the last muddy overshoe onto its mat.

"Very good, miss."

"Evans?"

"Yes, miss?"

She summoned a small smile. "Thank you for waiting up for me."

His chest puffed out, and he tilted his chin in a regal nod. "My pleasure, miss."

Her initial irritation drained as she climbed the stairs, turning at the top. Evans stood at the foot, waiting to extinguish the hall lamps. Archie had spoken at dinner about having gas lighting installed in the house. Plenty of homes had gas lighting in Pittsburgh, but not too many in their neighborhood. So much change.

Emmie entered her room and closed the door. She lit her oil lamp and set it on the desk. Without even changing from her finery, she plopped onto the chair and drew out a sheet of her stationery.

March 15, 1867

First Baptist Church of Jonesville, Michigan

To Whom It May Concern,

It has come to my attention that your church is in want of a pianist. I would like to apply for the position. I have played the piano for more than twelve years, including four years of study with a music tutor and two more years while attending the Young Ladies Seminary of Pittsburgh. My father has recently passed, and I find myself in need of an occupation. I am unmarried and willing to relocate. My only requirement is a safe place to live, perhaps at a local boardinghouse. It is my hope that I will hear back from you.

Sincerely yours,
Miss Emmie Mason

There. She blew across the ink to dry it and then pulled an envelope from the desk drawer. She wrote the church's name and town, folded the letter, and sealed it. She'd mail it first thing Monday. It took two or three days to reach Jonesville, depending on the trains. She'd figure a week for the church to respond since they'd need to talk about her letter among the elders. Then another two or three days for a return letter to Pittsburgh.

She slouched against the back of her chair. There was no help for it. She'd have to endure at least two more dinners with Archie and his next selections for possible husband material. If tonight was any indication, it would be two exceedingly long weeks.

What had Archie been thinking? The man he'd paraded her in front of this evening couldn't have been more repulsive to her if he'd picked his nose during dinner. On second thought... but she still couldn't imagine being married to a man who owned a tannery, had permanently stained fingers with nails bitten to the quick, and smelled of dead animals. Maybe not dead animals, but certainly the chemical fumes had clung to his clothing. Fumes that did not go well with dinner.

Archie wasn't likely to choose a man who would appeal to her. A man who worked outside in the fresh air. A man who saw the beauty in simple things around him. A man gentle enough to help a sheep deliver her lamb and strong enough to guide a plow across a field.

What would Russ say if she told him about applying for the pianist position? Oh! She clapped her hand over her mouth. What if he held a position at the church and saw her letter? Would he be surprised? Did she dare wish that he'd be pleased?

Maybe she should warn him first. She'd already posted a letter to him yesterday afternoon. If she wrote him again, he couldn't receive it until his trip to town on the twenty-fifth. Then she couldn't post her letter to the church until...

No. She couldn't wait that long. She'd just have to trust that Russ would approve of her applying to his church.

Goblin jerked up his head, his nose pointed to the barn rafters, a rear hoof held off the ground. Russ gripped the halter, even though the tall animal threatened to pull him off his feet.

"What's the matter, boy?"

The horse brought his head down almost to his chest and snorted, his eyes wide and the hoof still held aloft. Russ patted the shaggy gray neck, then side, and spoke soothingly as he worked his hand toward the hoof. Goblin leaned away when Russ cradled the hoof, but the stall wall stopped him.

"Of all the luck." Russ's breath hissed white vapor into the cold morning air.

A broken piece of wood was stuck on the bottom of Goblin's hoof, a nail head glinting in the lantern's light.

He gritted his teeth and shot a glance at the sheep pen, another board broken and hanging askew. One of the shards must have flown across the barn aisle and landed where Goblin could step on it.

The ram glared at him from the back of the pen. He should have shot that menace weeks ago.

"Easy, boy. This might sting a bit." He pulled the board and nail from the tender center of the horse's foot. Goblin jerked and quivered, but Russ kept hold of the hoof. He turned the piece of wood over and grunted. At least it wasn't a very long nail, so the puncture wasn't too deep. He pulled a hoof pick from his back pocket and cleaned the area. There was more than just the wound. The sole was bruised from the wood.

He let the foot go. Goblin held it aloft for a few moments before gingerly setting it on the ground. A snort and a head bob conveyed his thanks.

"I'll get some whiskey and pour a bit over that puncture. It'll hurt like the blazes, but it'll help it heal." He rubbed the scars on his face.

In the house, he rummaged around in a cupboard by the back door until he found the half-empty bottle. He wasn't much given to drinking, but whiskey came in handy from time to time. He'd need to pick up another bottle when he went to town next time.

Whenever that would be.

Disappointment weighed on his shoulders. There'd be no going to town today unless he walked. Five miles there and five miles back and the wind whipping up as if to blow in a new batch of snow. He pulled his muffler snug around his neck and headed toward the barn. Fetching Emmie's letter would have to wait.

From the foot of her bed, Emmie took in the contents of her room. Her curved-lidded trunk would have to hold most of her belongings, but she'd brought four large hat boxes down from the attic as well. She had two satchels she could fill with smaller things. She'd like to take her mother's trunk, but she supposed it belonged to Archie now.

Her fingers traced the edges of the emerald at her throat. She'd always have the deep green stone to remember her mother by. Not that she had any actual memories, of course. Still, it served as a connection to the woman who'd birthed her, as well as the grandmother who'd died many years ago in Ireland. Remembering Father's smile whenever he'd noticed her touching the stone was enough to make her feel loved.

A tapping on her door was followed by, "Miss?"

She pulled open the door, not worried about Evans seeing her packing. He'd think she was preparing to move in with Richard and Fanny. "Yes?"

Evans gave her a slight bow.

"Miss Edwards has come to call. I took the liberty of showing her to the music room and ordering refreshments."

"Thank you," Emmie called over her shoulder as she rushed to the stairs. She hadn't seen Helen since the funeral. They'd had time for nothing more than a quick hug.

She scurried down the stairs and to the music room, arriving out of breath. "You're here."

Helen stood from the chair she'd been seated on and laughed. "It has been a while, hasn't it?"

"A month at least." Emmie hugged her friend. "What brings you today? Not that it matters. Any time you can visit is just perfect." They sat, and Emmie all but squirmed on her chair. "Tell me all the latest news."

"I will, I promise, but first... how are you doing?" Genuine sorrow darkened the blue of her eyes.

"I'm well enough." Emmie swallowed a lump that threatened to block her throat. How she'd miss Helen. She'd love nothing better than to spill all her secrets about Russ, about the letter to the church, and about starting to pack her belongings, but something held her back. As much as Helen was an advocate for women's suffrage—she'd even spoken about studying to become a doctor herself—it might be best to keep her plans quiet. She desperately didn't want anyone, not even Helen, to have the chance to talk her out of leaving. "And I'm dying for news of the hospital."

Cook arrived with a coffee tray, and Emmie thanked her before pouring.

"I do have news that may excite you." The familiar gleam returned to Helen's eyes.

"Tell me."

"One of the night-shift assistant nurses has become engaged and plans to marry in a couple of months." Helen cocked her head and waited.

Emmie paused, then handed over a cup on its saucer. "Someone I know?"

"Emmie... are you listening?" Helen's brows drew together. "There will be an opening at the hospital when she leaves."

"Oh!" She almost dropped her cup. A way back into the hospital. But did she still want that? She gathered her bottom lip between her teeth.

"Don't tell me you've lost interest? Surely not."

"Of course I haven't." She searched for an excuse for her lack of interest. "It's just that with Father..."

Helen pressed her fingers against her lips for a moment. "I'm sorry. I shouldn't have barged in with such happy news so soon. It was thoughtless of me."

"Nothing of the sort." Emmie couldn't have her friend blaming herself for her own change of plans. "Let's start over. Tell me who it is and about the man she's to marry."

They spent the next hour and a half discussing the hospital and its employees, including some blushing admissions that Helen had caught the attention of the new doctor. Dr. Lawson may not have formed any romantic notions, but he'd requested Helen several times by name for assistance in his work.

A bubble of envy threatened to burst, but Emmie shoved it aside. As much as she'd loved her work at the hospital, her future lay elsewhere. If it landed in a certain small-town church that needed a pianist, all the better.

March 31, 1867

My dear Miss Mason,

I hope this letter finds you well. I cannot comment on the contents of your latest letter. I was unable to make the trip to town this past week. Goblin stepped on a piece of board fence that the ram had knocked loose from its pen. The wood had a short nail in it that pierced and bruised Goblin's sole. I've spent the week at home nursing his foot back to health. It's Sunday evening now, and I've just decided to write, as I'm sure Goblin will be sound enough to travel tomorrow.

It was a good week to stay home, as it happens. We had a terrific snowstorm that started Monday in the forenoon and continued until late Wednesday evening. The snow came with such wind as to be impossible to measure, creating huge drifts in some places while others were swept to bare ground. I fear I've lost a few shingles from the house that will need replacing. It was a fierce storm, and I hope the last of the season. As all farmers, I suppose, I'm eager to get into the fields and start planting.

There isn't much else to say. I look forward to finding your letter at the post office tomorrow.

Always your friend,
Russ Fields

Russ reread the letter he'd scribbled out the night before, then stuffed it in an envelope. At least Emmie would have something to open. He paused with his hand still inside his coat, envelope tucked into the inside pocket. Doubts washed over him again. What right had he to keep this correspondence going? None whatsoever. And yet, this past week, he could barely concentrate on his chores for thoughts of her letter sitting in the Jonesville Post Office. If not for the storm and then the drifts, he'd have walked to town to fetch it.

The next morning, the drive to town was uneventful. Other wagons had been on the road, probably for church yesterday, and the drifts had been broken through. Goblin didn't have to strain very hard to pull the wagon over them, and he showed not a sign of lameness.

As Russ entered the main street, a group of boys lounged at a corner, ratty clothing pulled up around their faces against the cold breeze. Only a couple of them wore hats. They were the same boys who had mocked Russ last month. The same boys the preacher had been talking about, no doubt.

He drew closer, and one of them spit into the street. One huddled against a post, his straw-colored hair uncovered and blowing in the breeze. It was the same scrawny lad who'd recognized Russ's scars as war wounds. While the rest made comments among themselves, the scrawny lad only watched as Russ's wagon passed.

Goblin stopped in front of the post office without any prompting. Perhaps Russ was becoming too predictable. He tugged off his hat and tilted his face as he entered the building.

"Mr. Fields. Oh, it's good to see you." Mrs. Russell leaned against the counter. "I've been worried, I have. If you hadn't come in today, I'd have sent someone out to check on you. That I would. It's not like you to miss a Monday. I was that worried, I was."

Heat crept up his face. "I didn't mean to cause you worry, ma'am."

She fished out an envelope from the slot behind her and used it to fan her face, as if him not coming had truly distressed her. "You living out there all alone, why, anything could happen and who'd know?"

"I'm fine, ma'am. My horse stepped on a nail and needed time to heal, that's all."

Her smile rearranged the deep grooves of her cheeks. "And you're here today, so all must be well."

"Yes, ma'am."

"Praise God for that."

He nodded and handed over the envelope, then fished coins from his pocket to cover the postage.

She gave him Emmie's letter and patted his hand. "Now, you mark my words, something good is going to come of all this letter writing." She gave a decisive nod.

He tightened down his hat as he left the building and walked into the wind. Once in the wagon and outside of town, he stopped Goblin and set the brake. He tore off his gloves and ripped open the envelope.

His stomach dropped as he plowed through her words. Her oldest brother was wasting no time in finding her a husband. The sheets fluttered, and he stuffed them back into the envelope and tucked them in his coat pocket.

Dinner with eligible young men at least once a week. The up-and-coming business types, no doubt. Smart, mannerly, poised to make their mark in the world.

Handsome.

Not a farmer with dirt under his fingernails who couldn't stand to look at himself in a mirror.

CHAPTER 11

"I PUT THE MAIL on the table in the hall, Miss Emmie." Cook looked up from her sink, half-scrubbed potato in her hand. "There are two letters for you."

Two? Emmie's heart stuttered. She dropped her dirty gardening gloves on the bench by the back door and hung her ratty old shawl on its peg, then stepped out of her muddy boots before hurrying down the hall, her stocking feet whispering against the polished wood floor.

She stared for a moment at the envelopes and their return addresses. Jonesville, Michigan, but only one had Russ's hand. The other must be from the church. Her stomach twisted between hope and dread. What if they weren't interested in her? What if they were sending her a polite refusal? What if they'd filled the position weeks ago?

She picked up the envelope as if it harbored a spider, grabbed Russ's with the other hand, and then ran upstairs to her bedroom. She wanted to be alone, unsure what the church's letter contained and her reaction to it. Seated in the chair by the window with the envelopes in her lap, she stared at the sunny daffodils she'd been loosening the soil around that morning. Like little rays of sunshine, they poked their heads through the damp earth and into the chilly air. Beacons of hope that spring was almost upon them.

Could this letter be another beacon of hope?

With fingers that trembled, she slit the envelope and removed a single sheet.

March 31, 1867

Dear Miss Mason,
    We are writing to extend you an invitation to come

and play at our church at your earliest convenience. We are still searching for a pianist who can serve our church on a long-term basis. We look forward to receiving your answer and setting up a date for your visit.

Sincerely,
Pastor Stanley Anderson and the Elders of First Baptist Church

A tempest of emotions tumbled through Emmie. She glanced at the calendar on her wall. Her next required dinner with Archie was tomorrow. With any luck, it would be her last. The trunk at the foot of her bed was half-packed. It shouldn't take long to fill it with her necessities. She wouldn't be able to take much, just a few small mementos. Her fingers curled around the emerald at her throat. Those that meant the most to her were small anyway.

She picked up the other envelope and caressed the bold letters of her name on its front. Soon, she might see the hand that had crafted them. Soon, she might see the man who had captured her heart letter by letter. Dare she hope that he felt the same? Or was she simply the silly girl Archie thought her to be?

No. She was a strong young woman willing to stake her future on her own initiative and not the wealth of her family. Surely there was merit in that. Perhaps even something more, something Russ would find admirable.

The hen squawked and ruffled her feathers as Russ shooed her away from the empty nesting box. No eggs. Again. He stood and scratched the back of his neck. This was the third time in a week. It was spring, and egg production should be increasing, not decreasing.

What was it the preacher had said about folks having stuff stolen? He suspected it was the boys from the Orphan Train. But that didn't make sense. Russ's farm being a full five miles from town, why would a group of hooligans hike all the way out here just to filch a few eggs?

He still had two dozen eggs to trade at the general store. He ought to sell half the chickens. There were too many for just him and Jigs, but somehow he couldn't bring himself to. Becky had raised this batch last spring.

Leaning against the door frame of the henhouse, he could almost see her. Blond hair escaping the kerchief on her head, apron dragging in the dust as she knelt, hand out with scratch feed in it, and circled by a flock of half-grown chicks, a smile curving her lips even as she talked to the birds.

He wiped his sleeve over his eye to erase the picture. Loneliness weighed on his shoulders for a few minutes until he pushed away from the door and entered the barn.

Goblin nickered, ready to be out of his stall.

Russ milked Song first, noting that he didn't get as much milk as normal. It had been falling off some days. Just like the egg count. Come to think of it, he seemed to be either short of eggs or milk every day. This morning, he was short on both. Hmm. He poured the milk into a can and set it on the wagon.

With smooth, practiced motions, Russ harnessed Goblin and backed him between the shafts. He climbed onto the seat and felt the front of his coat. No envelope crinkled against his chest.

"It's for the best, Goblin." The gray twitched his ears. "Her brothers want better for her than a scarred farmer who talks to his horse. And I don't blame them. A lady like her is used to servants and dinner parties and stuff we know nothing about."

He looked at his homestead. He'd purchase the shingles while in town today. The general store had had to order them in. His wasn't the only house or barn to lose a few in the storm. But other than that, the place was neat as a pin. He'd even fixed the fence where that fool ram had broken another board. He really ought to shoot that critter and get it over with. The thought of picking up his rifle... He'd have to eventually.

He'd have done it already if not for the nightmares. They'd slowed down over the months since the war ended, but picking up the gun would likely set them off again. He dreaded that more than the ram.

With a click of Russ's tongue and a gentle slap of the reins, Goblin started for town. The horse must have been feeling spring in the air, and they made good time. He was clipping past the church when someone called his name.

"Mr. Fields!"

He pulled the reins and halted the wagon at the side of the road, setting the brake. The preacher jogged in his direction. Russ squelched a sigh.

"Mr. Fields, I'm glad I happened to see you." The man puffed a moment and caught his breath. "How are you this morning?"

"Fine. What do you need?"

"Yes, well. Remember our discussion a few weeks ago about the gang of boys?"

"I do."

"One of them has gone missing."

"Missing?"

"Yes, and I believe him to be the youngest of the bunch."

"The scrawny one with hair the color of straw?"

The preacher's face brightened. "You know him?"

"No, but I've seen him around. Doesn't look like he rightly belongs with the others."

"It doesn't, and I fear they may have done him some mischief."

"Have you talked with the boys?"

The preacher took a step back and shook his head. "They aren't likely to speak with me."

"You've tried?" The ruddy hue filling the man's face answered his question. "You've been out to my farm three times now—uninvited—and you haven't tried to talk to the boys right here in town?" He didn't even try to keep the scorn from his voice.

"Yes, well. You're right, of course. It's just that..." His sentence ended with a shrug.

Russ knew what the preacher didn't say. There were some in the church who might find it unseemly that their preacher was getting involved with that gang of boys who were causing trouble and breaking laws. Might think it reflected badly on the church itself. Rumors would soon fly through the congregation. Because sure as night followed day the preacher would try to get those boys into the pews. But Russ wasn't going to make it easy for him. "What?"

After a couple of shifting steps, the preacher raised his eyes, and determination shone at him. "I believe I'll have that talk with them now."

"What about the elders? Will they back you if those boys start attending services?"

"Some of them will. Most, really."

Russ knew the ones who wouldn't. The same ones who had made him feel unwelcome. The ones whose wives had gossiped about him. They'd even badgered Becky. It was one thing to shun him, but to involve his sister—

"Would you go with me?" the preacher asked.

He pinned the man with a stare, unable to believe he'd even asked.

The preacher took a step back. "I just thought—"

"No. You didn't." Russ released the brake and snapped the reins over Goblin's rump. The startled horse practically jumped into the street.

He'd no call to take his anger out on Goblin, but today wasn't going his way. He knew the lack of a letter in his pocket was the major source of his discontent, but being reminded of the hypocrisy in the church didn't help. And knowing there was a missing boy—to go with his missing eggs and milk—only added one more burden to carry. He'd have to find that boy.

But first, he had to drive past the post office—without stopping.

Emmie entered the post office, her neatly written forwarding address in her hand—Miss Emmie Mason, Jonesville, Michigan, general delivery.

This was it. She was packed and already had her train ticket for tomorrow morning's departure. A strange little thrill passed through her, not for the first time since she'd made her plans and begun her preparation. She was going to do this. She was taking control of her life.

And she was scared to death.

Determination lifted her chin, and she stepped forward when the line moved ahead of her. Why was the post office so busy this morning? She refused to tap her foot even though her rebellious toes practically screamed for the exercise.

Then the same question that had plagued her for the past five days returned. Should she have written to Russ? Normally, she'd have posted him a letter last Friday, but she'd feared she couldn't stop herself from telling him she was coming. And she couldn't risk him wiring and telling her to stay away. If only she were more sure of his regard for her.

The bell over the door jingled.

"Emmie?"

Oh, no. The blood rushed from her face leaving a chill behind. She summoned a smile while tucking the paper she clutched into her skirt pocket and then turned.

"Hello, Archie. I'm surprised to see you here." What was he doing here? Why now? Why wasn't he at work?

He lifted an envelope. "I told Caroline I'd drop this off for her, but I'm in a hurry." He held out the envelope. "Do you mind?"

"Not at all." Relief surged through her.

He dug into his pocket, but she held out her hand. "No bother. I'll cover the postage."

His smile was brief but genuine, causing her heart—or was it her conscience?—to twist. He nodded his thanks and was gone.

Would that be the last time she ever saw him? She blinked when the closing door wavered in her vision. No, that wouldn't do. She couldn't think that way.

The lady behind her gave her a pointed look, and Emmie moved forward to keep her place in line. She pulled the paper from her pocket as well as three pennies.

The postmaster weighed the envelope and took her money before Emmie slid her paper across the counter.

"I'd like my mail forwarded to this address, please." Her last word ended with a quiver, and she cleared her throat. "Until further notice."

"Yes, miss. We can do that." He placed the paper on a ledger at his side and then waited for her to move out of the way of the next customer.

That was it. No fanfare, no questions, no fuss. There was nothing else for her to do. She thanked him and left, the little bell jingling over the door.

Did the post office in Jonesville have a little bell over its door? The thought of something so unimportant but familiar brought a moment's comfort.

She dawdled on the walk home, taking note of the spring flowers flaunting bold yellows and dashing purples. Despite the damp day and gray clouds, the delicate scent of daffodils and hyacinths carried a bit of cheer. Horses pulling work drays clomped along the cobblestones. A maid shook a rug from an upstairs window. A workman climbed a ladder onto a nearby roof.

Had Russ replaced his shingles yet?

In a couple of days... she might see for herself.

What Russ needed was a young farm dog, maybe another collie who would work the sheep. Jigs had been Becky's dog more than his, him being gone for years during the war. Jigs was still a good dog, but too old and too hard of hearing to be much help with the sheep. Russ leaned against his shovel and stared at the henhouse. If he had a good dog, he'd leave it in with the chickens at night and catch that scrawny lad who was pilfering his eggs. Jigs would likely sleep right through it.

No eggs again this morning. Not a one. That boy must be hungry to eat raw eggs. It was doubtful he had any way to cook them. The boy hadn't even owned a hat.

A hat. Hungry.

He left his shovel sticking in the half-turned garden plot and headed for the house. He rummaged around and found an old felt hat he never wore anymore. He slapped it against his leg, beating out the worst of the dust. Then he pulled a couple tins of food from his pantry, one of peas and one of salmon. He started to reach for a can of peaches but stopped. Those were his favorite. Egg thieves could make do with peas and salmon.

The chickens couldn't get into the cans, but could the boy? He picked up an old ice pick. That ought to do it. If the boy was as hungry as Russ thought, he'd find a way to make it work. Russ wasn't about to lose his only can opener.

No doubt the boy was cold too. That ragged coat he'd worn surely wasn't enough to keep him warm. Russ headed for the attic. Frank had been smaller than he, so Russ rummaged through a trunk with some of his brother's old clothing. He found a coat, not in great shape, but a far sight better than what the boy had. Holding the coat for a moment, he almost put it back. Parting with anything of Frank's hurt. It'd been almost six years ago that Frank and so many others had fallen at First Manassas. Russ pulled in a long breath, then laid the coat over his arm. His brother would have given it to the boy. Frank had been like that. Generous to a fault.

After placing the items in the henhouse, he finished turning the garden patch. Entering the barn to hang the shovel on its hook, he heard a high-pitched *baa*. The flock was outside, so he ran around the barn to the pen behind. A wobbly-legged lamb stood next to a doting mother, her tongue washing the little one as she grumbled encouragement to it. The first lamb.

Spring had officially arrived on the farm.

Russ climbed the fence to check over the newborn when the ram came around the edge of the flock. Maybe he'd wait a bit. Russ dropped to the ground outside the fence.

If he put that ram in the henhouse, he'd get the boy for sure but would probably kill him. Not to mention destroy the henhouse.

Russ glanced at the house and back to the ram. He really ought to shoot the thing before someone—him, most likely—got hurt.

He rubbed his palms on his pant legs. He'd spent more than two years on the back of a horse with a rifle in his hands. He'd shot men. Too many men. He'd had a bullet taken from his lower leg, not to mention the shrapnel that had destroyed his face. Why couldn't he shoot one nasty ram?

Because the nightmares would start again.

CHAPTER 12

T HE TRAIN CHUGGED INTO the station, steam hissing and billowing in the cool morning. Coal smoke belched black embers into the air, some settling on the platform next to Emmie. She clutched her two small satchels to her stomach to settle the doubts fluttering there. Evans's dour countenance didn't help as he stood beside her trunk and stack of hat boxes.

"It'll be all right, Evans. You'll see. Just give the note to Archie or Richard, and they won't cast any blame upon you."

"It isn't right, miss, you leaving this way." He'd said exactly the same words at least five times that morning, and the sun was barely above the houses.

She'd been right not to tell him last night. He'd have gone for one of her brothers for sure. As it was, he'd likely head straight to them the moment her foot landed on the train's step.

She pulled in a shaky breath filled with the stench of burning coal. What if one of them hired a fast horse and rode to the next station? Could they intercept her there? No. Both were at work. It would take time for Evans to reach them. Besides, even the fastest horse couldn't catch a modern locomotive.

The screech of metal against metal ended as the train came to a stop. The great iron beast spewed its passengers from several narrow doors. Oh, my. Why had she thought this would be easy? She'd never been on a train. Had never thought about what it would be like. That it would be... frightening.

"There's still time to change your mind, miss."

Evans's voice put a little starch into her back.

"No. I can do this. I must do this."

"It's not proper, miss, you traveling without a chaperone." His voice dropped to a whisper. "What will people on the train think?"

What would they think? She looked around the platform at other people waiting to board. The only other women she saw were all with men. Perhaps some were there only to see the others off. Maybe. She swallowed and held her chin high.

"They will think I am a very capable woman who can manage her own affairs."

One man nearby turned and smiled at her. Oh, why hadn't she kept her voice down? Heat flooded from her collar to her ears.

A porter came by and collected the trunk and hat boxes onto a cart. He tagged them and ripped off half the tags, handing them to Evans, who gave them to her. She ignored the raised eyebrows of the porter.

"Goodbye, Evans. I'll miss you." Pressure built in the back of her throat at the truth of her words.

He nodded, at an apparent loss for words, and blinked several times.

She put down the satchels and threw her arms around the startled butler. It took only a moment before his arms came around her.

"You'll do well, miss. I know you will."

He didn't, of course, but she loved him for saying so.

A porter shouted above the noise of the crowd. "All aboard!"

She gathered her satchels and hurried to one of the narrow doorways. With one last glance over her shoulder at the stoic butler, she climbed onto the train.

Footprints pressed into the soft earth around the henhouse. Russ bent and examined them. The boy would need a new pair of shoes soon. He opened the door. The hat, coat, and tins of food were gone, but the ice pick and eggs remained. He grunted. He'd never had eggs taken two days in a row, but the boy had come back the very next day for the hat, coat, and food. What would make the boy strike here two days in a row?

He must have seen Russ put the stuff in the henhouse yesterday.

An itch worked its way up his back and over his shoulders. The same itch that had kept him alive several times during the war. He didn't like being watched. Didn't like it at all. His fist tightened around the metal handle of the egg basket. This had gone on long enough.

He stomped outside and shouted, "Boy!" He searched the area, but the boy could be hidden behind any tree or dip in the land. "Boy! Come out where I can see you. I wouldn't have left that stuff for you if I meant you harm."

The wind rustled the willows down by the creek, but there was no sound of frogs. Not a croak. This time of year, the water's edge should be singing with frogs. He started walking in that direction. Halfway there, the fair-haired lad emerged from the trees, the old felt hat in his hands. If anything, he was even scrawnier than Russ remembered.

He stopped and waved the boy forward. The lad's shoulders dropped, and he dragged his feet, but he finally reached Russ, head bowed.

"Look up, boy." Russ made no attempt to angle the damaged side of his face away. The boy might as well know what he was getting into—or at least who he was getting into it with.

The boy raised eyes the color of a pond at twilight, somewhere between blue and gray. His face was dirty, his hair hadn't seen a comb in ages, and he smelled just slightly better than the manure pile behind the barn. He raised a hand and scratched his side. Likely covered in vermin. But he met Russ's eye straight on without flinching.

"Still hungry, boy?"

The chin dipped once in a tentative nod.

"Got a name?"

"Mickey."

"Got a last name?"

"Not that I ever knowed. The woman at the orphanage said it was Smith."

Russ grunted again. "I'll toss you a bar of soap and some clean clothes. You get yourself free of dirt and vermin, then come into the house. I'll fry some ham and eggs. I expect you'd enjoy a cooked egg about now."

The head bowed again.

Russ put his hand on the boy's shoulder. "I know what it's like to be hungry. There were times during the war when we'd get too far ahead of any supply lines. Been times I'd have sucked a raw egg if I could have found one." He gave the shoulder a gentle shake. "Being hungry isn't a crime."

"Stealin' is," came the muffled reply.

"You're right. It is. But I figure you can work off the cost of a few eggs. And the milk."

The boy raised his head again and straightened his pitifully thin shoulders. "I'll do it, sir. I don't know nothin' about farmin' nor animals or such, but I can learn. I ain't stupid."

"Never thought you were."

But Russ wasn't so sure about himself. Who was he to take on the care of this underfed, underwashed city boy?

The sun slanted its rays into the crowded train car, casting long shadows over the interior. A child cried across the aisle, its mother doing her best to shush the infant on her lap while two older children pressed against her sides. Emmie had attempted to help the woman several times, but she'd refused and pulled her children closer. Probably concerned about the moral character of a woman traveling alone.

The porter came down the aisle, the aroma of pipe smoke embedded in his coat a welcome scent. He'd watched over her as if she were his own daughter, moving several men along to different seats when they'd tried to join her.

"Next stop is Jonesville, miss."

"Thank you." She grasped the handles of her two satchels.

"It'll be a few minutes yet, but we'll stop before full dark. Is someone meeting you?"

She swallowed. "I believe so. I posted a letter with the date of my arrival, but there wasn't time for a response."

He rubbed his fingers over his graying beard. "I might be able to—"

"No, sir. You've done more than enough. I'll be fine." She hoped. But she couldn't allow this kind man to risk missing the train when it pulled out again. "I'm certain someone from the church will meet me."

He nodded, but the creases on his forehead didn't ease.

She offered her best reassuring smile as the train lurched in what she'd learned was its initial braking for a stop. They'd stopped and started at cities, towns, and tiny little villages all along the way. She knew every sound, smell, and motion involved in the process by now.

More lurching, bursts of steam, and coal smoke, with its ever-present cinders, flowed past the window. The ear-splitting squeal of metal on metal, and then the train shuddered to a complete stop.

Emmie stood, swaying for a moment as she found her balance. She'd gotten off the train at several of the longer stops, but each time she'd had to adjust to the floor under her feet not moving. It was an eerie sensation. At least she hadn't suffered from motion sickness as a few of her fellow passengers had. The humiliation of hanging over the metal railing and emptying her stomach would have been too much.

The porter came to her side. "Need help, miss?"

She shook her head. "Thank you for all you've done."

"It was my pleasure, miss. Good luck with your new position. If we should ever have a Sunday layover here, I'll come to the church to hear you play."

If they accepted her. She hadn't told him that she was here on a trial basis only. She nodded and smiled, then shook the worst of the wrinkles from her skirt before picking up her satchels and exiting the train.

The stink of coal smoke clouded the area. A wide dirt street led into the town, its wooden structures the same dull colors as Pittsburgh's brick buildings. Where were the green hills? The pretty colors of spring? The setting sun lent the only colors to be seen. She shoved aside a wave of disappointment that threatened to overwhelm her and looked closer at her surroundings.

Jonesville's train station was a wooden building in need of paint. Porters hustled to off-load trunks and crates as passengers stretched their legs on the platform or entered the station building. People waiting on the platform called and waved to those disembarking.

Oh, why had she never asked Becky what her brother looked like? Why hadn't Becky ever said or written about him that way? For the same reason she'd never shared about Richard or Archie. They were only her brothers, after all. But now she almost stamped her foot in frustration. Not that she was sure he'd meet her himself, but surely if he'd heard she was coming—

"Miss Emmie Mason?" The speaker was a younger man, tall and a bit gaunt, his drab brown hair longish at the sides of a face free of beard.

"Yes." She took a step forward, satchels clutched in front of her. From the corner of her eye, she spied the old porter, who tapped the brim of his hat before disappearing inside the train.

"I'm Pastor Stanley Anderson." The man swept his hat from his head and gave a short bow. "Welcome to Jonesville."

Relief and disappointment mingled as she gave a brief nod in return. Relief that someone had met her, especially as the train station was a healthy walk from the town proper, and disappointment that it wasn't Russ.

"Your letter arrived on Tuesday. I can't tell you how happy I am that you've come." He took her in from the top of her wilted hat to the toes of her dusty shoes. She must look a sight. "You're an answer to prayer." His smile widened.

Oh. How did one answer something like that? "I am... pleased to be here." She mustered a weary smile.

"And worn out from traveling, no doubt. I borrowed a rig to see you to Aunt Maggie's boardinghouse. You'll like Aunt Maggie. She's a dear woman and as fine a Christian as you'll find anywhere."

He was a talkative man, which probably suited a pastor. "My trunk and hat boxes are over there." She pointed to the items.

"Yes, well. I'll just load them on the rig." He had the items loaded in short order and then handed Emmie up onto the seat before joining her. The "rig" was an ancient sort of wagon, nothing like the fine carts or carriages she was used to in Pittsburgh. An old horse with a swayed back plodded forward when Pastor Anderson slapped the reins on its rump.

She steadied herself on the high, open seat. "Thank you for meeting me."

"It's my pleasure, I assure you." He pointed at the spire of a church rising from the thickening dusk. "That's First Baptist Church. I hope once you've rested, perhaps on Saturday, that you can come and play for the elders. They'd like to hear you before services begin on Sunday."

She nodded as she stared at the austere wooden building with its spire. Was Russ an elder? Probably not, being younger and unmarried. At least, all the elders in her church back in Pittsburgh had been older, most of them grandfathers.

"You've nothing to fear, I assure you. Old Mrs. Calhoun has been playing for us these past weeks. The dear woman's fingers are gnarled from rheumatism, and she can't hear much at all." He twisted on the seat to see her better. "In short, you've no competition for the position."

"Oh." Was that supposed to reassure her? It didn't. Why wouldn't any of the other local women play for them? Were the elders such a fearsome lot?

"You might wonder why we have no other pianists."

She almost jumped at his echo of her thoughts.

"The fact is, we have no piano teacher in town. I'm fairly new here myself, but it's my understanding that Mrs. Calhoun gave up teaching when her hearing faltered at least a dozen years ago."

That made sense. She relaxed a bit against the seat but said nothing. Words required more effort than she had in her. The jarring of the rig over the rutted dirt road only added to her bone-deep weariness.

They stopped in front of a two-story house with a wide porch. The whitewashed siding and lighted windows gave it a welcoming appeal.

"Here we are." He set the brake and jumped down.

An older woman in a full-length apron came out the front door. "You've fetched her then?"

"That I have, Aunt Maggie." The pastor handed her down from the seat. "Meet Miss Emmie Mason, the prospective pianist of First Baptist Church."

"Welcome, dearie. You shall call me Aunt Maggie, everyone does. My last name is O'Dell, but there're not many who remember it. I've been Aunt Maggie to the whole town for more years than I'd like to own to."

"Thank you."

"Let's whisk you right upstairs. I've saved a charming room with a view out the back. You'll have the sunrise to wake you each morning." She had Emmie's arm in her firm grip and was leading the way into the house before calling over her shoulder, "Hurry with the baggage, Pastor, this girl is dead on her feet."

Emmie smiled her gratitude. She'd had first the porter and now this woman to watch over and take care of her. Now she only had to find Russ, or better yet, for Russ to find her, before Archie and Richard could track her down.

CHAPTER 13

S UNLIGHT STREAMING INTO THE long, narrow window cut through the fog of sleep that had ensnared Emmie almost as soon as her head touched the pillow. She tried to stretch her aching muscles, but they protested each movement. Sitting up, she pushed tangled locks out of her face. What time was it? How long had she slept?

Her bare feet hit the worn wooden floor with a smack. She pulled on her dressing gown, the only thing she'd unpacked other than her nightdress before falling into bed the night before. She had one hand on the door handle when she stopped.

There was no water closet.

Instead of a short walk down the hall, she'd have to go down the stairs and out the back door to use a privy. A privy. In this day and age. She bent and spied the chamber pot under the bed, right where Aunt Maggie had said it would be. No. She wasn't going to use that.

With practiced hands—having had no maid because her father wished her to be as self-sufficient as possible for a gently-reared young woman—she fastened herself into a simple day dress still wrinkled from her trunk and fled down the stairs.

A light drizzle met her at the back door to the boardinghouse. If only she'd unpacked her overshoes. Grimacing, she stepped onto the muddy path from the house to the privy. Once inside what amounted to nothing more than an oversized packing crate, she held her breath while she finished her business.

Back in the house, her shoes scraped free of mud, and safely in her room, she peeked under the bed again. Maybe the chamber pot wasn't such a bad idea after all.

She poured water from the pitcher into the porcelain basin on the dry sink and washed off the last of the travel dirt. A long soak in a tub would be lovely, but without a proper water closet, she'd no idea how to go about it.

Her hair finally captured into some semblance of order, she descended the stairs and into the parlor Aunt Maggie had shown her the evening before.

"Ah. There you are." Aunt Maggie sat near the window. She stuck a needle into her mending and set it on the decorative side table near her chair. "Did you sleep well?"

"I did. And I fear I slept much too late."

"Only to be expected, my dear, after that long train ride. I had Penny put a breakfast plate aside for you." She lifted a little bell and gave it a shake.

Emmie took the seat across from Aunt Maggie. "What time is it?"

The old woman pointed at a tall clock across the room. "That was my grandfather's, so it's an honest-to-goodness grandfather clock." She slapped her knee and chuckled. "And it keeps time just as well as the day it was made."

Emmie almost gasped when she turned. It was after ten o'clock. Other than when she was ill, she couldn't remember having slept so late. Many of the girls she'd attended school with had talked of sleeping until noon, but Father would never have permitted her such a slovenly habit. As with the idea of a personal maid, his working-class roots had made him more pragmatic than that.

Penny—who she barely remembered meeting the night before—breezed into the parlor with a tray. She whisked the mending off with one bony elbow and slid the tray onto the little table. "There ye be. I hope you won't be disruptin' the house routine every mornin'." She bobbed a graceless curtsy. "Miss."

Emmie's face heated as her mouth dropped open, even though she hadn't a clue what to say.

"Penny, where are your manners?" Aunt Maggie's mouth firmed into a straight line. "The poor girl was on a train for a day and a half."

"Well, she's offen it now." Penny faced Emmie. "Breakfast is at six-thirty every morning. Dinner at noon. You're on your own for supper. There's cold meat and cheese in the icebox. If that ain't good enough, the cafe's open till eight." The maid shook her apron as if removing unwanted dirt, then did an abrupt turn before marching out of the room.

Aunt Maggie waved a hand at Emmie. "Don't bother about her. What she lacks in manners, she makes up for with her cooking. You won't find a better meal anywhere in town. And she supervises the day help to clean and keep the house." The old lady scooped her mending off the floor. "Under all that bluster is a heart of gold."

"I'm sure there is." That seemed to be the best answer, all things considered. Emmie uncovered the plate of biscuits and jam and a few slices of bacon. She slathered half a biscuit with the pinkish-colored jam and bit into a taste of heaven. She pressed her fingers to her lips to finish chewing and savoring the small bite.

Aunt Maggie broke into a grin. "I told you so."

"I've never tasted anything quite like it."

"The jam's her own recipe, and she'll take it to her grave, I'm sure. I'm not even allowed in the kitchen when she makes it. In my own kitchen." The old lady chuckled.

Emmie ate slowly, as she'd been taught, but she couldn't resist licking her fingers after the last morsel was swallowed. What would her father have said about that?

Someone knocked at the front door.

"Keep your britches on, I'm comin'." Penny tromped down the hall.

She came back to the parlor with Pastor Anderson in tow. "Preacher man's here to see you, ma'am."

He stepped around the little maid without so much as a raised eyebrow at her brusque manner. Apparently, everyone was used to the frizzle-haired little woman's temperament.

"Hello, Aunt Maggie." He nodded toward the old woman. "I'm actually here to see Miss Mason." He turned to Emmie. "I thought I might show you around town this afternoon if that suits you. And perhaps give you a few minutes to acquaint yourself with the church's piano. I could return to collect you at—"

Emmie stood. "Now would suit me fine. I'll run upstairs and fetch my shawl and hat."

"That's a good idea, my dear," Aunt Maggie said. "Don't let the April sunshine fool you. It's still chilly this far north."

Emmie dashed to her room and dug through her trunk for her heavy shawl. She twisted it around her shoulders before digging a straw hat with a silver bow from one of the boxes. She pinned it in place, then pinched her cheeks. The looking glass reflected a slightly disheveled person. She'd have to find out who did the ironing at the boardinghouse and get her other dresses properly pressed, but this would have to do for now.

Russ might be waiting at the church.

Russ pulled on the reins and brought Goblin to a halt. He pushed his hat back and wiped his forehead. A cool breeze bathed his face, but the sun beat down as if summer were already here. The tilled ground at his feet released its earthy fragrance as exposed worms wiggled to return to its concealing darkness. Several bold robins followed along in the plow's wake, picking up any stragglers. How many years had he and Frank followed after Pa and plucked the worms before the birds so they could spend an evening fishing?

Laughter pulled him back to the present. That fool boy was running three steps in front of the ram. Fear spiked through Russ, and he took a step toward the fence, but the boy was already there and vaulted over. Was he trying to get himself killed? The ram crashed into the bottom board, but it held firm. This time.

"Boy!"

The boy swiveled around, the laughter drying up and his shoulders drooping. "Yes, sir?"

Russ wished he knew what to do about the boy. By law, he probably belonged to someone, but Russ hadn't asked and the boy hadn't offered. Maybe it was better that way. Underfed, clothed in rags, and acting as if he'd been handled roughly, he'd tugged at Russ's sympathy.

"I told you to stay out of that pen. That ram's bad news."

The boy straightened up a bit. "I won't get catched by the likes o' him. I'm quick on my feet."

"Are you finished with the stalls?"

The boy nodded. He needed something to do. All boys needed to keep busy, but they didn't need to be worked to death.

"Fetch a bucket from the workroom in the barn. Just a small one. You can pick up worms behind me."

"Worms?" The boy's face pulled into comical lines as if he thought Russ meant to fix them for supper.

"Can't go fishing without bait."

The boy's body went tense as a bowstring. "You mean it? We gonna go fishin'?"

"Do you enjoy fishing?"

"I ain't never done it."

Never done it. The boy had to be twelve years old, maybe older. How old had he been when Pa first took him fishing? He couldn't remember. Likely Pa had toted him along before he could even walk proper, Frank running along ahead.

He snugged his hat back in place. "You fetch that bucket, and we'll see what we can do about catching our supper."

"Yes, sir!" The boy scampered into the barn.

"And stay out of the sheep pen!"

Mickey didn't slow down but acknowledged the command with a wave over his shoulder that didn't convince Russ the boy would heed him.

He flicked the reins over Goblin. "Get up there, we need some worms."

They were both hot and dirty by the time they reached the bank of the pond at the far corner of the farm. Russ showed Mickey how to bait the hook and set the bobber, then gave a flick of his wrist to put the line right where he wanted it.

"Might take you a few times to get the hang of it, but just let it rest there a bit. That's as good a spot as any."

"Yes, sir." The boy clenched the pole as if it might try to get away.

"Relax, boy."

Instead, Mickey fidgeted from foot to foot, then dropped onto the ground.

Russ sank to the grass beside him. "Something eating at you, boy?"

"My name's Mickey." His voice was low but clear. "I don't much like bein' called boy."

Russ rubbed his chin. "Been calling you that, have I?"

"Yes, sir."

He paused but had the look of someone with more to say, so Russ waited. It didn't take long.

"I only got one name to call my own, I kinda like hearin' it." The boy—Mickey—met Russ's eyes straight on without a flinch for the mangled side of his face.

Russ dropped his hand to the thin shoulder and gave a squeeze. "It's good to be proud of your name, Mickey. I'll respect that in the future. If I forget, don't be bashful about reminding me."

The pole in Mickey's hand jerked. "I got one!"

It was a small bluegill, the size Russ would normally have thrown back, but one look at the—Mickey's face, and he knew he'd be cooking that little fish for supper. He showed Mickey how to unhook it and tossed it in the bucket they'd brought.

With Mickey's line back in the water, Russ baited and set his own. He leaned back against his elbows and watched the painted cork bobber drift with the breeze.

"Sir?"

"Hm?"

"Tomorrow's Sunday, iffen I did my figurin' right."

"It is."

Silence stretched, broken only by the frogs beginning their nightly chorus. Mickey shifted around on the seat of his pants as if he'd sat on an ant hill. Russ waited. Sometimes it took a while for thoughts to become words.

"Are we agoin' to church?"

Church. The word sent a mixture of emotions through him. As a child, it had been the highlight of his week. Pa never worked on Sunday outside of caring for the stock. The family spent the whole day together. Russ saw his friends after church service, and they romped and played while the adults visited before piling in the wagons for home. But after the war...

"I don't guess so."

Mickey relaxed beside him. It appeared he wasn't the only one who wanted to avoid the church. What could have happened to the—to Mickey to cause that reaction?

"I'm sorry we couldn't be here to greet you yesterday, Miss Mason."
The rather short, rather bald, and rather rotund elder took her hand.
"But we all have businesses to run, you understand. Can't drop every-
thing and go like the pastor here."

Pastor Anderson cleared his throat. "Yes, well. Miss Mason, would
you like to play something for us?"

This was what Emmie had come for, so why was her stomach
aflutter? She knew the hymns, could play most of them from memory.
The three elderly men were watching her expectantly. It wasn't just
nerves. There was that underlying disappointment that Russ wasn't
among them. She took a deep breath. She'd just have to get over that
and do what she'd come to do.

"Do any of you have a preference?"

The tallest of the elders half-raised his hand. "I'm partial to 'Tarry
With Me.'"

It was a favorite of hers as well. She sat on the piano bench and
poised her fingers over the keys. She emptied her mind of her doubts,
and then let the song flow from her heart.

Even with several keys in need of tuning, one of them badly, the
elders murmured happily together when she let the last chord die
away.

"We'll get the piano tuned just as soon as we can, miss," said the
elder with a shock of snow-white hair above a neatly-trimmed beard.
"To tell you the truth, we never noticed it needed tuning when Mrs.
Calhoun was playing—"

The short elder's elbow connected with his side, cutting him off.

Pastor Anderson beamed at her. "That was lovely, just lovely. We
have a hymnal, of course." He reached behind her and pulled a dusty
book from a shelf on the wall. "I'll be happy to let you know which
hymns I've selected on Wednesdays, so you'll have time to practice
before Sunday service."

"Don't appear she needs much practicing," the tall elder said.

"I'd appreciate that, Pastor," she said. "I prefer to be prepared ahead of time, to give my best for the Lord."

The white-headed elder nodded. "I say we offer her the position."

"I second that motion," said the tallest elder.

"Then we're unanimous." The short elder rocked from toes to heels, his thumbs stuck in the sleeve openings of his vest. "Pastor, we have our pianist. Guess we didn't need to keep her arrival a secret after all."

"A secret?" What did they mean?

"We didn't want to get anyone's hopes up before we'd heard you play," Pastor Anderson said.

Relief poured over her. Russ wasn't here because he didn't know. "That makes perfect sense," she said around a wide grin.

She played two more hymns before the elders filed out.

Pastor Anderson saw them to the door and then faced her. "What they didn't say, and probably should have, is that the church can't pay much."

Oh, dear. What if she couldn't afford to stay?

He raised his hands, palms toward her. "Now, before you turn us down, I want to assure you that there are mothers who will pay for their children to take piano lessons. I've personally spoken to a half dozen who are interested for at least one child. And Aunt Maggie has offered you a discount on your room and board if you take the position."

"I'll have to see the figures." Because if she couldn't make her own way— These were things she should have worked out before getting on the train. Perhaps she wasn't as prepared to be on her own as she'd thought she was back in Pittsburgh. Perhaps Evans had been right to worry over her. Perhaps she should have learned more about making her own way before she'd left Pittsburgh. Father had always provided for her in every way. So much so that she'd donated her wages from the hospital to various charities. The idea that she'd ever need to provide for herself had never occurred to her back then. She clenched her emerald pendant.

"Let me walk you back to Aunt Maggie's." Pastor Anderson extended his arm. "We'll wade through the particulars. You're free to use the church to give your lessons during the week, except for Wednesday evenings, of course. We have a prayer meeting then that you're welcome to attend. But I'm sure we can get all the little details worked out."

They'd better because she'd already burned her bridges.

CHAPTER 14

E MMIE HAD A GOOD view of the congregation from her perch on the piano bench. Her fingers brushed over the keys as if on their own while she watched the people filter into the church. Most came in as couples, many with children shepherded in front of them. There were plenty of older couples too, some sitting with what must have been their grown children and grandchildren. It wasn't unlike her church back home.

Then a single man entered. It was difficult to tell his age beneath the dark beard. He was tall and lean with skin darkened by the sun even this early in the year. Surely he'd be a farmer. Her pulse increased. She had to concentrate to keep the mellow hymn she was playing at its solemn pace. Another single man entered. He was older, maybe, than the first. His dark blond hair was as shaggy as his beard, and his coat buttons strained across his middle. As she started the last hymn, another single man entered. He was as tall as the first but had a rugged look. Broad shoulders stretched his coat to its limit, and lines grooved his shaven cheeks from top to bottom. Even from her seat, his piercing blue eyes drew her attention. A formidable man. A tiny bubble of doubt crept in. Was that Russ? A small shiver worked between her shoulder blades as she finished the hymn.

Pastor Anderson stalked to the pulpit. Did pastors all learn to walk at that same stately, measured pace at seminary? He bowed his head and delivered the opening prayer, but Emmie's mind couldn't follow it. She caught a few words, but Pastor had said he'd like her at the back of the church to greet the congregation with him after service, and she couldn't help thinking about the three single men in the group. When Pastor announced the hymns they'd sing together, she almost started with the wrong one.

Wouldn't that have been a fine introduction?

With the congregational singing done, she left the bench and slid onto the empty front pew. Pastor began his sermon, and her thoughts returned to the three men. The first one was surely a farmer, or at least someone who worked outdoors. That he was more attractive than the others wasn't swaying her opinion. Much. But appearances shouldn't matter. She'd been exchanging letters with Russ for almost half a year. She knew him as well as any girl could know a suitor—not that he was—of course. Not yet. Her cheeks heated and she kept her head bowed until that feeling passed.

What would Becky have said about her sitting in church mooning over a man she'd yet to meet? The pinch of grief always present when she thought of her dear friend was even sharper here, in the very church Becky had grown up attending. She sat straighter and fixed her attention on Pastor Anderson, trying to focus on his words. At the end of the sermon, he nodded to her, and she moved to the piano again. The congregation produced a boisterous version of "All Hail the Power of Jesus' Name."

When the song ended, Pastor said, "Instead of playing while we file out today, I've asked Miss Mason to accompany me down the aisle so that you'll have a chance to greet her and welcome her to our community."

He waited for her at the head of the center aisle, and they walked together in a somewhat awkward silence to the large double doors at the back of the church.

A frail old woman approached first, clinging to the arm of a much-younger, iron-haired man.

"Miss Mason," Pastor Anderson said while the rest of the congregation hung back, "May I introduce you to our former piano player for many years, Mrs. Calhoun."

In the hush that followed, Emmie's hands were taken by a pair gnarled and spotted with age, covered with paper-thin skin. Blue eyes clouded by a milky layer peered at Emmie as Mrs. Calhoun's face crinkled into a smile. "Bless you, my girl."

"Thank you, Mrs. Calhoun."

The old woman looked at the man beside her.

"She said 'thank you,' Ma," he bellowed.

Mrs. Calhoun turned back to Emmie and gave her hands one last pat. "Bless you." Then the man helped the old woman over the threshold and outside.

"And so the torch is passed," whispered Pastor Anderson.

The congregation surged forward and the next person to greet Emmie was another older woman. "My dear, you played so well." She touched Emmie's arm and leaned in. "Such a pretty thing, too. I have a nephew..."

And so it went with person after person, a flurry of names she'd never remember. The women offered to have her for dinner some evening, to introduce her to someone they knew, to stop by for a chat. Respectful nods, murmured greetings, and touched hat brims came from the men. She listened closely to each male name, but no Russ appeared. When the line ended, she stretched forward to look around the pastor into the empty church. Surely someone was still inside?

"Are you looking for someone, Miss Mason?"

She snapped back. "No. Not at all." Was lying to a pastor a special sort of sin? If so, she'd be scorched on the spot. "I was just wondering if everyone has left."

"I'm sure you're a bit overwhelmed."

"Yes." She huffed out a small sigh. "That's it exactly."

"In that case, I'll see you back to Aunt Maggie's."

He shut the church doors and then offered her his arm. She took it, giving the building one more glance. Where was Russ? She couldn't outright ask anyone without raising eyebrows. After all, it would look as if she'd come here just to meet him. Which wasn't the... well, it wasn't the only reason.

Goblin clopped along through the fog, his hooves squishing on the soggy road. Russ stifled a yawn and glanced at the boy beside him. Mickey's shoulders hunched, he tucked his chin and hugged his arms to his sides. He was doing a pretty good impersonation of a turtle. He'd wanted to stay at the farm, but Russ didn't know enough about buying clothes to guess at sizes, and Mickey needed clothes. What wasn't stained was worn through and, even after a soaking, still smelled worse than the rags Russ kept in the barn. And Frank's things didn't fit him. A boy couldn't work if he was constantly tripping over pant legs and rolling up sleeves.

Why was Mickey so against going to town?

Russ shrugged and clicked to Goblin, who'd slowed to a walk. The gray gelding tossed his mane in protest but picked up his feet. Unlike his passenger, Russ was anxious to get to town and check the post office, where a letter should be waiting from Emmie. A letter Russ knew he shouldn't answer—but probably would. This past week, knowing she'd been disappointed by his lack of reply...

He chirped to the horse again.

Mickey slouched lower on the seat.

"You might as well tell me what this is all about," Russ said. "We're almost to town."

The boy turned his face away. "Nothin'."

"*Nothing* doesn't make a man try to fold himself in half."

Mickey straightened up a bit. "I ain't a man."

"Seems to me you're closer to than not." He cocked his head. "How old are you, anyway?"

Mickey slouched again, then cast a glance at Russ before sitting up. "Don't know."

"You got a guess, don't you?"

One shoulder lifted and fell.

"I haven't asked many questions. Don't expect you need to tell me your life story. Man's entitled to his own past." He rubbed his hand along his scars.

"The fella on the train, he said I was thirteen."

"How long ago was that?"

The shoulder lifted again, but the boy's blue eyes met his. "Been through two winters out here."

Russ nodded. "About fifteen then."

"I guess."

Russ doubted it. The orphanage probably thought if they presented the boys as older than they were, it was more likely they'd be picked up as farmhands.

"I was twenty-two when I mustered into the Seventh Michigan Cavalry, and I'd been doing a man's work for quite a few years before then." He pulled on the reins and stopped the wagon, then waited in silence.

Mickey fidgeted for a moment, then glanced at Russ. "It's that gang in town."

"They threaten you somehow?"

Mickey nodded.

"And?"

"They wanted me to steal somethin', and I wouldn't do it."

Russ nodded, keeping his face forward, not hurrying the boy even though he knew a letter was waiting for him. "You stole my eggs."

"I was hungry."

"I know. That's why I wasn't angry. But you'd have done better to come and ask for work. That's what a man would have done."

"Ain't never had a man teach me nothin' but..."

Russ waited while the fog lifted, the sun burning through the dampness. Mickey sat straight, the muscles in his jaw flexing, a sheen of moisture behind his blinking. No sense upsetting the boy over a past neither of them could change. He slapped the reins on Goblin's rump.

"I'll teach you what I can."

They rolled into town and stopped in front of the general store. Mickey sprang from the seat and hurried inside. Russ followed, casting a glance up and down the street. No sign of the gang.

He pulled a list from his pocket and slid it across the counter to the clerk. Then he cocked a thumb at Mickey. "Mickey here needs some clothes. Two sets of everything including gloves. And a sturdy pair of boots."

"But—"

Russ clamped his hand on the boy's shoulder. "You'll work it off. We'll be planting next week if the weather holds. The gloves and boots are a necessary part of the job." He nodded to the clerk. "Toss in a good pair of braces to keep his britches up. The b—Mickey's as skinny as an eel."

The clerk looked back and forth between them.

"I need to fetch a part from the blacksmith, then stop at the post office. Why don't you wait here with the wagon?" The gang wasn't likely to venture into the general store to make trouble.

Mickey nodded, hat brim flopping over his eyes.

"Pick out a new hat while you wait."

Russ strode to the smithy for the mended spade, then headed for the post office. When he stepped inside the small building, he had to squeeze to the side to shut the door. Three people stood in front of him. Mrs. Russell chatted with a lady wearing a feathered hat. The postmistress handed her a piece of paper and pen, then the lady stepped aside to write something. The next two people completed their business before the lady finished her writing, so Russ stepped forward.

"Oh dear, you're here for your mail, I suppose." The little lady wrung her hands at her waist. "I haven't a single thing for you today." The poor woman acted as if it was her fault.

He nodded to her. "Have a nice day, ma'am."

"Perhaps the mail was held up somewhere. You know those trains, always breaking down between here and there. I'm sure that was it."

"Likely you're right, ma'am." Russ tapped his hat brim before he stepped outside. A ruckus down the street caught his attention. Several of the gang stood around someone lying in the mud. He slammed the door and took off at a run.

"I've completed this—" Emmie's words were left hanging in the room as the scarred man took off down the street.

"Whatever is happening?" The old woman hurried from around the counter.

"I'm sure I don't know, he just ran—"

"Oh, those boys. Those good-for-nothing boys are at it again. The sheriff needs to do something. Something drastic. I ask you, what's a town to do when a gang of boys hangs around causing trouble?"

Emmie blinked at the skinny finger the old lady shook in her direction.

"I'm... I'm not sure." Pittsburgh had such gangs roaming their streets, but it was a big city. One avoided them by staying out of the bad parts of town. Apparently, Jonesville wasn't large enough to have separate districts.

The old lady stood beside Emmie watching the commotion through the glass in the door. The scarred man had two of the boys by the backs of their collars, toes of their shoes barely reaching the muddy street.

"I'd heard he'd taken in one of those boys." The postmistress shook her head. "I could have told him no good would come of it."

The scars were no doubt a result of the war. Emmie had seen many like it while working at the hospital. If anyone could help a boy out of a bad place, surely it was a soldier. They knew about discipline, and unruly boys needed that.

"Who is he?" she asked.

"That's Cyrus..." The old woman stood on her tiptoes and craned her neck to follow the man's movement down the street. "Very good." She gave a stiff nod. "He's taking them to the sheriff's office. Didn't I just say that's what was needed?"

"Yes, ma'am. I believe you did."

The postmistress returned behind her counter.

Emmie slid the paperwork in front of her. "I've completed this—"

The door's bell jingled, and a well-dressed man entered.

"Why, Mayor, you're early today. You're here for your mail, I suppose."

"Good morning, Mrs. Russell. Has it come in?"

"Indeed it has." The postmistress turned to Emmie and took the paperwork. "I'll check this over and, if there's a problem, I'll let you know. You're at Aunt Maggie's?"

"Yes, ma'am."

Emmie stepped onto the boardwalk. The scarred man gone, and only one boy was in sight—a lad sitting on a wagon behind a gray horse. The obvious discoloration of his face and his mud-covered clothing attested to his involvement in the fight. Why had he not been taken to the sheriff's office? Not that it was any of her business.

She'd best get back to the boardinghouse. Aunt Maggie had invited several women to tea to talk about piano lessons for their children. Emmie'd figured things out last night, and if she signed on at least four students she'd be able to remain here and support herself.

Barely.

"Where's the one they beat up?" the sheriff asked after Russ had described the ruckus he'd broken up in the street in front of the general store.

"Back on my wagon. I'll take him home and see to him."

"Should he see Doc Perkins first?"

"No." Russ ignored the sheriff's raised brow at his terse answer. "He's bruised, but nothing's broken."

The sheriff nodded. "Guess you've seen enough to know the difference."

Russ grunted, then turned to leave.

"You keeping that boy?" the sheriff asked. "There's been talk."

He stopped with his hand on the doorknob. "I hired him. Needed a hand on the farm."

"Wish I could find work for all these boys."

He straightened and met the sheriff's eyes. The man didn't flinch. "Men. They are young men. Treat them that way and they'll come around."

The sheriff rubbed his hand over his jaw, cutting a glance at the two muddied fellows behind bars. "You might have something there. Men caught in a public brawl like that... the justice of the peace would give them a few weeks in jail. I'm sure I could find them plenty to do around town to work off their time."

Russ left and made his way back to the wagon. Mickey huddled on the seat.

"Get the stuff loaded?"

"Yup."

One glance over the side confirmed it. He climbed up beside Mickey and loosed the brake. He glanced at the boy, from his muddy hair to his shoes.

"Find a pair of boots that fit?"

"Yup."

"Why aren't you wearing them?"

Mickey sighed and clenched the edge of the seat, his knuckles white even through the mud. "They took 'em."

"Who?"

"The fellas who run away."

"Well, if that don't—"

"I'll pay you back." The boy raised eyes filled with misery.

Russ felt an almost physical nudge and resisted the urge to turn and look. There wasn't anybody behind him on the wagon, but a man's conscience sometimes couldn't be ignored. He set the brake again, rested his feet on the wagon's kickboard, and dropped his elbows to his legs, reins dangling from his hands.

"Go get another pair. The exact same if they've got it."

"But—"

"Go. Man needs a pair of work boots if he's going to do a full day's labor." He met the boy's open-mouthed stare with a grin. "And I got a feeling that the fellow who stole those boots is going to be needing them." He winked. "Sheriff seems to think a bit of hard labor will do wonders to straighten that bunch out."

A slow grin spreading over his muddy face, Mickey jumped off the wagon.

Russ's grin slid away as he looked down the street at the post office. Why hadn't there been a letter from Emmie? Because he'd not written, or because her brothers had found her a husband by now? The ache in his chest was a match for the bruise on Mickey's face.

CHAPTER 15

S TRAIGHTENING THE MUSIC SHEETS, Emmie hummed to herself. The next student was due in a few minutes, her sixth and last this week. She clasped her emerald pendant and allowed herself to enjoy that thought. Six students meant not only that she could pay her rent and afford to eat, but she'd have extra money to put away for a rainy day. Money to add to what she'd brought with her from Pittsburgh. There would be no need to return to Richard or—no, never Archie. She'd starve first.

She grimaced and let go of the pendant. It was all well and good to think such things when her belly was full and she had a roof over her head.

The church door creaked open, and a boy entered, followed by a woman with fiery hair and the pale complexion of so many red-haired women. They approached the piano at the front of the church where Emmie stood.

"Are you Miss Mason?" the woman asked.

"I am. And this must be Robbie McCann."

"Yes, miss." The dark-haired boy crossed his arms over his chest, his lips in a firm line.

"I'm Alannah McCann, Robbie's aunt. He lives with us." She jostled the toddler on her hip. "This is Alice, and the one behind me is Stewie." An adorable dark-eyed boy peeked around at her.

"It's nice to meet you all." Emmie focused on Robbie. "Why do you want to learn to play the piano?"

"I don't."

His aunt bumped his shoulder and frowned at him. "Mind your manners."

"I don't, miss."

"Is it because you think playing the piano is for women?" She'd already heard that from several other students. A regional difference from Pittsburgh, for sure.

He nodded, his mulish expression doing nothing to hide a charming dimple on his cheek.

"I see." She stood and walked to the piano to fetch a hymnal. "How old are you?"

"Almost thirteen."

She widened her eyes to feign surprise. "Is that so? I would have said you looked a year or two older."

His aunt turned her head, but not before Emmie caught sight of a smile. Good. She was on the right track then. She opened the hymnal.

"What's your favorite hymn?"

He crinkled his brow for a moment. "I don't know, maybe 'The Solid Rock.'"

She opened to the page of that song and held it out to him. "Tell me who wrote it."

He leaned over the page. "Edward Mote."

"Do you have another favorite?"

He shifted his feet. "At Christmas, I like 'Joy to the World.'"

"That's one of my favorites too." She flipped to the page and held the book out. "Who wrote that one?"

"Isaac Watts."

"Do you have another?"

He shrugged and glanced at his aunt. "I suppose if I do, it'll be written by some other fellow."

His aunt nodded. Robbie's shoulders sagged in defeat. Emmie stifled the urge to grin. He wasn't the first reluctant boy she'd taught the piano. She'd taught lessons the two years she'd lived at the Young Ladies Seminary. She'd also taught Becky to play. If only Becky were still here...

"I only came to meet you, Miss Mason," Mrs. McCann said, "because I wasn't able to attend the tea on Monday. Robbie can make his own way to and from lessons from now on."

"I'm glad you came. I don't know many people yet."

"We haven't lived here very long either. My husband took the job as station manager for the railroad last year. If you need anything, don't hesitate to call. We live on Fayette Street. It's only two blocks from Aunt Maggie's."

"Thank you."

Mrs. McCann strode toward the door, turned, and waved before she walked out. Before Emmie could fully savor that offer of friendship, something crashed behind her.

"I'm sorry, miss. I backed into it."

The piano bench had spewed its contents across the polished wood floor. Robbie's chin hung to his thin chest while he stared at his feet. Large feet he obviously hadn't grown into yet.

"It was an accident." She gave his shoulder a light squeeze. "Let's right it and get started, shall we?"

They lifted the bench, and she did her best not to wince at the cracked corner of the seat. It was just a bench, after all, but would the elders rethink her giving lessons here in the church now?

And if they did... how would she earn enough money to stay?

Another Sunday morning service and no Russ. Where was he? She knew him to be a church-going man. After all, Becky had shared plenty of stories about her family's Sundays before the war and... oh. She shifted on the settee in Aunt Maggie's parlor. What if he'd stopped going after the war?

Memories of men in the hospital filled her. Men who believed that no God would have let what they'd seen happen. A stark contrast to other men who had found God on the battlefield.

"I say, are you listening to me, Emmie?" Aunt Maggie's sharp question broke through her thoughts.

"Yes, ma'am. That is, I was distracted for a moment." Heat climbed from her collar to her ears.

The old woman's wrinkles relaxed into a smile beneath her rather fierce eyebrows. "Daydreaming, no doubt. What young woman doesn't? Especially on a pleasant Sunday afternoon."

"Yes, ma'am, that's what happened."

Aunt Maggie leaned closer, excluding the room's four male occupants from her whispered, "Dare I hope that our handsome and very single Pastor Anderson took part in your daydreams?"

Emmie straightened and leaned away from her landlady's knowing expression.

"No, ma'am. Nothing like that."

Aunt Maggie gave a huff and sat back. "I don't see why not. It would be an advantageous match, our pastor married to our piano player." A crisp nod accented her words. "Most advantageous."

To whom? Emmie gathered the thought before it could escape her lips. The town might be advantaged by such a union, but not her. Not when her heart belonged elsewhere.

Russ, where are you?

How could she inquire without looking the fool, or worse, the harlot? She'd been over her options a hundred times. She'd almost inquired about Becky, but it would have been dishonest to pretend she didn't know of her friend's death. What if Russ found out later that she'd used some sort of subterfuge to find him?

Of course, that wouldn't be an issue if she never discovered his whereabouts.

Maybe she could speak with Alannah McCann about it. She'd come up to Emmie after services and told her that Robbie had returned from his lesson in a better frame of mind about learning to play the piano. They'd chatted for a while, and she'd met Mr. McCann.

But somehow speaking with Mrs. McCann about Russ didn't sit well either. What if she got the wrong impression about Emmie and her move to Jonesville? No. That wouldn't do. She'd need to come up with something else.

At least she could check at the post office again tomorrow. Russ's letters often mentioned his Monday trips to town. After the kerfuffle in the street last week that had drawn the sheriff's attention, she'd hurried back to the boardinghouse. Surely tomorrow she could invent some honest and worthy reason to hang around the post office and general store. Perhaps she'd have a letter from Russ that she read on the bench outside the post office. While keeping one eye on the people walking around town.

"Aunt Maggie," one of the gentleman boarders said. "Is music on a Sunday against your house rules?"

The woman's eyebrows drew together for a moment as she looked at Emmie. "I see no reason not to enjoy music on a Sunday, providing it honors the Lord."

"Some hymns then?" he asked.

The men standing at the opposite end of the parlor nodded toward Emmie. She smiled and moved to the piano in the corner behind her. That was what she needed, music to take her mind off of everything else for a while.

"Hurry up, Mickey," Russ yelled at the barn. That boy was dragging his feet as if they were going to his lynching. He blew out a breath and stopped fiddling with Goblin's reins. He couldn't blame the boy, considering his face was still discolored from last week's beating. After all, he knew enough about people staring and making judgments based on one's looks.

If Russ were being fully honest with himself, it wasn't the boy's tardiness that had him on edge anyway. It was going to the post office knowing there wouldn't be a letter. Not from anyone who mattered. His fingers pressed against his coat pocket. Nothing crinkled within. Should he have broken the silence? Should he have written, even knowing that her brothers were looking for a husband for her? No. How would he feel if he found out his future bride was keeping correspondence with another man? Not that he had the chance of a future bride.

Mickey appeared at the barn entrance. "I don't see why—"

"Get in the wagon."

The boy slunk over and climbed onto the seat beside him.

Russ slapped the reins on Goblin's rump and they jerked into motion, birdsong and the chink of horseshoes striking rocks breaking the silence between them. The boy wasn't much for small talk and neither was he, but the sullenness of Mickey's silence bothered him this morning.

"You said we didn't need much from town," Mickey said. "Why pull the wagon in? Why not just ride to town and back? It'd be faster."

Maybe the sullen silence was better after all.

Russ rubbed the scars on his face. The boy'd been with him for about ten days, and still Russ knew nothing about his background. And he had no hankering to share much of his own, either. He'd stopped riding the day he boarded the train home from the war, and he never intended to climb on a horse again.

"Never know. There might be something at the general store I want that's too big to bring home on horseback."

Silence settled back over them for a mile or so.

"I wish I could learn to ride," Mickey said.

Russ flinched, and the boy must have noticed, because he turned toward him.

"I ain't seen a saddle around nowhere."

Nor would he. "Don't have one."

Mickey slouched against the back of the seat.

Why didn't a boy his age know how to ride? Russ remembered sitting on his pa's plow horse, hanging onto the knobs of its work collar while Pa walked behind the plow. He'd practically grown up on the back of a horse. And look where that had gotten him. Flashes of battle scenes danced in front of his eyes, the scream of horses being hit, the stench of gunpowder so thick he could taste it. He pulled Goblin to a halt with hands that shook. Something moved behind a row of trees, and he pulled the boy behind him.

"Hey!" Mickey squawked.

The high-pitched shout shook Russ out of the memory. He looked at the boy, whose blue-gray eyes threatened to swallow his narrow face. Russ swung back to face the trees that lined the shallow creek. A deer flicked her tail once, twice, and then bounded away with her tail high in the air.

A deer. Just a deer. Not a Johnny Reb.

Russ let the boy go.

Mickey slid to the far side of the bench seat. "You okay?"

He must look a sight if he'd rattled the boy that badly. He sucked in a couple of deep breaths and nodded toward the creek.

"That deer startled me."

Mickey half turned to where the deer had disappeared into the brush, keeping one eye on Russ.

He'd have to tell the boy something. Normal people didn't act like that. But then, it wasn't a normal person who'd taken him in. He dragged off his hat and wiped his forehead with his sleeve before pulling the hat back low over his brow.

"Sometimes things bring on the memories." How could he explain it so that a fresh-faced boy who'd never seen war would understand?

But the boy nodded. "I know."

Russ shook his head, but Mickey grabbed his sleeve.

"I do. Sometimes I remember the night my ma was killed and it... it..." He hung his head.

How had his ma been killed? The boy must have witnessed it. How old would he have been? Well, if the boy wanted him to know more, he'd tell him.

Russ grabbed the boy's far shoulder and pulled him closer. "Yeah. Like that."

Mickey didn't move away. Russ gave the bony shoulder one last squeeze and then picked up the reins he'd dropped when he grabbed Mickey and blocked him from the... deer.

It'd been a deer. Nothing but a deer.

He slapped the reins, and Goblin jerked his head up from the grass beside the road. At least the horse had enjoyed their unexpected stop.

Silence returned for the rest of their ride, but it was a more comfortable silence now.

Russ pulled up to the post office first. Might as well get it over with.

"Good morning, Mr. Fields." Mrs. Russell viewed him from her perch on a tall stool behind the counter. "You're here for your mail, I suppose."

Just like every Monday morning. Mrs. Russell was as regular as a stout cup of coffee. "Yes, ma'am."

"I have a letter for you." Her wrinkles pulled into solemn lines. "Not the one you're looking for, I'm afraid." She handed over an envelope addressed with a bold hand. The return address was from the farming cooperative. No doubt with arrangements to pick up his sheared wool. Nothing to lift his spirits as Emmie's letters had. He tucked it in his pocket.

"Thank you."

"Have you heard about the new pianist at church?"

"No, ma'am. I haven't." And he didn't care to.

"Such a talented young thing. Single, too. Not a striking-looking woman, but one can hear her sweet spirit through her music." She blinked up at him.

He nodded, unsure what she expected him to say.

"Someone to keep in mind should the letters have stopped." Her gray head tilted, rather like a chicken eyeing a fat worm.

He backed toward the door. "Good day, ma'am." Then he fled for the wagon.

Of all the days to oversleep, why did she have to do it today? Emmie hurried along the dusty back streets, a letter to Helen in her grasp. She knew why she'd overslept. She'd lain awake half the night debating a letter to Russ. The thought that he knew she was here and was purposely avoiding her had taken root and refused to budge, no matter how many ways she tried to dislodge it. The church's new female pianist, who was single, no matter how plain, would of course be the gossip of a town as small as this. He must have heard.

Her only hope that it wasn't true was clinging to the fact that he didn't live in town and, it being spring, may have been too busy on the farm to come in for his usual once-a-week trip. She didn't know the first thing about farming, but even a ninny knew that crops were planted in the spring and harvested in the fall. And she was no ninny.

She squared her shoulders as she rounded a corner of the main street and stepped onto the boardwalk. If no letter from Russ awaited her today, she'd write to him. That very evening. She'd mail it tomorrow and... her steps faltered. How could she mail it from this post office? The postmistress, while a very pleasant elderly lady, would surely recognize her handwriting when she handed it over. She'd know that it was Emmie who had written to Russ so often in the past months.

Emmie stopped a few shops down from the post office. A wagon with a gray horse hitched to it and a stripling boy slouched on the seat was parked outside the post office. Wasn't that the same wagon that had been in front of the general store last week? Last Monday? Could it be?

Her heart hitched, and she clutched her letter to her waist. Why hadn't she seen the owner last week? The boys fighting in the street had distracted her, even frightened her a little. She hadn't thought to look closely at the farm wagon. Surely that's what this was, a farm wagon. Wasn't it?

Hurrying along the boardwalk, she had almost reached the door when a man exited. His strong profile was shaded by the large-brimmed hat he had pulled low across his brow. He half-turned toward her, and she slowed. The left side of his face was scarred in a manner that left no doubt he'd served in the war. He was the same man who'd been here when the ruckus in the street had started. He'd run into the fray to stop the fighting. As any soldier would.

But he wasn't Russ. The postmistress had called him Cyrus.

CHAPTER 16

N O WEEK SHOULD'VE SPAWNED as many problems as the past week had managed. Russ leaned his elbows on the kitchen table with a groan. He sank his forehead into his palms and breathed deeply of brewing coffee and sizzling bacon. The comforting scents didn't help.

Some critter with four legs instead of two had gotten into his hen-house, killed two of his best layers, and frightened the rest enough that eggs had been scarce all week. The ram had broken through a spot in the fence, and half a dozen of the ewes with their lambs had followed him out. It'd taken him, Mickey, and Jigs the better part of Wednesday to flush them from the thickets along the creek and herd them home. He really needed a young dog. Jigs had barely been able to rise the next morning.

Mickey'd whacked his thumb with a hammer while fixing the fence. He'd been doing chores mostly one-handed since, but at least it wasn't broken. And as if that weren't enough, right before dusk last night on the backside of the cornfield, the plow had broken. One of the braces between the handle and beam had snapped. There was no way to repair it, so if the blacksmith didn't have a spare, Russ would have to fashion a new brace from one of the hickory branches stored in the barn. Time spent that he didn't have if he were going to get his crops in on time.

The fact that he hadn't heard from Emmie since the beginning of the month... facing adversity with a heavy heart didn't help.

Hadn't he had enough troubles for one man?

He growled low in his throat. Feeling sorry for himself wasn't going to fix the plow, catch the critter, shoot the ram, plant his fields, or summon a letter from Emmie.

Mickey came into the kitchen, his hair standing at odd angles around his face. The lingering yellow of his bruises accented the lean lines of his jaw. The boy had filled out some in the two weeks he'd been eating regular meals at Russ's table.

Scorching bacon shot Russ to his feet. He grabbed a towel and pulled the hot pan away from the stove.

"It's ready."

The boy's eyebrows wrinkled in a dubious frown. "Burnt again?"

Russ shrugged. "Never said I was much of a cook, but it fills your belly."

Mickey grabbed clean plates off the shelf and slid them onto the table. Russ filled two cups with coffee, then grabbed their last loaf of bread. It was almost as dry as a cracker, but they'd get fresh in town tomorrow.

He sat and then broke a piece of the bread and handed it to Mickey. "Been some week."

The boy slid a few pieces of slightly charred bacon onto his plate and rubbed the bread in its trail of grease. "Makes ya wonder if God's got it out for us, don't it?"

Russ stopped mid-chew. Did it? Was that what all this was about? He slurped some coffee to wash down the mouthful. "You think so?"

Mickey nodded. "I reckon. I ain't never been good enough for God to pay no attention to, what with my ma earnin' her money like she did and all." His eyes, round and uncertain, met Russ's.

So that was it. "I was told that God doesn't hold our family against us. Preacher said that once."

"You figger it were true?"

"Got no reason not to."

Hope warred with skepticism on the boy's face.

Russ chewed another mouthful, then swallowed. "Ever been to church?"

Mickey jerked. "No. Never." He pushed his half-finished meal away. "Not no place for the likes of me."

Russ pushed his plate away too. Nobody should feel like that. But didn't the boy echo his own thoughts about church since returning from the war? Yes, but that was different. He'd been through something the people in those pews couldn't understand. Mickey, he'd... what? Been raised in a way the people in those pews couldn't understand.

Maybe it was time they did.

The sun poured over the horizon outside the window. Sunday morning. He might not go to church, but not because he'd turned his back on God. It was God's people who'd turned their backs on him. Yet there sat Mickey, his arms crossed, looking down at his lap as if he'd turtle in on himself again.

Russ remembered being Mickey's age. There were good lessons to be learned in church. Things a boy ought to know about living life right, keeping your nose clean, and treating folks with respect. And plenty more things a war-weary soldier couldn't explain very well.

"Pull on your cleanest clothes and find a comb for your hair."

"Huh?"

"We're going to church."

"We ain't."

"We are."

"Why?"

"Because I said so."

"I don't want to."

Neither did Russ. But deep inside, he knew it was the right thing to do. For the boy for sure... and it was probably time he faced the townspeople again. He wouldn't be a good example to Mickey until he did.

The piano keys beneath her fingers were cool and smooth, a comforting contrast to the uproar in her thoughts. She'd been in Jonesville for almost three weeks and was no closer to finding Russ. Playing hymns she knew by heart left her free to glance over each person who entered the church. Alannah McCann smiled and nodded after she took her seat. Emmic responded in kind, her fingers never pausing, the music never wavering.

But it wasn't filling her soul like it usually did. The man in the blue jacket, had he been there before? Yes, she recognized his wife beside him although she couldn't remember a name. And that fellow in the back, shadowed between the windows, could he be new? She tried not to stare, but when he moved, his sheriff's badge glinted in the light. The rest of the congregation looked familiar, although she couldn't claim to know more than a dozen names. She let the final chord die away.

Pastor Anderson approached the pulpit. Movement caught her eye. It was the scarred man from the post office and the skinny boy from the wagon. A father and son, no doubt. She bowed her head while the pastor prayed, but she asked for wisdom and courage instead of listening to his prayers.

She intended to learn the whereabouts of Russ's farm today. Exactly how hadn't come to her yet, so she added an extra thought onto her prayer. To have Russ so close and not be able to see him... it was getting ridiculous. Maybe he didn't want to meet her in person, but she was going forward with her plan anyway. If he spurned her, she'd drive back to town and no one would be the wiser.

After all, how hard could it be to drive a single buggy?

The sermon came from the Book of Ruth. Could that be a sign? It had been Ruth's determination to be noticed by Boaz that landed her a husband. A husband. Emmie bowed her head to hide the wash of heat across her face. She was getting too far ahead of herself. But there'd be no chance of anything if she didn't meet the man.

Back in her dresser, tied with a ribbon, was the stack of letters that had come to mean so much to her. Letters written by a man of compassion and wisdom. A man willing to share in her grief. The exact type of man she could see herself with years in the future. But still a man without a face.

Would it bother him that she was so plain? It hadn't seemed to put off any of the men Archie had paraded in front of her, but then, they were doubtlessly looking at the size of her dowry rather than her too-long nose or too-narrow mouth. Archie would've settled a tidy sum on her.

There'd be no dowry now. Her brother was probably furious.

She almost missed her cue to return to the piano for the closing hymn. Pastor walked down the aisle as the congregation sang. He'd greet everyone at the door as they left, but she wasn't expected to join him since she'd already shaken hands with everyone the past two Sundays. The music died away, and a subdued chatter began as neighbors greeted neighbors.

Emmie wove between people until she reached Mrs. McCann's side near the door. Pastor Anderson was shaking hands with the scarred man, who kept his head down and tilted. What a shame that he felt the need to hide his deformities. Perhaps, once they were introduced, she could share with him some of what Helen had told her about the great work being done with the new technique called plastic surgery.

"Another morning of beautiful music," Mrs. McCann said.

"Thank you. I enjoy playing."

"It shows," her husband said as he drew his wife's hand into the crook of his arm. "Have we thanked you enough for coming and rescuing us from Mrs. Calhoun's playing?"

"Stewart." Mrs. McCann poked him in the ribs. "Behave yourself."

His grin lacked even a touch of contriteness. "Isn't that why you've insisted that Robbie play? To spare us another round of Mrs. Calhoun should someone come and sweep the lovely Miss Mason off her feet and out of our church?"

"Stuff and nonsense, and don't you dare embarrass Miss Mason." She turned back to Emmie. "Please say you'll come back to the house with us for dinner. I promise to make Stewart behave." Her eyes sparkled with genuine friendship and good humor.

And maybe Emmie'd find a way to ask after the whereabouts of Russ's farm during the conversation.

"I'd love to."

After he finally extracted his hand from the preacher's, Russ moved into the yard and toward his wagon. Mickey strode beside him. They probably looked like a pair of rats scuttling from a burning ship.

"Whoa, there, son." Old Jack stepped out from behind his wagon, which was parked next to Russ's. "What's the rush?"

Russ slowed to a stop and shook the old man's hand. "No real rush other than filling our bellies."

"Who's the youngun?"

"Mickey. He works for me now."

"That's a fine thing." The old man eyed the boy up and down. "Not much meat on his bones, but them wiry ones can get a lot done betwixt sunup and sundown."

"Yes, sir. He's learning fast."

"How's that ram done for you?"

How honest should he be? He hated to cast a bad light on the old man's bloodstock.

"Meaner than sin," Mickey piped up. "Um, sir."

A belly laugh was the last thing Russ had expected. "The best of 'em always are, and that's a fact. How do his lambs look?"

"No complaint there," Russ said. "We're almost done lambing, and this crop is as good as any year's I've seen."

The old man thumped him on the shoulder. "What'd I tell you?"

"You were right, sir."

"Good to see you here again, son. Your ma and pa would be pleased."

"Yes, sir." He couldn't argue with that.

"Saw the preacher about wring yer hand from yer arm. He's a good one, though. Him and that new piano player. She ain't much of a looker, but she can sure play."

Russ rubbed the back of his neck. "Reminded me of Becky."

The old man nodded.

They stood in silence for a moment, that awkward kind of silence that follows the mention of someone who'd died.

Mickey's stomach rumbled.

"I guess I better get the boy home and fill him up. It was good seeing you, Mr. Keen."

"Likewise, son. Until next week." The old man touched the brim of his hat and climbed onto his wagon.

Russ untied Goblin and backed him away from the hitching rail before taking his seat next to Mickey. They wove through the other wagons, buggies, and people walking. The new pianist walked out of the church with the fellow who'd taken over at the train depot and his wife.

Black hair gathered in the back, a wide forehead, and a small, rounded chin. She was a dainty little thing. She glanced at him as they passed. Eyes the same color as the inside of a black-eyed Susan met his without flinching.

He'd seen her before.

She smiled, and he snapped his attention to the road before him. Caught gawking like a gangly boy at his first dance, but she hadn't turned away from his scars. Heat that had nothing to do with the midday sun warmed his face.

"She don't look so plain to me," Mickey said, twisting in the seat to get a better look.

"Don't stare. It's rude."

"But—"

Russ glared at the boy, and Mickey slouched back into his sullen pose. Which was just fine. Better not to think of things like ladies who played the piano.

Like Emmie.

"Whatever brought you all the way to Jonesville from Pittsburgh?" Mrs. McCann asked as she set a slice of rhubarb pie in front of Emmie.

It was a question she'd been asked almost daily since her arrival, and it no longer made her nervous. She'd perfected her speech.

"My father passed away, and I needed an occupation. When I heard about the opening at the church, I had to apply." The dinner all but over, it was time to shift the conversation to the whereabouts of Russ's farm. "I was somewhat familiar with this area."

"You were?" Mr. McCann asked, a forkful of pie suspended between plate and mouth.

"Yes, you see, my roommate at school was from here."

Mrs. McCann resumed her seat once everyone had their pie. "I haven't heard anyone mention knowing you. Who was your room-mate?"

"Becky Fields."

"Oh." Mrs. McCann sighed. "I'm sorry. We didn't know her well. She passed away just a few months after we arrived, but she seemed a wonderful young woman."

"She was." Emmie swallowed and dabbed a napkin to her lips, both to subdue the urge for tears and to gather her courage. "I never was able to visit, with my father's lingering illness, but I'd love to see the farm she wrote me about so often."

"It's easy to find," Mr. McCann said. "It's northeast of town on the Chicago Road. Not an overly large farm, but well placed and with a nice stream running through it."

"So says the man who was raised on a vast plantation in Virginia." Mrs. McCann shot her husband a fond glance. "We drove the Chicago Road last fall when the colors were peak. Mr. Field's farm is a beautiful place. We turned around shortly after passing it. What was it, Stewart, five miles?"

"Something like that."

"I suppose there are many such farms out that way." Emmie did her best to sound nonchalant.

"Not so many as you'd think," he said. "I believe the Fields' farm is flanked by state-owned land both behind and to the east."

"That's why we turned around, wasn't it? There were no more farms past there," Alannah said.

He nodded.

Chicago Road to the east to the last farm. Even a city girl like Emmie could find the place with those simple instructions. She'd visit the livery on West Street tomorrow and see about hiring a horse and buggy. She pressed her hand against the base of her throat, where a knot of nerves had gathered.

Tomorrow, she and Russ might finally come face to face.

CHAPTER 17

E MMIE PICKED UP THE reins and smiled at the liveryman. "I'll be fine."
Nothing was going to deter her after waiting three whole days for
the rain to quit. She had no piano students today. It was her last chance
to make the trip this week.

"Miss, wait a minute." The liveryman leaned forward and took the
reins, then laid them across her gloved hands. "You had 'em crossed.
The horse weren't gonna know what you wanted of him."

"Yes, of course. Thank you." He must think her a total incompetent.
Which she might very well be, and for a brief moment she wished she'd
asked Mrs. McCann to accompany her.

"He's a gentle one, miss, but any horse can get headstrong if they
think you're not in charge. Keep a steady hand on them reins. Just give
a tug on the right one to turn right, left one to turn left. Haul back on
the pair and he'll stop."

"Yes, I understand." She sat straighter. "Let's go, horse."

The large red animal swiveled an ear but otherwise ignored her.

"I said, let's go." She jiggled the reins in her hand.

Nothing.

Something like a smirk ticked at the corner of the liveryman's
mouth. "Miss, he ain't gonna move till you slap them reins on his rump.
Give him a good smack."

She frowned at the man, then raised the reins and brought them
down with a loud crack. The horse jerked forward, and she fell against
the seat's wooden back with a shriek.

"Miss!" the liveryman's shout followed her as she righted herself in
the buggy.

"I'm fine. I've got the hang of it now."

She couldn't turn to see if he'd heard her. She had to concentrate on steering the horse along the street. Thank goodness it was still early and there weren't too many people about.

The horse slowed to a steady trot and turned in the correct direction onto the Chicago Road. Tension in her shoulders eased once they left town behind and fields opened up ahead of her. Flowering trees of some sort lined part of the road and added a heady fragrance to the breeze washed clean by three days of rain.

Driving the buggy wasn't too difficult after that rocky start. It was better than having Mrs. McCann along. After all, how could she have explained Russ's reaction to seeing her?

The horse snorted, and Emmie tensed. "We're doing fine, horse. Just fine."

What would Russ's reaction be? If he truly didn't know she was in Jonesville, perhaps he'd be shocked. But surely, after the initial shock wore off, he'd be happy. Or would he be scandalized that she'd driven out by herself, knowing that he was a man alone on his farm?

And what if he knew she was here and had been avoiding her? What would his reaction be then?

It was a very good thing Mrs. McCann hadn't joined her.

She might as well practice her greeting. It would pass the time and maybe settle her nerves.

"Russ, I'm so happy to finally meet you." That sounded friendly without being too forward.

"Mr. Fields, I've looked forward to this meeting." The horse cocked its ears back.

"I agree, much too formal."

An approaching wagon kept her silent. She nodded to the driver as they passed, a young boy barely out of short pants, who was no doubt much more experienced at driving than she was.

"Russ, I'm sorry to arrive without notice." No, that wouldn't do, she wasn't a bit sorry. She was... she was... she didn't know what she was. Somewhere between excited and terrified. Leaning more toward excited.

"Russ, may I call you Russ? I feel as if we already know one another." Definitely too forward.

The miles flew past and soon she saw a farm nestled in the curve of a hill. It was just as the McCanns had described it, with forest stretching behind and to the east. This had to be it. The horse slowed to a walk.

"Not now, we're almost there." She flicked the reins, but the horse ignored her. Then, it swung to the left as if to turn around in the middle of the road.

"Oh, no, you don't." She hauled back on the right rein. The horse half-reared, but straightened itself back on the road. Then she did like the liveryman had said and smacked the reins on the horse's rump. As before, it charged forward, but this time—it didn't slow down.

"Whoa! Whoa!" They barreled down the road. Clods of mud flew up and struck the front of the buggy as it bounced and lurched and threatened to throw her from its seat. The tassels decorating the hood swirled and swooshed above her head. "Whoa!"

Didn't this horse know anything? The buggy tipped onto two wheels, and her heart sank as she dropped the reins to hold onto the seat with both hands.

Oh, what had she done?

Goblin's ears perked, and he thrust his nose into the air while blowing a snorty breath. Russ stopped in the doorway to the barn, Goblin's lead rope loose in his hand. A buggy careened down the muddy road from the direction of town. A feminine shriek and a froth of blue skirts and white petticoats set a stab of fear through him. Before he could think about what he was doing, he leaped onto Goblin's bare back and thumped the gray's sides with his heels.

Not used to a rider, Goblin half ran and half jumped for the first few steps. Russ clung like a burr and thumped his heels again.

Goblin got the message. He stretched out his neck and took aim at the runaway horse.

The buggy crashed into a rut and bounced, all four wheels leaving the ground. Another shriek cut the air.

The wind snatched his hat as he leaned further over his horse's neck, black mane hair whipping his cheeks. They met the red horse at the end of the lane. He shifted his weight and swung Goblin beside the red, grasping the horse's bridle.

"Easy, boy. Steady," he spoke to the horse as it slowed next to Goblin. The steady old gray acted as if he'd done this type of thing every day, dropping to a trot and then a walk. Goblin swung his head and took a half-hearted bite at the red horse, as if to make it behave.

Russ twisted on Goblin's back. "Are you all right, ma'am?"

The blanched-out face of the new church pianist stared back at him with those dark eyes he'd noticed now wild with fear.

She brushed at her skirts, covering the glimpse of her knee that had him swiveling back to face forward.

"I think... I think I'm fine." Her voice was reedy and thin. He glanced back again. She was sitting upright, holding onto the seat with both hands.

"That's my place up the lane. I'll lead your horse that way. He'll have to cool down before you can go any farther."

Her mouth dropped open and, if possible, her eyes got even larger. He'd forgotten to shield her from the worst of his ravaged face. He turned his back to her, wishing he hadn't lost his hat. He tugged on the red horse's bridle and aimed the buggy at his barn. The lady might not care for his looks, but her horse needed a rest.

She'd just have to put up with him for a half hour or so.

The scarred man from the post office was Russ Fields? But how could that be? The postmistress had called him Cyrus. Oh. Cy—*Russ*. Of course. He'd been at the post office her first two Mondays in Jonesville. How had she not figured that out? He'd been in church last Sunday. He'd seen her, heard her play.

Shock at the discovery overrode her terror of moments before.

He must have known who she was.

She stared at the straight back and wide shoulders that tapered to lean hips and long legs hugging the gray beast beneath him. He rode the animal without a saddle. He'd charged to her rescue like the cavalryman she knew he'd been. What must he think of her pitiful attempt to drive this buggy by herself?

Oh, she'd made a terrible mess of everything. In abject misery, she sat as he slid from his horse and tied the livery horse to a hitching post near the barn. She couldn't look at him. She just couldn't.

"You might as well get out of the buggy."

Was that disgust in his voice? She ventured a peek in his direction, but his face was turned away. She cleared her throat.

"Russ?"

He stiffened but didn't turn.

"Russ Fields?"

"I suppose someone at the church told you my name."

"No. Nobody did."

He turned his head to the right, until she could see the undamaged side of his face. His hand lingered on the head of the black-and-white dog at his feet. It had to be Jigs. Becky had written about the aging sheepdog. Its tongue lolled out the side of its face in a halfway grin like Becky had described more than once. At least something looked like she'd thought it would. And the gray horse—that must be Goblin.

"Then how do you know my name?"

She sucked in a breath. Was that hostility in his voice? She hadn't allowed herself to think that he might be angry with her for coming. She blinked furiously and lifted her chin. She wasn't going to cry.

"Untie the horse, and I'll be going. I didn't mean to—that is—I didn't think..."

"Your horse isn't ready."

"He's not *my* horse."

Russ turned a little more, looked at her. One light-brown brow rose above a piercing blue eye.

"I rented him from the livery stable."

"They aren't going to be happy if you bring him back all used up, ma'am. Let him rest a spell. You're welcome to wait in my house if you prefer. I've work to get back to."

He took a few steps away while her mind spun. Why was he calling her ma'am?

"Russ?"

This time he turned completely around, the sun on his face high-lighting the ridges and valleys of his scars.

"You're free with my name, ma'am, seeing as we've never met."

She climbed out of the buggy, steadying herself with one hand on its side.

"I know we haven't met face to face. That's why I'm here. I didn't expect that you'd..."

A moment of silence spread between them while she stared at hoof prints in the soft ground.

"You know my name. How about you tell me yours."

She lifted her eyes and searched his face. Didn't he know? Of course he didn't, or he wouldn't have asked. He wouldn't be calling her ma'am. She smiled, her breath leaving in a little rush of air.

"I thought you knew."

He shook his head.

"It's me. Emmie—Emmie Mason."

If she'd reached into the heavens, grabbed a lightning bolt, and hurled it at him, Russ couldn't have been more shocked. He staggered back a step. How could this be? What was she doing here? His heart hammered against his ribs.

His hat lay on the ground several yards away where the wind had blown it. He stomped over and grabbed it. Cramming it onto his head, he tugged it low over his brow. He kept his back turned. She'd already seen him, but at least he could spare her having to look at him again.

Spare her? Or spare him? He thrust that question away.

His swirling emotions centered on anger and focused there. This wasn't supposed to have happened. She was supposed to be back in Pittsburgh. She was supposed to find a handsome husband to love and care for her. And she sure wasn't supposed to be here looking at the remains of his face.

"Russ?"

He startled at the soft trembling of her voice, but he didn't turn.

"Why are you here?" He regretted the words as they tore from his throat in an anguished rasp.

Her silence was broken by a lamb bleating in the pasture. The breeze carried the scent of honeysuckle. Goblin snorted and shifted his hips as he dozed in the sun. It should have been an idyllic morning. It would have been an idyllic morning if not for the woman standing behind him.

The woman he'd dreamed of meeting.

He whirled around, keeping the left side of his face tilted away from her, his hat shading it.

She stood with her head bowed and her hands clasped in front of her.

"Emmie?" It didn't seem right to call her Miss Mason when she'd called him Russ. And her name came out so easily. So naturally.

She looked up, her brown eyes clouded.

"Why? Why did you come?" He needed to know. His chest hurt with how much he needed to know.

"After Father died"—her shoulders moved under the deep breath she drew in—"I didn't want to stay and be foisted off on some man my brother chose for me. You'd mentioned the position with the church, so I wrote to them."

She'd come for employment, a way to frustrate her brother's plans. She hadn't come for him.

"And your brothers allowed this?"

"I haven't told them where I am."

He leaned his hip against the hitching rail. "They must be worried sick." He would be, if he didn't know where she was, what she was doing, or who she was with. Her near accident in the buggy would have terrified them. It'd scared him before he'd even known who she was.

"I suppose they are." Was that defeat in her tone?

They faced each other, a half-dozen yards and a world of differences separating them. Still, she didn't move.

"You shouldn't be here. Folks would talk if they knew."

She stiffened and glanced toward town.

"Your horse has cooled off. If you go slow, he'll be all right to drive back."

She crossed her arms, hands grasping her elbows, shoulders hunched. Was she afraid? Of course she was. She'd almost been in a wreck.

He should drive her, but it was a long walk back from town. As if he wasn't losing enough work time today with Mickey off fishing. The boy had earned the break and had been excited to try his hand at fishing again since Russ had shown him how. But why was Russ thinking about farm work or Mickey with Emmie standing in front of him?

Because he wished she wasn't there. He wished she'd never seen him. And he wished he could forget ever seeing her.

She was perfect.

Goblin snorted and shook his mane. The wild ride down the lane hit Russ like a charging ram. He'd ridden the horse. His legs went rubbery. He ran his hand down Goblin's neck. He could tie the horse to the buggy and ride him back to the farm after seeing Emmie safely home.

Home. Emmie was living in Jonesville.

His rubbery legs threatened to dump him onto the muddy ground.

"Miss Mason—"

"Emmie."

He cleared his throat. "I'll drive you back to town."

He moved Goblin to the rear of the buggy and tied him securely, then untied the red horse. Emmie hadn't moved, not an inch. He extended his hand.

"I'll help you in."

She gave the tiniest nod just before her gloved fingers touched his. He stepped into the buggy and sat beside her, the normal side of his face to her. He didn't look at her, didn't have to, her presence filled the tight space until he fought to breathe through it.

"Go back to Pittsburgh, Miss Mason. Go back where you belong."

He ignored her gentle gasp and smacked the reins on the horse's rump. It lurched forward and Emmie gasped again.

This wasn't how anything had happened in his dreams. But he couldn't live in a dream.

CHAPTER 18

H OW COULD EMMIE TEACH piano lessons when her heart was broken? Totally, completely, and thoroughly broken. And the worst part of it was... she'd said nothing. Nothing. The entire ride to Jonesville in the buggy, not a word had passed between her and Russ. It was as if she'd sat beside a total stranger.

Well, hadn't she? Other than his letters and his sister, what did she know about Russ Fields?

Those scars. What must he have gone through? She'd seen scars like his at the hospital, but men came to Pittsburgh only after they'd been treated in the field hospitals, usually weeks or even months after their injuries happened. What Russ had lived through... she shuddered despite the midday sun warming her shoulders as she walked to the church.

Her first pupil would arrive soon. She toyed with the emerald around her neck. She had to get her mind on the music. Off Russ. Her heart squeezed until drawing a breath was painful.

She'd made a mess of everything.

He hadn't known she was in Jonesville, but it was clear he didn't want her here either. He didn't want *her*, period. Shame heated her face as she turned the corner and headed for the church's side door. If anyone found out what she'd done, practically chasing a man across the country and then showing up on his doorstep unannounced and unaccompanied, they wouldn't let her teach their children anymore. She'd be dismissed as the church pianist. There'd be nothing to do but pack up and return to Archie.

Would Russ say anything?

Not the Russ she'd come to know letter by letter. Not the Russ who had given her wise encouragement and sympathy when she'd needed it most, but the Russ who'd driven her to the livery stable. Could she trust that Russ with her secret?

She stopped on the top step. What about the lanky boy she'd seen with Russ in town? Where'd he been yesterday? Had he witnessed everything? Would he talk?

"Miss Mason!" The cheery greeting slapped her like cold water on a hot day, bringing her back to the present. Her first student raced across the yard, pink ribbons streaming behind her, eyes sparkling with eagerness.

Emmie needed to focus on the things at hand. She forced a smile, opened the door, and waved the girl into the church. Shoulders back and head held high, Emmie followed. The music should shut out her doubts, fears, and broken heart for the next couple of hours.

At least, she could hope.

He'd made a hash of everything. Even tonight's dinner. He slapped the plates on the table and then grabbed the heavy skillet with its burnt offering from the stove.

"Supper."

A muffled yelp answered. It could have been a word or not, hard to tell. Mickey bounced through the doorway and stopped. His nose wrinkled as the excitement drained from his face.

"You burnt my fish?"

"And the cornbread."

Nothing had gone right. Nothing might ever be right again. He all but tossed the pan of cornbread onto the table. It landed with a *thunk*. Fine. It didn't smell appetizing. It might as well sound unappetizing.

Russ sat in his chair and grabbed a fork.

Mickey slunk onto the other chair and stared at his plate.

Russ slid another fork across the table. The clatter brought Mickey's head up.

"I'm sorry, son. I can't seem to do anything right today."

"It's okay." Mickey retrieved the fork and shoveled some of the un-burned cornbread from the middle of the pan, then he picked through the fish and found some edible-looking pieces. After he'd taken a bite and chewed, his grin returned. "It ain't half bad."

Russ grunted. It wasn't half good, either.

Mickey gobbled down his portion and reached for more, stopping when he looked at Russ's bare plate.

"Ain't you gonna eat anythin'?"

"Not hungry, I guess." Not for any of this slop, anyway. If Becky were still here—

"Want me to fry you some eggs?"

Russ stared at the boy's eager eyes.

"You can cook?"

"Some." He pointed the fork at the pan of blackened fish. "Better'n this."

Russ waved at the stove. "By all means." Why had the kid not said anything until now?

Mickey hopped off his chair and set to work like he knew what he was doing. Within minutes, bacon was sizzling in the pan, its aroma clearing the stink of burned fish from the room. Well, that and Mickey had opened the windows.

With an awkward half-shrug, the boy slid a plate of perfectly pre-sented bacon and eggs in front of Russ.

"Looks good." He picked up his fork and took a bite, then nodded to Mickey. It *was* good. Better than good. It didn't hit his stomach and threaten a revolt. He pointed his fork at the boy. "You're the new cook around here."

A grin broke across Mickey's face, making him look even younger than he was.

"I ain't cooked much more than bacon, eggs, and biscuits—"

"You can make biscuits?"

"If you got the right stuff, I can. Some of that white powder stuff in the tin. Ma'd run out of it sometimes, and they ain't so good without it."

White powder stuff. Becky had kept all kinds of white powder stuff in the corner cupboard. Emmie might know which one to use—

Emmie.

The eggs lost their flavor, but he continued to eat anyway. He couldn't disappoint the boy. Heaven knew he'd disappointed Emmie. But that was for her own good. She didn't belong here. She didn't belong with him. She belonged in Pittsburgh, married to a man her brother had chosen. A man who could give her the type of life she was used to.

A man without scars.

He hadn't come to church yesterday. Emmie rubbed her temples even though the ache that bothered her was in her heart, not her head. She'd been awake and dressed for over an hour. It was Monday, Russ's day to come to town. She'd been sitting there working up the courage to walk to the post office, hoping she'd have a chance to speak with him.

Or more to the point—that he'd speak to her.

"Still here?" Aunt Maggie shuffled into the room, her hair tucked under a black bonnet. "I thought you were going downtown."

"I am."

The old lady's formidable eyebrows rose.

"There's no hurry. I don't have any students on Mondays."

"Do you mind if I walk with you, then?"

Emmie's heart dropped to her heels. How could she speak with Russ if Aunt Maggie was with her? But how could she say no without raising more than her landlady's eyebrows?

"Of course. I'll fetch my hat."

How had this morning managed to go from bad to worse when it hadn't even gotten started yet? She pinned a straw hat to her hair and pulled on a pair of gloves. A quick glance in the mirror showed a plain young woman with a smooth face, not a hint of the turmoil brewing beneath the surface. Good.

The walk to the shops was slow with Aunt Maggie leaning on her cane.

"I wonder, should we invite the pastor to dinner next Sunday?" Aunt Maggie asked.

"I'm sure that would be nice."

The old woman stopped. "Would you enjoy his company, then?"

"Of course. He's been very kind to me." Why did Aunt Maggie look at her like a robin eyeing a June bug?

"He's also very single, and a man in his position should have a wife. Someone to look after him properly. You know these men of the cloth, nose always in the Good Book, barely taking time to see to their own needs."

Emmie's mouth dropped open, but words failed her. It was one thing to hint at something so personal, it was quite another to discuss it on a public street.

"Don't look so surprised, girl." She started walking again. "He's been singing your praises to anyone who'll listen since you stepped off that train."

Emmie stared at the woman's back for a moment, then hurried to catch up to her.

"I'm sure he's just being polite, and I can't think he'd be—"

"Of course he's interested."

"Oh, no."

"Confound it, girl, you don't get to be my age without knowing a thing or two. If you'd give him the slightest encouragement, he'd be yours for the taking."

The slightest encouragement? Nothing could be further from her mind. Nothing.

They turned onto the main street, and there stood Goblin and Russ's wagon, parked in front of the general store. Heartbeat echoing in her ears, Emmie searched the street for any sign of Russ.

"Let's stop by the post office first." Aunt Maggie fished an envelope from her beaded black reticule. "I have a letter to mail to my sister."

Maybe Russ was already there. Emmie swallowed, or tried to, her throat so dry nothing moved. She opened the door for Aunt Maggie and followed her into the small building.

"Aunt Maggie, how good to see you out and about this morning." The little postmistress sang out her greeting from behind the counter.

"It's good to be out on such a fine day," Aunt Maggie said.

"You're here for your mail, I suppose."

"Yes, of course." Aunt Maggie said. "Why else does anyone come to the post office?"

"To check the wanted posters, of course." The elderly postmistress laughed and waved her hand toward the back wall where the posters were displayed.

Aunt Maggie laughed too, and Emmie got the feeling that there was a joke in there somewhere, but she wasn't privy to it, and nobody else was in the post office. The two old women nattered on, but Emmie couldn't focus on what they said.

Where was Russ? She fidgeted from foot to foot, her fingers pleating and unpleating the ribbon sash at her waist.

"I have a letter for you, too, miss."

"Excuse me?" Emmie brought her attention to the postmistress.

"It came this morning on the early train. Why, I was just slotting it when you walked in with Aunt Maggie. Here you go. Such a pretty envelope."

Emmie took it and flipped it over. It was from Helen. Relief flooded her. For just a moment, she'd feared that Archie had found her. Guilt pinched, and she stuffed the envelope in her pocket. She'd let him know where she was eventually, but not until she'd had a chance to speak with Russ. Really *speak* with Russ.

"We'll be on our way, then." Aunt Maggie wrapped up her chat with the postmistress and stepped out onto the boardwalk.

"Let's go to the general store next," Emmie said.

"What do you need there?"

"Oh, nothing in particular, but I like to see what they've gotten in that's new." She offered Aunt Maggie a bit of a smile.

The old woman cut a sharp look her way, then gave an equally sharp nod before setting off, her cane thumping on the wood.

The wagon and Goblin remained outside. Emmie opened the door and waited for Aunt Maggie to enter. The scents of oiled leather and liniment greeted her as she stepped inside. Several people milled around, but one lanky boy caught her attention. The same one who had been on the wagon when she'd seen it before. There was no sign of Russ. Perhaps he'd sent the young man in here while he went into another store. She positioned herself near the front window while Aunt Maggie poked around in the button display at the back. It was going to look odd, Emmie standing in front of a display of harness parts and men's boots.

The boy picked up a wrapped package, nodded to the clerk, and made his way to the wagon. He untied the horse, climbed onto the seat, and released the brake before shaking the reins across the animal's back. They drove away. Without Russ.

"What's so all-fire important about that boy?"

Emmie jumped half out of her skin at Aunt Maggie's quiet words. "N-nothing. I was just looking out the window. Such a beautiful day, don't you think?"

Aunt Maggie's piercing look said she wasn't buying a word of it. Well, let her think whatever she wanted. Emmie peeked out the window one more time as the boy disappeared down the street. Heading back toward Russ's farm. By himself.

Russ hadn't come to town.

The tension she'd been carrying since she awoke that morning settled into a hard knot of disappointment and despair, lodging in her middle. How could she talk to him if he wouldn't come into town?

Russ hacked at a weed in the pitiful excuse for a garden. Sparks flew when the hoe connected with a flinty piece of rock. He resisted the urge to heave the hoe as far as he could fling it. Ma and Becky had always made gardening look simple. He was a grown man who could plow, plant, and till a field full of corn or wheat, but the art of the kitchen garden was beyond him.

The row of beans had come up just fine, only to be eaten off by some critter or another. He glanced at Jigs snoozing near the back door of the house. Another reason he needed a young dog. Then that dad-blasted ram had got out again and trampled the tomato plants Mickey had brought back from town on Monday. At the rate things were going, by January they'd have nothing but meat and corn to eat.

He chopped out another weed, then planted the hoe into the dirt and leaned against the top of the handle, looking toward town.

Was she still there? Or had she run back home to Pittsburgh?

A puff of dust shimmered from the road and against all logic, his heartbeat quickened. When a lone rider topped the hill, that fickle organ flattened out again. Why was he looking for her? He'd sent her away. She didn't belong here.

He watched the rider, a man who sat a horse like he'd been born on its back. Not the preacher then. He'd half expected that man to come nosing around since they hadn't attended last Sunday. He was a persistent fellow. But this man was closing in fast and he rode like a—

Russ looked away and closed his eye. The smell of dust mixed with the smoke from hundreds of rifles. Hoofbeats shook the ground. Sabers swung, slicing the air and anything else in their path. A horse screamed, men swore, someone cried out for his mother. He jerked his eye open. The hoe was clenched in his fists like a rifle, halfway to his shoulder.

A lone black horse with three white stockings cantered up the lane.

Russ dropped the hoe and left the garden, walking toward the house.

The man reined in the horse and swung from the saddle before the black had come to a full stop.

"Russ? Russ Fields?"

Older, but not much, the clean-shaven face of John Henry Lewis grinned at him.

"I told you I'd look you up when I got out." John Henry pulled off his glove and stuck out his hand.

Russ wiped the dirt from his hand before taking it in a firm grasp. "You're looking well." The fresh-faced young man who'd joined the Seventh Michigan Cavalry toward the end of the war had filled out, his grip thickened with calluses.

"I'm still here," John Henry said, "no small thanks to you."

Russ pulled his hand back and stuck it in his pocket. He didn't want to talk about that.

Mickey came pelting full-bore around the barn, and Russ stiffened. Was the ram out and chasing him? The boy slid to a stop beside him, gasping for breath.

"I seen you ride up and jump off that horse. I wish I could ride like that."

John Henry laughed and shook the boy's hand. "Is this a younger brother?"

"This is Mickey, my hired hand. Mickey, meet John Henry Lewis. He and I served in the war together for a time."

"Just a few months, but long enough for your boss here to save my bacon not once but twice."

"Really?" Mickey's eyes rounded until Russ feared they might drop out of their sockets.

"It wasn't anything," Russ mumbled.

"Was to me. I like being alive."

"Will you tell me about it?" Mickey all but danced on his toes. "Russ don't never say nothin' about the war."

John Henry shot him a look. Russ shrugged and glanced away, then waved toward the house. "Might as well come in for a bite of supper. Mickey made biscuits this morning, and we got ham."

"Sounds like a feast to me. Been eating mostly canned beans and peaches with some jerked bear meat since I left Colorado Territory."

"You're all mustered out then?"

"I am. Army sent me as far as Jonesville on the train. Heading home and thought I'd look you up before I get myself all married and settled in on the farm near Somerset Center."

Married and settled in. John Henry could do that with his intact face. He and Mickey headed for the house while Russ took one more long glance toward town.

Was Emmie still there?

CHAPTER 19

Another Sunday and no sign of Russ. Emmie lingered over the final chord of "Blest Be the Tide That Binds." The congregation was filing down the center aisle, the men shaking Pastor Anderson's hand, the women nodding and shepherding their children out the door. Aunt Maggie and several of her elderly women friends chatted in a knot at the side of the church. Several of them threw speculative glances at her. What was Aunt Maggie saying? Not more of that nonsense about her and the pastor. She tidied her music and left the bench, intent on going home and... her steps faltered.

And what? What was there for her in Jonesville without Russ?

"Emmie, come join us."

Oh, no. Aunt Maggie's words weren't an invitation, they were a command. Emmie sucked in a fortifying breath and joined her landlady.

"I was just telling the ladies what an advantageous match we could make between you and Pastor Anderson. Wasn't I, ladies?"

Gray heads nodded and wrinkle lines deepened beside mouths and eyes, all kindly meant, and all so wrong.

"Aunt Maggie—"

"Of course, you'll need a little help. Most girls do." Aunt Maggie looked to her cronies and received another silent round of nods. "You without a mother and so new to our town, it's up to us to see to things."

"No, I beg you—"

"Pastor Anderson." Aunt Maggie waved him over as the last of the congregation left the building.

The man in question strode their way. His longish hair was slicked back, and his freshly shaven chin exposed the slight dimple that rested there. He was polished and handsome in his Sunday suit... but he wasn't Russ.

Emmie wished the floor would collapse beneath her, or maybe the church would burst into flames. Right. Then.

"Ladies, always a pleasure to speak with you."

Emmie summoned what she hoped was more smile than grimace as the older ladies returned his greeting.

"Pastor, I meant to mention this earlier, but why don't you join us at the boardinghouse for supper? We've plenty, and Penny is the best cook in town."

"As it happens, I've already been invited to the McCanns' for supper, but I am free any other day this week except Wednesday."

Aunt Maggie beamed. "Shall we say Tuesday then?" She patted the man's sleeve. "Bring your appetite." She swiveled toward Emmie as if just noticing her. "Come along. Penny will have the table set by the time we arrive. We shouldn't keep people waiting, dear."

Emmie nodded to the ladies and then to Pastor Anderson. The warmth in his eyes—or was it interest?—started a slow burn in her cheeks.

Oh, how could she get out of dinner on Tuesday?

A shout woke Russ. He sat bolt upright in bed, his long underwear drenched in sweat and twisted around his body. Rain pelted the window, adding to the gloom of pre-dawn. He ran his shaking hand through his damp hair. Footsteps pounded down the hallway until Mickey burst into the room, all wild hair and wide eyes.

"What's wrong?" Mickey shouted as he surveyed the room.

"Nothing." Only it wasn't nothing. The shout had been his. The dreams were back. He pulled his knees up and rested his forearms on them.

"You hollered loud enough to wake the dead. Liked to scared me out of my pants, were I wearin' any." The boy stood there in a shirt that hung halfway to his knobby knees.

"It was just a dream." Only it wasn't.

"A nightmare?" The boy's stance relaxed. "I use to get them sometimes right after Ma..." He shrugged. "They ain't good."

No. They weren't. Russ untangled himself from his quilt and stood, straightening his long underwear. "You might hear things... sometimes." How much should he tell the boy?

Mickey cocked his head. "It's from the war, ain't it." It wasn't a question. The boy knew too much for one so young.

"Yes."

"I reckon Mr. Lewis stopping by stirred things up."

Russ stopped mid-grab for his pants and studied Mickey across the murky room. "I reckon." That's the way it usually worked. Something would get him thinking about the war, and then the dreams would return. How he hated those dreams.

"I enjoyed his stories about the army, what he done out west with them Injuns and all, but I got a feelin' it ain't all like he said."

"No." John Henry had left out the parts about friends being blown apart. Cannonballs screaming overhead. The smell of blood, the taste of fear, and—

"Iffen you go to screamin' again, I'll know it's just that war thing botherin' you, and I won't be scared outta my gourd." Mickey left the room.

At least one of them wouldn't.

Russ tossed his pants on the tumbled bedding and shucked out of his long underwear. He filled the basin on the washstand with tepid water from the pitcher and scrubbed the worst of the sweat from his body.

If only he could scrub the dream from his mind.

He gripped the edge of the washstand. They'd been at the edge of the Blue Ridge Mountains. It'd been raining then too. Custer had told them to dismount and leave the horses behind. Russ had tried to get John Henry assigned with those who'd tend the horses, but his commanding officer hadn't listened.

John Henry had been greener than grass, just turned eighteen and mustered in only a few weeks before. Russ had told the kid to stay right beside him, but as was the way of things in battle, once the shooting started, even the best plans changed. They hit Early's troops at Rockfish Gap, attacking Early's left flank while Sheridan's cannon and the rest of his command battered the center and right. The smoke, the scream of cannon shot, the cursing of men, the slap of bullets into bodies and trees.

Breath rushed in and out of Russ as if he were still running through the trees.

John Henry had tried to stay with him, but the forest made it nearly impossible. Then a shout to his right. John Henry crashed to the forest floor, his gun dropping to the wet ground.

Russ'd yelled his name, fought his way through to the young man writhing on the ground. He'd tripped and twisted an ankle, but he wasn't shot. Russ stood over the top of him, hollering encouragement, firing his gun at the oncoming rebels. So many rebels. It was a rout, and it was coming right at them.

The *thunk* of wood hitting the cookstove below pierced through the memories. The rattle of the stove's damper. The *clank* of a frying pan on the stovetop. Jigs's toenails clicking on the floorboards.

Russ blinked. He was in his bedroom. The war was over—for most folks. John Henry Lewis might be going back to his old life to pick up where he'd left off. Maybe the dreams didn't haunt him. Maybe he'd find a nice girl, settle down, and start a family. Maybe he was one of the lucky ones.

Russ looked out his window toward town—toward Emmie.

If she was still there.

Emmie fiddled with the envelope while balancing an umbrella she'd borrowed from Aunt Maggie in her other hand. Helen had scolded her, none too gently, for not telling Archie and Richard where she was. Helen had been clever enough to figure it out, likely from badgering poor Evans with questions. Not that he'd known her destination, but he'd known of the letters.

Emmie couldn't tell her brothers, not yet. She needed at least one more chance to speak to Russ.

She snorted, then looked around to be sure nobody was close enough to have heard her. Young ladies did not snort on a public street... not even in Jonesville. She clutched the envelope tighter, hoping she'd written the proper words to convince Helen to hold her tongue.

She hurried along, turning onto the main street just a block from the post office. The Monday morning traffic greeted her, people on foot, some riding horses, and a mix of buggies and wagons splashed along the muddy street. She stepped onto the boardwalk and searched for the familiar gray horse. There were plenty of chestnuts, bays, and even a black, but no gray.

Where was he? How was she going to speak with him if he didn't come to town? The thought of driving herself out to his farm again didn't appeal. She'd almost gotten herself killed the first time.

Her heels beat her frustration into the boards as she entered the post office.

"Good morning, Miss Mason." The postmistress apparently had only one greeting be it fair, rain, or, doubtless, snow.

"Good morning."

"You're here for your mail, I suppose." And only one question.

"I've a letter to post today."

The postmistress took her envelope, weighed it, and affixed the proper postage. "Such a fine hand you have, miss. I could swear I've seen it somewhere before."

Emmie froze. What if Mrs. Russell connected her handwriting to the letters Russ had been receiving? She had to derail that train of thought.

"I learned at the Young Ladies Seminary in Pittsburgh. We were instructed to conform to a certain style of writing. I'm sure many women have learned to write in the same way." She was babbling.

The little birdlike eyes searched Emmie's face as if looking for a flaw. Or a lie. Oh, that wasn't good. That wasn't good at all. Perhaps she should have someone else post her letters from now on. Emmie pushed her pennies across the counter and swung around to leave, almost running over a young man coming through the door.

But not just any young man. It was the same one she'd seen on Russ's wagon.

"I'm sorry, ma'am." He dragged his hat from his head, sprinkling Emmie's dress with rain droplets, his face registering chagrin.

"No, it was my fault," she said. "I wasn't looking where I was going." She let him pass and then exited the building. Goblin stood with his head bowed against the rain right in front of the post office, but there was no Russ in sight. Emmie stepped to the side and leaned against the building, the porch roof shielding her from the rain.

What should she do? She couldn't exactly waylay the young man and demand he tell her where Russ was. Before she could formulate a plan, he came out the door and headed for the wagon.

"Pardon me."

The boy stopped and turned toward her. "Oh, ma'am. I am sorry I done got you wet—"

"It was no bother at all. Tell me. Isn't that Russ Fields' wagon?"

"Yes, ma'am. I work for him." The narrow chest puffed out a tad. "Name's Mickey."

Russ had a hired hand? He'd never mentioned it.

"I was hoping to run into him today." She tilted her head at the boy. He wasn't much more than half-grown, but still half a head taller than she.

"Oh, he stayed back at the farm." The chest swelled another notch. "This is the second time he's trusted me to bring the wagon in by myself to run the errands."

"I see." So the boy was newly hired. "He must have a lot of faith in you." If only Russ'd had a little faith in her.

The young man's grin widened. "Yes, ma'am. Do you want for me to tell him you was askin' after him?"

Did she?

Yes.

No.

Maybe?

Before the silence could stretch into something awkward, she shook her head. "Perhaps I'll see him in church on Sunday."

The boy rubbed the side of his chin. "I dunno. We tried that a couple of weeks ago, but he ain't wanted to come back since." He shrugged. "I thought it were pretty good, 'specially your music. That were something fine, ma'am."

Oh dear. He'd recognized her. "Thank you. I'll just be going about my errands now." She hurried away. Why wasn't anything as simple as she'd thought it would be? Would he tell Russ she'd been asking after him?

Did she want him to?

What could she do? Emmie stared at the looking glass. She was already plain, and her dress was nothing special. Maybe she should pull her hair back in a more severe style? The last thing she wanted was for the pastor to think she was trying to garner his attention.

Far from it.

Not that he wasn't a nice man, and reasonably good looking, but her heart was taken. Taken by a man who didn't want it. Or at least, who didn't know he wanted it. Yet.

She squared her shoulders and wrinkled her nose at her slightly wavy reflection. The dinner had been Aunt Maggie's idea, not hers. She'd be polite, but nothing more. If Aunt Maggie wanted to attract the pastor, she'd have to do it herself. Her reflection dissolved into a giggling girl. Just the thought of Aunt Maggie—

"Are you done primpin' and preenin' up there?" Penny's voice rose from the staircase outside Emmie's door. "Time to eat is time to eat, whether you're at the table or not."

Despite the maid's crusty comments, Emmie smiled. Penny was nothing like the soft-spoken and kindly Cook back in Pittsburgh. She had a cranky kind of spunk. For whatever reason, it was rather refreshing. Fitting for life in a place like Jonesville, a place populated with working-class people.

Like her.

She stopped with her hand on the doorknob, looking back into her rented room. Some would say she had fallen down society's ladder, but there was a simple dignity about doing for oneself.

"Miss Emmie!" Penny's voice rose to a bark.

Emmie shut her door and hurried down the stairs. The rest of the boarders and Pastor Anderson were already seated. There was one empty chair.

Right next to the pastor.

Aunt Maggie smiled and nodded toward the chair.

Emmie always sat next to Aunt Maggie. As the only female boarder, Aunt Maggie had made a point of that. But now... oh, the old woman's maneuvering would have to be addressed. And soon.

She sat and tried not to scowl. Ladies never scowled.

"Pastor, would you give the blessing?" Aunt Maggie asked.

He bowed his head, and everyone else followed. The prayer was short, and then dishes were passed from right to left. She took a bowl of mashed potatoes and scooped a small dollop onto her plate.

"Are you feeling at home here yet, Miss Mason?" Pastor Anderson asked as he took the warm dish from her.

"Yes, I am."

"It must be very different from Pittsburgh."

"It is, indeed."

He filled his plate from several other dishes, and Emmie took a thick slice of turkey before passing the platter on.

"I hear nice comments from your students and their mothers regarding the piano lessons."

"They're good students."

He cleared his throat. Good. Maybe he'd get the hint if she stuck with three-word answers. Aunt Maggie, however, had her formidable brows pulled into a straight line and aimed right at her.

Pastor Anderson leaned slightly in Emmie's direction. "I wonder if you'd be interested in accompanying me on a round of visits on Thursday. I could rent an open buggy, so it would be very respectable. There's a family new to the area, one shut-in elderly couple, and a special case whom I've been trying to bring back into the fold."

"Oh, I..." Couldn't possibly spend the whole day with him. What would he think then? But what could she say with Aunt Maggie glaring at her?

"You've nothing going on Thursday, Emmie," the old lady said. "It would do you good to see some of the countryside."

"And you might offer me a bit of advice," the pastor spoke more softly. "The last visit will be to a veteran of the war. You may have seen him a couple of weeks ago. His face is terribly scarred from his injuries."

Emmie turned toward the pastor for the first time. He must mean Russ. "How could I help?"

"You mentioned having worked in a hospital. Perhaps you know more about dealing with wounded soldiers and their issues. I don't seem to be making much headway with Mr. Fields."

She clutched her napkin under the table, fingernails digging into the linen.

"Why, yes. If you think I can be of assistance. I did quite a bit of work with those recovering from the war." Thursday. She was going to see Russ on Thursday.

Aunt Maggie may be smiling, but Emmie wanted to shout and sing.

CHAPTER 20

A DOE BROKE FROM a small thicket near the road, its white tail waving in the air. Behind her pranced a spindle-legged fawn, its bright spots shining in the sun.

"Ain't that a sight?" Mickey said.

"It is." One Russ never tired of. He leaned against his hoe. Spring on the farm brought renewed life. Downy fluffs drifted on the breeze, sent forth by the willows that lined the creek, new leaves so green they almost hurt the eye. Monday's rain had washed everything clean. The air smelled of the warm earth in the cornfield and budding wildflowers that lined the sheep pasture.

The rattle of a buggy's wheels caught his attention. The road was still damp enough that no dust announced its arrival. The strike of horseshoes on gravel reached him next. Lots of wagons crawled along the Chicago Road hauling freight from the railroad depots all along its path. Riders rode by frequently too, but buggies and carriages were not as common.

His pulse beat at the base of his throat. Every buggy reminded him of the same thing. Emmie. But she wasn't coming back. He'd told her not to. He'd been very firm about that. Very... firm.

"Wonder who it could be?" Mickey stretched to his full height as if he could see the buggy before it crested the hill.

"Nobody who's going to help us with these weeds."

The boy flashed him a chagrined look.

The words had come out harsher than he'd meant them. "I wouldn't want anyone else helping me. You're doing a fine job, son." Mickey might eat his weight in groceries every week, but he was a quick learner and applied himself to every task Russ set. Even hoeing weeds in the cornfield.

Russ rubbed the scarred side of his face. It was time to start paying the young man a wage. He'd more than worked off the food he'd stolen and the new clothing, and he knew enough now to be a genuine help around the farm. Russ watched the buggy come over the rise. What sort of wage should he—?

The buggy slowed near the lane to the farm.

"Hey." Mickey pointed. "They are comin' here."

Two people sat under the shade of the buggy's top, a man and a woman. It wasn't a buggy he recog—oh, yes it was. It was the livery's buggy that Emmie had driven out, pulled by the same red horse. His heart sank as they got close enough to recognize the faces.

"It's the preacher man and the piano lady." Mickey grinned, looking at Russ. "Let's go say hello."

"Sure." Mickey took off for the barnyard, but Russ didn't try to keep up. Why was Emmie with the preacher? What had she told him? He tugged his hat down on his brow. He didn't want her to see him, but he couldn't take his eye off of her.

He'd been so flustered the last time that he'd not thought about what she looked like. Of course, she'd arrived in a rather disheveled state, having been tumbled around inside the buggy.

This time, she sat erect on the buggy seat, a fashionable straw hat perched on her head. Her green dress mimicked the new leaves on the willows by the creek. Her forehead was broad, her nose a little long, and her face tapered down to a rounded chin now held at an angle that dared him to deny her a greeting.

The preacher had tied off the horse and was helping Emmie from the buggy when Mickey puffed to a halt.

"Ma'am, preacher." The boy bobbed his head, then belatedly jerked his hat off.

"It's Mickey, isn't it?" Emmie asked.

Mickey's head bobbed, and a flush crept up from his collar.

"You two know each other?" the preacher asked.

"I met Mickey outside the post office on Monday," Emmie said.

Russ stopped beside the boy but didn't remove his hat. He kept his face angled away from Emmie. "What can we do for you two?"

"I'm making the rounds, Mr. Fields, and thought I'd bring Miss Mason with me to meet more of the congregation. She's a wonderful addition to our church family." The man practically beamed at Emmie.

Russ forced his fingers to relax. "Pleased to meet you, miss."

A flicker of something passed across her face. Was it relief? Had she not confided in the preacher? Or had she thought he'd toss her off his property?

"Pleasure to meet you too, Mr. Fields. Pastor Anderson has told me a bit about you."

"I thought you knowed each other," Mickey said. "You was askin' after him on Monday."

Emmie flushed and dropped her eyes. "We haven't been properly introduced."

"Miss Mason attended school with my sister." The two of them spoke over the top of each other. Mickey and the preacher both looked confused.

Oh, what a tangled web we weave...

Why had she thought this would go smoothly when nothing else had? Emmie did her best not to squirm under Pastor Anderson's accusatory raised brow. Once again, she'd made a mess of things.

Before she could spill her whole sordid story about chasing after a man who had only been writing to her out of politeness—which she now realized was the case—Pastor Anderson turned to Mickey.

"You look quite at home here on the farm. I trust you've settled in well?"

The boy nodded and jerked his head toward the barn. "Russ has put me in charge of the bummer lambs now."

"Bummer lambs?" The pastor's puzzled face probably mirrored her own.

"Yup, them's the ones what got rejected by their mommas." Mickey shrugged. "Sheep ain't that much different than some folks in that way."

"Yes, well," Pastor Anderson said, "God often refers to us as His sheep in the Bible."

"He does?" Mickey wrinkled his nose. "I ain't sure that's a good thing. No offense, Pastor, but sheep do some mighty dumb things."

Pastor Anderson chuckled as he looked from Russ to Emmie and back again. "That's true enough. Why don't you show me your... bummers, was it?"

They headed for the barn, Jigs beside them, but Emmie couldn't move. Russ seemed to have the same problem.

Oh, for Pete's sake. They weren't going to continue in silence again, like that interminable buggy ride, were they?

"You should write to your brothers, or send a wire."

She jumped at his voice. "I will, when I'm ready."

"They must be frantic. If it were Becky who'd run away—"

"I didn't run away." How could he say that? She'd come for the employment—mostly. She'd come to be independent—sort of. She'd come... she'd come to see him. She blinked and looked away, the green corn seedlings swimming in front of her for a moment. She blinked again. Twice. She would not cry in front of him. "I left my brothers a note."

"Did you tell them where you were going?"

"No."

"Emmie." His voice was little more than a whisper.

"What?" She couldn't look at him. Not yet.

"Write to them. Tell them that you're fine, that you've got a safe place to live and are working for the church here."

"But—"

"It's the right thing to do."

"Archie will come."

"Just as I would have gone after Becky. He can't make you leave, you know. You're of age to make up your own mind." Russ sighed.

She looked at him then. He still kept his face angled away. Did he fear that she was repulsed by his scars?

"Russ?"

"Hm?"

"You're right."

"Hm." He cast a glance toward the barn, his unblemished profile toward her. The firm line of his jaw, straight nose, high cheekbones... he was a very handsome man. Had that made enduring the scars even worse for him? Perhaps being plain wasn't such a bad thing. One didn't think much about her appearance when it'd never been anything to brag about.

"Thank you," she said.

He snapped his attention back on her.

"You've been giving me good advice for months now. I should have listened when you told me to write my brothers before, when I came..."

He let loose a gusty sort of sigh that might mean he was disgusted, or it might mean he was aggravated, or it might even mean he was sorry.

"I'm sorry for how that turned out... when you came that first time."

A giddy relief washed through her. "I am, too."

"It was so unexpected."

She could see that now. It would have been better had she written him a letter and invited him to come to her. Not to mention much more proper. Speaking of proper...

"Do you think Pastor Anderson suspects?" she asked.

"Yes. And they'll be coming back soon, so let me say this now, and we'll part as friends."

Her heart dropped. Part as friends?

"I'm glad I had the chance to meet you, Emmie. I am. But I'm sure now you understand why your brothers have been trying to find you a suitable husband. It's not an easy thing to be on your own. When Archie comes for you, you should go back to Pittsburgh with him." He grasped her upper arm for a moment, gave a light squeeze.

Then he walked away.

Her suddenly weak knees wouldn't let her follow him, even though she wanted to. Oh, how she wanted to. He flipped the latch on a nearby gate and then closed it behind him. The farm looked just how she'd always dreamed it would. Russ walked through the lush green field while white sheep dotted the gentle rise of the hill. A cow—that must be Song—lifted her brown face in Russ's direction, her bottom jaw swinging contentedly. Two birds flushed from the grass in front of Russ, their wings a blur against the blue sky.

Then another blur, a white one, barreled across the idyllic scene heading straight for Russ's blind side.

"Russ!"

Her shout came too late. The sheep launched itself, head down, straight at him. The crack of impact was jolting, sickening even at a distance. Russ was tossed to the side and landed in a heap. Jigs shot from the barn, his staccato barks drawing the sheep's attention for a moment. Then the ram squared up and ran at the dog. Jigs dodged sideways but didn't get completely out of the way. Bumped hard, the dog still sank its teeth into the sheep's hind leg.

"Jigs! Russ!" Mickey pelted across the pasture holding a hayfork like a spear. The sheep swung around and butted Jigs, dislodging the dog's hold before it faced Mickey and charged. The young man leaped aside at the last minute, swinging the handle of the hayfork and catching the sheep's back legs. The sheep rolled and landed on its back. The boy was on top of it in a flash, grabbed a rope from his back pocket, and tied the animal's legs together. It struggled, but it couldn't hurt anyone now.

Emmie flew across the pasture, unaware of how she'd gotten through the gate. Pastor Anderson was also running, his hat flying off on the way. He reached Russ first.

"Lie still. Mickey has the beast under control." The pastor had his hand on Russ's shoulder, keeping him from trying to rise. "Where did he hit you?"

"Leg." Russ panted out the word.

Emmie fell to her knees beside him. Even through his trousers, the limb was obviously broken, his foot at the wrong angle to his hips. "Someone must fetch a doctor."

"No!" It wasn't a word, it was a roar that burst from Russ's lips.

"Steady, man." Pastor Anderson increased the pressure on Russ's shoulder. "She's right. Your leg is broken."

"No doctor." The words were ground out through his clenched teeth.

"We need to get him to the house." Emmie turned to Mickey. "Have you a loose door? A wide plank? Something we can move him onto? It'll hurt less if we can secure him to something before we move him." Her nurse training kicked in.

"I know what'll work." The boy raced toward the barn.

The angry sheep bawled and bucked against its restraints. Jigs lifted his head and growled but didn't rise.

"Should have shot that blasted ram weeks ago," Russ said.

Emmie glanced over her shoulder at the struggling beast. "Your new ram?"

Russ nodded, his eye glazed with pain. It wasn't going to get better until the bone was set and immobilized, and even then...

"Don't worry about that now," said Pastor Anderson. "Let's worry about getting you to the house."

Mickey came through the gate pulling a long, slender something behind him. Russ turned his head when Mickey got close. "The hay chute. Good thinking, son."

"We have to move him while keeping his leg as still as possible." Emmie stepped into her old, familiar nursing assistant's role. "Pastor, you slide your arms under his hips. Mickey, you take his shoulders. I'll get the chute as close to him as I can, then I'll hold his leg." She maneuvered the chute into position. "Slowly and smoothly, at the count of three, we slide him sideways. Ready?"

Pastor and Mickey nodded, Russ gritted his teeth.

"One, two, *three*."

Russ passed out before they'd finished the move.

"Russ?" Mickey blanched as white as the sheep. "Is he—?"

"He passed out from the pain," she said. "That's a blessing. Let's get him into the house before he comes around. One of you get on each end, and I'll open the gate and door to the house."

"You know what you're doin', miss, and I'm right glad of it." Mickey's face had a bit more color. Good. Couldn't have him passing out too.

"I worked in a hospital during the end of the war until a few months ago."

Pastor Anderson shot her a thankful look. "A woman of many talents."

"I just did my part." She opened the gate and held it while the men brought Russ through.

"That why his scars don't bother you none?" Mickey asked. "I notice when we're in town, most women look away from him. But you don't."

She closed the gate, turning her back so they wouldn't see her flush. "I've seen plenty worse."

Hurrying around them, she made it to the house first and opened the door. If only she were entering under different circumstances. She'd so wanted to see the house Becky had written of. A house filled with love and laughter. Or at least, it used to be.

"Where should we put him?" she asked Mickey.

"His room's up them stairs, but I don't know—"

"Is there a downstairs bedroom?"

Mickey lifted his chin to indicate a door to her right. "Through there."

She led the way. The bed was wide and high and unmade. "Have you any idea where to find bedding?"

"Maybe in that trunk at the end of his bed."

She glanced toward the bed.

"No, miss. His bed upstairs. Second room."

Oh, of course. "Can you two hold him while I get the bedding?"

"Hurry if you can," Pastor Anderson said, sweat popping out on his forehead. Russ wasn't a small man. He wasn't fat, just tall and well-muscled from farm work. And no doubt heavy.

She raced up the stairs and burst into the second room. Resisting the urge to look around his private sanctuary, she flung open the trunk. A uniform lay on top. She pawed through the layers but found no bedding. What was she thinking? She left the trunk and pulled the bedding off the bed, grabbed some toweling from the washstand, wadded it all together, and hurried back down the stairs.

"I'll have it made up in a jiffy."

As soon as the sheet was tucked under the mattress, she spread the toweling where his leg would rest. They laid the chute on one side of the bed and reversed their earlier maneuver, sliding Russ off the chute and onto the bed. He groaned but didn't awaken.

Emmie worked at removing the boot from Russ's uninjured leg. "We need to get his trousers off and clean the wound site." Silence followed her order. She glanced up. "Mickey, do you know where to find the doctor?"

He shook his head.

"Then you'll need to go, Pastor. Mickey can help me here."

"Miss Mason." Pastor Anderson shook his head.

"There's no time to waste. When he awakens, he'll be in tremendous pain. He'll need the doctor, no matter what he said in the field."

"Perhaps you could leave the"—he cleared his throat—"the undressing until the doctor arrives."

"No. It'll be better if we do it while he's passed out." She tossed the boot to the floor and started on the other one.

Russ moaned.

"There's no way to do it without causing him pain," she said.

Both men stared at her. She straightened and planted her hands on her hips. "Move! There's no time to linger." She pointed her finger at the pastor. "You go fetch the doctor." She swung her finger to Mickey. "You go upstairs and find a second blanket, and then go release that animal bawling in the pasture." Neither moved. "Now!"

They scattered, and she turned back to the patient. For now, that's what she must force herself to see him as.

She entered the kitchen and grabbed a knife that looked sharp. Cutting the trousers was the best way to remove them. Yet even that would hurt him if he regained consciousness.

Mickey clomped down the stairs, a blanket in one hand and a rifle in the other.

Emmie froze.

Mickey's face flushed, and his mouth pulled into a grim line.

"You're going to shoot the ram." Of course he was. She may be a city girl, but she knew that dangerous animals were put down.

"Yes, miss." His face was pale but the slant of his mouth determined. "And maybe Jigs too."

She took a step back, bumping into the stove. "Jigs?"

"He didn't get up to follow us, miss. I fear..." The nob in the boy's thin throat bobbed.

Becky's dog. One more link to his sister that Russ might lose.

Because of her.

He'd never have been caught off guard if she hadn't shown up unexpectedly. Again. Disrupting his world. She wanted to cry, but there wasn't time.

She returned to the bedroom and was cutting through Russ's trousers when a shot broke the silence. The ram's bawling stopped. She wiped her forehead on her sleeve.

The second shot started her tears.

CHAPTER 21

S OMEONE GROANED IN THE distance. Mickey? Russ tried to open his eyes, but they refused to obey. His head pounded, and his mouth tasted as if someone had shoved a dirty sock in it. Felt like it too. He couldn't work up enough spit to swallow. With a groan that sounded familiar, he raised himself onto his elbows. Pain shot from his leg to his head and back again. His eye popped opened, but the room tilted, and he slammed it shut again.

"Russ?"

Becky? No, she was gone. Grief weighted his chest.

"Russ?"

Who was that? Why wouldn't his brain function? He hadn't felt like this since the hospital when they'd fed him laudanum. He forced his eye open again. Where was he? This wasn't his bedroom. His heart sped, and he gasped for air against the pain in his leg and head.

"You must lie still. The doctor said—"

"Doctor?" The word left his dry throat with little more than a croak.

"Lie still and let me get you a drink of water."

Water sounded like heaven at the moment. The woman's hand slid beneath his head, fingers cool and strong. Emmie. It was Emmie. What... what had happened?

She tipped the cool liquid into his mouth, and he swallowed as much as he could before she took it away.

"Not too much at first. I know you're thirsty from the medication, but your stomach might not accept too much just yet."

Her voice was cool and impersonal but once he could focus, he knew it was Emmie.

"Where?"

"You're home. In the bedroom downstairs. There was an accident. The good news is that only one of your lower leg bones was broken, and it was a clean break, it didn't rupture the skin. The doctor set it—"

"Doctor?" She'd said that twice now, hadn't she?

"Yes. We needed the doctor to set the bone. Now you must lie still for your leg to mend properly. The doctor said it should as long as you don't try to rush things."

A doctor had been here, in his house? Anger added to the pounding in his head. He rubbed his scalp.

"You hit your head when you fell. It's probably not a concussion, but you may have a headache for a few days."

"He's awake?" Another woman entered the room. She looked vaguely familiar.

Emmie turned to her. "He is, but the laudanum has him a bit fuddled still. I told the doctor he was using too much."

Laudanum. They'd doused him with that at the army hospital. It had given him a headache then, too. Better a headache than what happened to others, to those who became dependent on the stuff like a drunk needing a drink. He wouldn't take it again, and he'd demand Emmie throw the rest away. As soon as he could keep his eye open.

Would she still be here when he awoke? He hoped so. He shouldn't, but he did.

"I don't know what I'd have done if you hadn't come." Emmie poured the coffee, handing a cup and saucer to Mrs. McCann. "When Pastor Anderson suggested it..." Insisted was more like it. Although how her staying with Russ to nurse him back to health could be improper when the man couldn't even get out of bed was a bit beyond her. And the doctor had been firm that Russ could not get out of bed for at least two weeks, and even then he'd require help with his splinted leg.

"I'm glad I could. With Stewart in Chicago for the week and maybe longer, the children and I had little else to do."

"I so appreciate it."

"Stewie has missed living in the country. Mickey's good to allow him and Robbie to tag along while he works."

"I don't think Mickey's much older than Robbie." Emmie took a sip of the strong brew. "You said you were newly moved to Jonesville. Where did you come from, Mrs. McCann?"

"You must call me Alannah, please. Stewart ran a Pony Express station in Wyoming. We met there." She shook her head with a funny sort of half-smile. "That's a long story for another day. We stayed after the Pony Express stopped running, and he managed the telegraph post there until last year. That's when Robbie's father—Stewart's brother—finally succumbed to his injuries from the war." Sorrow clouded her blue-gray eyes. "We came across the country to collect Robbie. His mother had died of tuberculosis more than a year past. Before we could return to Wyoming, the position in Jonesville came open, so we decided to move here."

"I'm sorry for your loss." Emmie had seen too much of that at the hospital in the years following the war. Men who had lingered for months, even years after their injuries, only to lose their final battle at home. She looked toward the bedroom.

"He probably doesn't think so," Alannah said, "but Mr. Fields is one of the lucky ones."

He was alive, but was he truly living? Or had he buried himself here on the farm with little contact beyond his weekly trip to town? Did he push everyone away... or only her?

She took another sip of her coffee to hide the tremble of her lips.

"Forgive me for asking, but is there something special between you and Mr. Fields?"

Emmie choked on her drink. Alice, the toddler, stopped banging her blocks together and stared while Emmie coughed and wiped the tears from her eyes.

"I'm sorry. I shouldn't have asked." Alannah handed her a handkerchief. "It's certainly none of my business."

Emmie mopped her eyes and steadied her breathing. "No, it's all right." She sighed and glanced out the window. "It would be nice to have a friend to talk to again."

Alannah nodded and waited.

"I told you about Becky and me going to school together. It was a shock when Russ wrote to tell me that she'd passed away. After a few days, I wrote him back and thanked him for letting me know. After that..." She shrugged. "We kept writing."

"So you agreed to meet?"

It would be easy to let her new friend think the best of her, but she couldn't do that, not if they were to be true friends. And there was something to the fiery-haired woman that drew Emmie to her. An openness and an honesty that reminded her of Helen.

"I'm afraid it didn't happen that way. You see, he'd mentioned the opening at the church for a pianist, and then I applied."

"Without telling him?" Her new friend's eyes grew rounder.

Emmie gripped her emerald and plowed on with her story. "No, I didn't. When my father died a couple of months ago, my brothers were intent upon finding me a husband." She raised her eyes to Alannah. "They are much older than I and have very different views from mine on what my life should look like."

"Do they know about Mr. Fields and his letters?"

"No."

"Oh, Emmie. Do they know where you are?" Real concern mixed with a tinge of shock in Alannah's voice.

"Not yet." Her voice reflected her shame even to her own ears. "Russ told me that I must write to them, and I will."

Alannah reached across the table and grasped her hand. "That's good. It's the right thing to do. Now tell me, how did your meeting with Mr. Fields go?"

The words poured from Emmie like water from a fountain. The horrid buggy ride, his rescuing her, his shock, the silent return to town... She barely drew a breath until the whole sordid story lay between them.

"Had you any idea of the extent of his scars?"

"Becky had mentioned him being injured but not how. And that doesn't matter to me."

Alannah squeezed her hand. "Perhaps it matters to him."

Clunk. Clunk. Clunk.

Russ tried to focus on the sound. *Clunk.* Wood banging against wood. The ram. He struggled to sit upright only to gasp and fall back against a pillow. He breathed deeply until the pain evened out.

He was in bed. Not his bed. *Clunk.* He swiveled his head just enough to see the open doorway. A toddler in a faded pink gown sat on the floor. She smiled at him and knocked a wooden block in her chubby hand against the door frame. *Clunk.*

"Alice, how did you get clear over there?" A woman with striking red hair bent and scooped the toddler off the floor. Then her eyes met his. "Mr. Fields, you're awake. I'm sorry if this one bothered your rest."

"Who are you?" Was that his voice or a rusty hinge? He tried to swallow, but there was nothing to go down.

Emmie bustled into the room in a flurry of green and gold skirts. She slipped her hand beneath his head and lifted a cup to his lips. The water revived him. He swallowed until she took it away.

"This is Mrs. McCann and her daughter Alice." Emmie eased his head onto the pillow. "She's come to help me nurse you back to health."

The scene came rushing back. "The ram hit me."

"Yes. Your leg is broken, and you must remain still for it to heal properly." Her voice was so crisp, cool, and professional. That's right. She'd been a nurse. How had he forgotten that? Because he never wanted to remember anything to do with hospitals or doctors.

She picked up a brown bottle from the bedside stand. "The doctor left laudanum for your pain—"

"No."

"But—"

"No."

She set the bottle down and clamped her hands on her hips. "The doctor said—"

"I don't care. No laudanum."

"The pain—"

Anger bubbled up from deep inside him. "I can handle pain. Trust me. I've had plenty of practice." He turned his head so she'd have a full view of his scars.

She cupped his damaged cheek with her palm, shocking him into silence. Shocking him to his core. Then her tender fingers prodded the skin he worked so diligently to hide.

"You healed well. Do the scars itch? I could make you a lotion—"

He pushed her hand away and turned his head until the scars were hidden against the pillow. "No."

"Russ. I only want to help."

"Then leave me be."

"You need nursing."

"Mickey's here. He can do the chores and cook. We don't need any help."

He hadn't turned his face enough to miss the frown that marred her smooth brow.

"If you think I'm leaving you here like this, with only a half-grown boy to tend you, you're sadly mistaken, Mr. Fields."

He closed his eye and fought the urge to grab her hand and hold on. He needed her to go. He couldn't let himself become dependent on her. Couldn't let himself dream of the possibility that she'd stay.

For always.

"I'll send Mickey into town for supplies." Emmie cleaned off the table, setting the breakfast dishes into the washtub already filled with hot water. The lingering smells of fried ham and eggs were whisked away by the scents of wildflowers when she pushed the window open.

"I'll make a list while you wash the dishes." Alannah untied her apron and opened the drawer where they'd discovered paper and pencils the day before.

Wash the dishes. Emmie plunged her hands into the water, then grimaced and dried them off on her apron. She needed to shave in the soap first. The lump of white soap on the shelf above the washtub crumbled into bits when she ran it across the grater. She plunged her hands back into the water and sloshed it about until bubbles formed.

Such a simple thing, really, but she'd never washed a dish until she'd come here. Cook did the washing up at home, and Penny at the boardinghouse. Alannah had covered her shock—mostly—when Emmie'd admitted she didn't know how to wash dishes.

It must seem strange to her new friend—whom Emmie'd already learned could do anything that needed doing—to meet someone like her. Someone so ill-equipped for life on the farm. The life she'd been dreaming about for months—years. Long before she'd started writing Russ, she'd already fallen in love with the simple country life Becky had painted with her words.

Becky had never mentioned washing dishes or clothing. Why would she have? It was just part of her daily routine. She'd made gathering eggs sound charming, which hadn't prepared Emmie for getting pecked by a broody hen. She rubbed the back of her hand before swirling the washrag across another plate. And who knew that frying pans couldn't be soaped? Well, she did now. And she'd learned that sanding off rust was something to avoid in the future. She washed the last cup and set it on the rack to dry.

Alannah sat at the table, the stump end of a pencil to her lips. "Check the flour barrel, will you? I think I should order another fifty-pound bag."

Emmie lifted the lid. It was almost half full. She'd no idea how large a fifty-pound bag was, but she didn't feel like showing her ignorance this early in the morning. The past three days had included enough of that.

"Yes. I think you should."

"There's flour in the cellar," Russ called from the bedroom.

"There's nothing wrong with his ears," Alannah said as she crossed off the word from her list.

Emmie sighed. She took off her apron and pasted on the smile that had worked with so many patients over the years. Even though it hadn't worked with Russ yet. Then she entered his room.

"Breakfast is cleaned up. The boys are taking care of the livestock. It's time to check your leg."

"You check it every morning, and it's always the same." He tucked the edge of the blanket under the wooden splint.

"And I'll check it again this morning. Doctor's orders."

A low sound, something between a growl and a groan, escaped from Russ. She ignored it and pulled the blanket away, being careful not to jar his leg. The skin was a mottled combination of colors from black to blue to purple, even turning greenish near the edge of the bruising. She laid the back of her hand against it, giving a nod at the warmth. Not too hot, not too cold. Then she pressed her fingertips along the surface. Russ sucked a breath through his teeth. There were no watery pockets beneath the skin.

"I'll have Mickey stop by the doctor's office and give him a report. You're healing well."

"So you keep saying, but you won't let me out of bed."

"Broken bones need time to mend. You're otherwise strong and healthy. You'll do well if you follow the doctor's orders."

A grunt was his only response, his head turned away from her. She wanted to touch the wounded side of his face and turn it toward her, to show him that she wasn't put off by his scars, but the memory of his reaction to her touch the last time kept her hands at her sides.

"I could read to you for a while. What type of books do you prefer?"

"Don't trouble yourself."

"It's no trouble. I'd be happy to—"

"Send Mickey in before he goes to town."

She knew a dismissal when she heard one. "Yes, Russ."

Alannah's eyes met hers as she returned to the kitchen. *I'm sorry*, her friend mouthed the words. Emmie shrugged. What else could she do? Even though he needed help, the man didn't want her around. She'd been a fool to come across the country thinking anything good would come of it.

Now she was a broken-hearted fool.

"Come in, Mickey," Russ said when the boy hung in the bedroom doorway, twisting his hat in his hands.

Mickey walked to the bed, his face pulled into long lines.

"I'll be fine."

"Reckon you will, leastwise, the doc says so. And Miss Mason is determined you'll get better."

Russ didn't want to argue. He'd done enough of that with Emmie, so he ignored the mention of the doctor. "You know where my rifle is?"

"On the wall rack upstairs."

"I hate to ask it of you, but I need you to shoot that ram before he hurts you or anyone else."

"I already done it."

"You did?" The boy knew how to handle a gun?

"Yup." Mickey's boots scuffed against the floorboards. "Pastor, he stayed long enough to show me how to use the gun before goin' for the doc. I hadn't never shot one before."

"You did good. I'm grateful." Why was the boy so downcast about shooting a rogue ram?

"Thing is, I had to shoot Jigs, too."

Pain stabbed at Russ's chest. A vague remembrance of the old dog's frenzied barking came to him. "The ram got him?"

"Yup. Busted old Jigs up bad. I knowed there wasn't nothin' anyone could do. Pastor thought his back was broken 'cause he couldn't move his legs none."

Russ closed his eye but reached out and grasped the boy's forearm. "Thank you. You did the right thing, and I know it was hard."

Jigs. He'd been too old, too slow, to handle that ram. And now he was dead. One more link to Becky, gone. It was Russ's fault for being cowardly.

He should have shot that blasted ram weeks ago.

CHAPTER 22

T HE WOMEN'S VOICES DRIFTED through the open window, swirling in with the scent of apple blossoms from the tree near the house. The clothesline hung near that window of his parents' room. He hadn't been in here much since Pa died. It was all tidied up now, the women having thought it needed cleaning. Emmie seemed to be obsessed with cleanliness, even though she hadn't a clue how to achieve it.

He smiled at the memory of Mrs. McCann's lessons. Emmie was used to other people doing the washing and cleaning, but she was plucky enough and willing to learn. He gave her credit for that. She'd tackled each task the other woman set for her. Even now, the yeasty scent of bread rising made his stomach tighten. He could almost picture Emmie bent over the table, flour to her elbows, the green stone she wore around her neck dangling, and a smile on her face. His stomach tightened in a different way.

He should force her to leave. Those thoughts, those *feelings*, they wouldn't do him any good. And they wouldn't stop with her here.

He'd be fine with just Mickey. The boy was a passable cook and knew how to do all the basic chores. The cornfields were planted, and the hay wouldn't need cutting for a few weeks yet. Mickey would be able to handle it, and Russ'd be up hobbling on crutches by then and of some use at least. If things weren't as clean and orderly as they were with Emmie here, he and Mickey would get on well enough.

"Can we come in, sir?" Four-year-old Stewie stuck his head around the corner of the door, a shock of red hair over his round face.

Russ nodded.

The boy entered with a book in one hand and his little sister's hand in the other.

"You read us a story, sir?" the boy asked.

Little Alice took her thumb out of her mouth, pointed at his face, and said, "Boo-boo?"

His heart contracted for a moment in a rise of panic. He'd not kept his face turned away.

"Hurt?" the little girl asked.

"Naw, Ma says he fighted in the war like Robbie's pa. Got hurt just like Robbie's pa did."

Before Russ could gather his wits, Stewie pushed little Alice from behind, trying to scoot her onto the bed. Russ grabbed a handful of the back of her dress and lifted her up. She grinned and snuggled against his side, her thumb poked back into her mouth.

She wasn't afraid of him. Or his scars.

Stewie climbed up after her and sat near the edge of the pillow. "I brung a book." He thrust it at Russ. *The Story of a Dog* by Mrs. Perring. A lump formed in Russ's throat. The book he'd bought to give to Becky last Christmas. A book she'd never had the chance to read.

"Will that do?" Stewie asked.

"It'll do." The crisp pages crinkled as he opened them.

Alice cuddled against him, and Stewie snuggled on the edge of the pillow, little hands tucked behind his head, elbows jack-knifed on each side like oversized ears.

Russ's voice drowned out the two women talking while they hung wash on the line.

Was this what it would be like to have a family of his own? He paused a moment, then read on when Alice turned her baby-blue eyes his way.

His voice thickened with a combination of longing and regret.

Emmie followed Alannah into the cool house, wiping sweat from her brow. Not that it was terribly hot, but summer had arrived, and hanging laundry wasn't as easy as one would think. Her friend gestured wildly from near Russ's bedroom door. A spark of fear shot through Emmie until she saw the grin on Alannah's face. She set her empty basket on the table and crept closer.

Russ's deep voice came from the bedroom in a cadence as if he were... reading? She looked at Alannah, who nodded vigorously and pointed toward the open doorway. Emmie eased closer and peeked inside the room. She jerked back, her hand tight across her mouth.

Alannah grabbed her arm and all but hauled her back outside.

"I'm no nurse, but surely that's a good sign."

"I have to agree." Emmie looked back into the house, even though she couldn't see into the bedroom. Russ was interacting with the children. She pushed away the small stab of hurt mixed with a thread of jealousy. What mattered was that Russ had opened up to someone.

Even if it hadn't been her.

"It must have been the children's idea." Russ hadn't spoken to anyone unless necessary for the past four days.

"That would be Stewie. Neither Stewart nor I are very outgoing, but that boy makes up for it. I'd bet my bottom dollar that he just marched in and asked to be read to. But where did he find the book?"

"There were several in the sitting room when I dusted yesterday." Emmie had lingered over the titles, imagining Becky enjoying them. "Becky was an avid reader."

"Perhaps her brother is too, and we just didn't know."

She'd offered to read to him but hadn't thought to offer to fetch him a book. She resisted the urge to slap her forehead with Alannah watching.

The rattle of wheels and jingle of harness was followed by the doctor's buggy coming around the house. Alannah hurried to tie the horse while Emmie waited for the doctor to step out.

"How's the patient?" he asked, his voice the same gruff tone he'd used on his first visit. Maybe the man couldn't speak any other way, but to her mind, it wasn't the best for a soothing bedside manner.

She crossed her arms. "He's resting well, no fever, and the leg is warm to the touch with only normal bruising to discolor it."

He grunted and looked her up and down. "You were a nurse, eh?"

She straightened, smoothing her apron. "Not a full nurse, a nursing assistant."

"Well, that'll do. I'll check on the patient as long as I'm here, but it sounds like you've got everything under control."

Was that grudging admiration? She followed him into the house. Alannah had tied the horse and was right behind her. There was no sound of anyone reading now. Stewie and Alice stood just outside the bedroom door. The doctor patted the boy on the head as he passed.

"You can leave." Russ's voice lashed through the house. Alice scurried to her mother, who picked her up. Emmie shooed Stewie away from the door, entered the bedroom, and closed the door behind her. She marched past the doctor and stopped beside the bed. Russ glowered at her, for once not turning his face away.

"You've scared the children."

His eye snapped to the door, and the belligerence faded from the angle of his mouth. "Didn't mean to."

"Let's have a look at you," the doctor said.

The belligerence returned in a heartbeat. "No."

"Young man, I have three other people to visit yet today. I've no time for nonsense."

No bedside manner at all. Emmie balled the sides of her apron in her fists. "Let him look at your leg, and then he can be on his way."

Russ focused on her. "You've already checked it. You said it's fine."

"I'm not a doctor."

"I don't care."

"Well, I do." She cared very much, more than she should, more than he wanted her to, but she wasn't backing down.

Something of her thoughts must have reached him, because he turned his face to the wall and jerked the blanket from his leg.

The doctor stepped forward. Russ's jaw muscles bunched as the man poked and prodded, more than was necessary, as far as she could tell. They both needed a smack. One for being stubborn and the other for being uncaring and unkind.

"As you said, everything appears to be healing well." The doctor stepped away from the bed and faced her. "Continue as you are, complete bed rest for another week. Send someone for me if he develops a fever or you find any sign of infection." He looked around the room and grunted. "You've a good handle on things, I see. If you ever decide to take up nursing, let me know. You appear to be trainable." With that, he stalked from the room.

"Insufferable man," she muttered under her breath.

"Him? Or me?"

Emmie whirled to the bed. Russ kept his head tilted but not completely turned away. She cocked her head at him. "Both."

A slow smile relaxed his mouth. She sucked in a breath and wished she had something to do with her hands other than mangle her poor apron. "Can I get you anything?"

He shook his head and tried to cover his leg. She grabbed the edge of the blanket to assist, and their hands met. Their eyes met for a brief moment and something flared between them. The piercing blue of his eye faded as he buried his hands under the blanket and faced the wall again.

But there had been something. Something real. She hadn't imagined it.

Sweat beaded on Russ's brow by the time he'd gotten himself into a sitting position on the bed. It had been a week since the disaster with the ram. A week of lying in bed, and already his muscles were turning to mush. He'd follow Emmie's orders and stay in bed, but he had to at least sit upright for a while. He maneuvered the pillows to cushion his back against the wooden headboard. That felt better. In fact, it felt better just sitting up again. He bent his good leg and rested his forearm on it. Much better.

"Mr. Fields is gettin' up," Stewie announced from the doorway, but before Russ could say a word—

"Oh no, he's not." Emmie charged into the room, color high and dark eyes flashing. Her hair was pinned up, but tendrils had escaped and clung to her damp brow and cheeks. It was an unusually warm day for late May, and she'd been cleaning. Again. It seemed she couldn't stop once she'd started. The whole house smelled of pine oil. He'd heard her talking to Mrs. McCann about some doctor and his theory connecting cleanliness and good health. She'd sure taken it to heart.

But at the moment, she was all but breathing fire at him.

"I'm just sitting up. I haven't left the bed."

"You're not going to, either." She dipped her chin and raised her brows, one hand planted on each hip, daring him to contradict her.

Some bedevilment took hold of him. "I don't think you're big enough to keep me here if I want to get up."

She stormed to the bed and loomed over him, as much as her petite form could loom. He clenched his teeth to avoid a smile. She might not be what some would consider a classic beauty, but she was more than pretty enough.

"I think you'll find that I've learned how to handle exasperating patients quite efficiently."

He'd bet she was right about that. Determination was written all across her features, from the tilt of her round chin to the high flush on her cheeks. What he really wanted to do was kiss her. It wasn't her fierceness, but his shock that made him look away.

Had he really just thought that?

"That's better." She backed away. "Can I bring you anything?"

She couldn't bring him what he really wanted. A whole face and a whole mind. "Nothing." The word came out flat. She opened her mouth but snapped it shut again. Instead, she turned and left the room.

What had come over him? How could he allow himself to feel so... so... like a normal man?

Come to think on it, he hadn't had a war dream—sleeping or awake—since he'd been injured. Why hadn't the injury or the doctor caused one? He stared out the bedroom door. The women were talking, a gentle murmur too low for him to catch the words. Alice jabbered, probably to that corncob doll her mother had fashioned for her. Pine oil and lye soap vied with the fresh breeze coming through the window.

Normal sounds, normal scents, normal... Was there a chance he was finding his way back to normal again? Or could it be that Emmie was bringing normal back to him?

Could he let her?

Nursing another red mark on the back of her hand and muttering under her breath about the broody hen, Emmie emerged from the henhouse to the clip-clop of a horse approaching. Mickey and Robbie were in the barn cleaning the horse and cow stalls. Alannah was hoeing in the garden while Alice and Stewie played beneath a nearby tree. Being the closest to the house, Emmie hurried to greet the visitor.

Pastor Anderson pulled the horse to a stop by the hitching rail. "Good morning, Miss Mason." His smile was pleasant, but maybe a little reserved.

"Good morning, Pastor." She cradled the eggs in her apron, so she nodded toward the door. "I'm sure you're here to visit the patient. Won't you come in?"

He tied the horse and opened the door for her.

"Sorry I couldn't come earlier," he said. "There was a house fire in town, and I've been working with the family to relocate and gather needed supplies."

"Oh, dear. Is there anything we can do to help?"

He cocked his head. "We?"

She turned her back and placed the eggs in a basket one at a time, letting the heat leave her cheeks. "Alannah and I. Mr. McCann has been detained in Chicago."

"Hm."

She turned and waited.

"Yes, well. Perhaps you could do some sewing? The little girls lost most of their clothing."

She took a deep breath and nodded. That was something she could do reasonably well. And she wouldn't need to leave Russ. Especially since things seemed to have settled down between them after yesterday. She should have insisted he sit up sooner, so marked was the change in his manner. At least, his manner toward her.

"I'm sure we can do that." She gestured toward the bedroom door. "Mr. Fields is through there."

"Yes, I remember." The pastor stepped into the bedroom.

While Emmie waited in the kitchen, she took a rag and cleaned around the windows. Pollen and flies made that a daily chore. It had probably been a daily chore at home as well, but she'd never noticed. The servants had taken care of all the cleaning.

She paused and gazed out at the sheep pasture. The woolly creatures moved together with their heads down, grazing the lush spring grasses. Nothing was gray here and the air smelled as fresh as she'd imagined. Maybe even fresher.

Something crashed. She jumped and whirled. Three steps toward the bedroom, a shout ripped through the house. She ran the remaining steps. Russ sat hunched over on the bed, his hands clasped over his ears, his eye closed. Another shout ended in a heart-rending groan.

Pastor Anderson turned to her, his mouth opened and shut. He gestured toward the plate she'd left on the side table. It lay broken on the floor.

Russ wasn't moving.

The back door slammed.

Mickey rushed in and glanced around. He shoved Pastor Anderson out of his way and dropped onto the side of the bed.

"It weren't nothin', Russ. Just a plate. Look at it there on the floor." He pointed to the broken shards. "Look, Russ."

Russ turned a fraction toward the boy.

"Just a plate, I promise."

Finger by finger, Russ loosened his hands from around his ears. He blinked a few times.

"That's right. Just a plate. See it there?" Mickey crooned the words.

What was happening? She flicked a glance at the pastor, who looked as confused as she felt.

Mickey bore at glance at her. "We'll just clear the room and clean that up now."

She knew a hint when it was tossed in her lap. She plucked at the pastor's sleeve and tilted her head toward the door. Once in the kitchen, they stared at each other a moment.

"What happened?" she whispered.

"I'm so sorry. He was sleeping, and I sat on the chair. I bumped the table, and the plate fell. Then he..."

She'd heard the rest. She'd seen men react that way before in the hospital. They called it soldier's heart. But it was her heart that hurt now... for Russ.

CHAPTER 23

"T HEY CALL IT SOLDIER's heart or irritable heart." Emmie sat across the table from Mickey and Alannah. Robbie had the younger children occupied outside. Russ was sleeping, no doubt worn out from the incident. Pastor Anderson had left, still shaken even though she'd assured him it hadn't been his fault.

She laid her hand over Mickey's. "You've obviously seen him like that before."

The lanky boy nodded, looked at their hands, and then back to her. "Wakes me in the night cryin' out like that sometimes. Liked to scared the pants offen me the first time."

"It's happened more than once?"

He nodded.

"What do you do when it happens?"

"Like I done just now." He pulled his hand from under hers and gestured to the bedroom. "Talk to him slow and easy like. Tell him to look around and see what's there. I guess he's seeing things that ain't. And maybe hearin' 'em. Always covers his ears like that."

Alannah leaned forward. "Why hasn't it happened before while we've been here?"

Emmie shrugged. "The doctors don't know enough about it. The patients' heart rates increase, breathing becomes rapid, there can be severe chest pain. Sometimes it goes away on its own. Sometimes they try medication." She shook her head. The medication didn't help as much as it drugged the men into oblivion. Like alcohol, it stole their wits. She didn't want that for Russ.

"What can we do to help him?" Alannah asked.

"I have a dear friend who's a nurse back in Pittsburgh. I'll write to her today. She knows more about this than I do. Maybe she can give us some advice."

Alannah rose and fetched the paper, ink, and pen. She set two sheets and two envelopes in front of Emmie. "I think it's time you wrote that other letter as well, don't you?"

Emmie searched for another reason to put it off, but the caring and concern in her friend's eyes had her nodding. She picked up the pen as Mickey and Alannah stepped outdoors. She'd write Helen's letter first, since that was the easy one. Within minutes, she'd scratched out questions about soldier's heart. Then she paused, the handle end of the pen pressed against her bottom lip.

What could it hurt? Helen was working with Dr. Lawson, who was a student of Surgeon McKee's new techniques. She bit down on the pen. Maybe Alannah was right. Or partly right. Maybe it was the scars and the soldier's heart that kept Russ from opening up to others.

Not just to her, but especially to her.

She dipped the nib in the ink, missing her fountain pen back at Aunt Maggie's, and scratched out another flurry of questions. Blowing on the ink until it was dry, she took her time folding the sheet and addressing the envelope.

She took another few minutes to check on Russ. He still slept, his fingers twitching on the covers, but a peaceful expression relaxed his features. His head was turned in profile, the handsome side toward her. He must have turned the girls' heads before the war. He'd never have looked at someone as plain as she back then. A tiny part of her cringed over that truth. He was scarred now, and others might look at him differently, but she didn't care. She'd fallen in love with *him* on paper, not with his face. However, if it meant that much to him, she'd do whatever she could, with Helen's help, to see him restored to some semblance of his former handsomeness.

The single blank sheet of paper on the table mocked her attempts to ignore it. She plopped down in the chair and picked up the pen. It was time to write to Archie... even if she didn't plan to mail it right away. After what she'd just written to Helen, she needed to buy more time for her friend to respond.

Since the preacher's visit two days past, Russ'd barely spoken to any-one, even the children. He cringed at the memory of little Alice's blue eyes filling with tears the last time she'd peeked into the bedroom, refusing to enter. What had he become?

A casualty of war. Not in the normal sense. He hadn't been that lucky. His comrades in battle who were buried in fields across a trail of states hadn't had to come home and deal with the aftermath. The stares, the whispers, the looks of horror—those were the easiest parts. The constant fear of the battlefield overtaking his mind was worse.

Far worse.

Emmie had seen it, yet she was still there. She hadn't even gone in for church with the rest of those now staying at his farm. She stayed behind. Stayed with him. Not that it could last.

He covered his face with his hands.

"Is everything all right?" Emmie's voice carried from the doorway.

Why hadn't she gone with everyone else? Why didn't everyone just go home and leave him alone? He clenched his teeth and dragged his hands from his face. He was being unreasonable and he knew it.

"Everything is just fine." He couldn't keep the surly edge from his voice.

Emmie stepped into the room. "Russ." She half-lifted one hand toward him and then let it drop to her side. "Is there anything—?"

"No."

She closed her eyes, then turned to leave.

He was worse than unreasonable. He was becoming the monster to match his face.

"Emmie."

She stopped but didn't turn. Didn't want to look at him, no doubt. Why would she? Why would anybody?

"I'm not myself right now." How he wished that were true, but it wasn't. This was who he was now... who he would be from now on.

"You're right." She turned, her dark eyes shimmering in the bright sunshine pouring through the window. "I would do anything to help you get back to where you were."

Impossible. Why couldn't she see that? He shook his head.

"There are things that can be done. Treatments."

"In a hospital?" He almost spat the last word, so vile it tasted on his tongue.

"Well, yes. But also here at home."

He folded his arms across his chest. "You don't understand."

"I know, and I don't pretend to. But I've seen through your letters—"

He issued a rude half snort, half bark. "That wasn't me."

She took a step back. "Russ..."

"That was who I might have been if—" He waved his hand at the damaged side of his face.

"I don't believe that."

"I don't care what you believe." He couldn't stop the snap in his voice.

She sighed and straightened. "I know you don't, so I'll just have to care enough for the both of us... for a while. I've written to a friend, a nurse—"

"Why can't you just leave me alone?"

Chin lifted and cheeks at high color, she swished from the room with a flick of her skirts. If only things had been different. If only they'd met before the war. If only...

If only he had the heart—the courage—to try.

Alannah folded the last of Alice's clothing and stacked it into the small trunk she'd brought when she'd arrived with the children.

"I'm sorry I have to leave."

"Nonsense. Your husband has returned, and your place is at home with him." A small twinge of envy tightened Emmie's throat for a moment. She swallowed. "I just can't believe that Aunt Maggie agreed to come out and stay."

"She didn't agree. It was her suggestion."

"And you said Mr. Keen will be driving her out?" Emmie had a vague memory of being introduced to an old man with gnarled fingers and missing teeth on her first Sunday at the church.

Alannah paused with her hands on the trunk's latch. "That was the odd part. Mr. Keen isn't known for his generosity of spirit, but he stepped up and volunteered when he overheard us after the service. He said he had something else to bring out to Mr. Fields."

"Any idea what?"

"None. He told Aunt Maggie he'd pick her up after breakfast today, and then he was gone."

"Maybe Russ will talk to another man."

Alannah gave her a sympathetic glance. "Maybe."

It had been too quiet since the incident of soldier's heart. Three long days of grunts and one-word answers from the man she so desperately wanted to help. If only he'd let her.

"Can you get the other end?"

Emmie nodded and took the handle of the trunk closest to her. They muscled it down the narrow staircase. Childish shrieks and giggles erupted from the bedroom off the kitchen. The two women looked at each other after they set the trunk down. Alannah shrugged, a smile pulling at her lips.

"At least he's opened up to the children again." She moved toward the happy sounds, and Emmie followed.

Russ sat up in bed, little Alice on his lap, her face half-buried in his shirt, while Stewie pretended to be a bear—or perhaps a wolf—and attacked the bed.

"Alice, dear, come off of there." Alannah rushed in and scooped her daughter off the bed. "Remember Mr. Fields has an injured leg." She looked at Russ. "I'm so sorry, did she hurt you?"

"No. She doesn't weigh enough to bother about."

He grinned and tickled the little girl under the chin, setting off another shriek. His face relaxed with his attention on the children. Emmie's heart squeezed at the thought of what might have been. What could be if only—

Robbie banged the back door open and rushed through the kitchen to the bedroom. "There's a wagon in the lane."

Emmie went to the window. The old man she remembered from church drove to the house, Aunt Maggie sitting ramrod straight on the seat next to him.

"It's Mr. Keen and Aunt Maggie," Emmie said.

"Come, children. We'll load our belongings on the wagon, then pop back in to say our goodbyes."

For the moment, Emmie was alone with Russ in the room. Their eyes met, and his grin melted away. "There's no need for you or Aunt Maggie to stay. The doctor said I can be up and walking with crutches in a few more days. Mickey can handle things until then."

"I know."

"Then why—?"

"Mr. Fields! Mr. Fields!" Stewie charged back into the room with a wiggling bundle of black and white fur in his arms, Robbie right behind him. "It's a puppy. That man said it's for you. Golly, you're awful lucky."

Emmie sucked in her breath. What would Russ say to that?

"Hand that puppy here," he said.

Stewie being too short, Robbie helped lift the squirming puppy onto the bed. Russ took it and settled it on his chest.

"Aren't you a sweet little girl?" Russ dodged the wet tongue intent on washing his face.

"She oughta be." Mr. Keen arrived at the doorway and glanced around the room. "Her pa's the best sheepdog I ever had, and that's a fact. Her ma ain't far behind him, neither."

"How old?"

"Three months. I figure she'll be ready to start training about the time you get your legs back under you."

Russ wiped his face and got the pup under some sort of control. "How much?"

The old man cleared his throat. "She ain't for sale. She's a gift."

"A gift?" Russ turned his head toward the old man, not even trying to keep his scarred side hidden.

Mr. Keen shuffled his feet and rubbed the back of his neck. "I heard it was that ram you bought from me what done this."

"It could have been any ram. You and I both know that."

"Aye, but it was that one. Iffen you'd had yourself a young dog like her, things might've been different." He looked away and wiped his hand across his chin. "You might not have lost the old dog."

The two men shared a look that seemed to say things neither would mouth aloud.

Emmie slipped from the room into the kitchen.

"So, this is where you've gotten off to," Aunt Maggie said, "leaving us to the mercy of Mrs. Calhoun at the piano. I figured I'd best come myself and see that man back on his feet before the whole congregation turns tone-deaf." She set two large, misshapen bags at her feet.

"It's good to see you, too. Let me take your bags upstairs."

"I suppose I'll have to walk the stairs, my old legs being somewhat better than his at the moment."

"Yes, I'm sorry. There's only the one bedroom downstairs."

Aunt Maggie waved a hand as if to brush away a pesky fly. "It won't be for long. I spoke to the doctor yesterday, and, by his calculations, Mr. Fields should be walking around soon."

"I suppose he will."

Her voice must have been too wistful. Aunt Maggie's eyebrows flattened into their formidable line. "I see." The old lady cut a glance toward Russ's room and the excited chatter within.

Alannah came back into the house with Alice on her hip. "We'll say our goodbyes and wait outside for Mr. Keen." A wry smile twisted her mouth. "I'll need to warn Stewart about the puppy. We haven't had a dog since Zeus passed away. I'm sure the children will be begging to see the rest of the litter."

"Thank you for everything." Emmie stepped forward and embraced her friend. "You'll mail my letters for me? One this week, and the other the next?" At her friend's understanding nod, Emmie relaxed. They'd talked long after the children had gone to bed the night before, and she'd convinced Alannah to hold the letter to Archie for another week to give Helen time to respond.

"Best show me to my room," Aunt Maggie said.

Emmie grabbed Aunt Maggie's bags and led the way up the stairs. "Alannah and I changed the sheets this morning, and the little children picked that bouquet of wildflowers for you." She set the bags on the bed's colorful scrap quilt. "This was Becky's room. Alannah's been staying here with the two smaller children while Robbie shared with Mickey at the end of the hall."

"And you?"

"I'm in the bedroom right next to this one." Russ's bedroom. She'd chosen that one over Becky's.

"His?"

Emmie cleared her throat. "I suppose it was."

The old woman snorted again.

"Why don't you take a little rest after the long ride out here?"

"I'll do that, and then we'll talk." Aunt Maggie looked around the room. "Seems there's been more than just nursing going on here for the past week and a half."

"I don't know—"

"Yes, you do. And we'll talk about it later. Go say your goodbyes to those children now. Go on."

Partly shooed away and partly beating a hasty retreat, Emmie stopped halfway down the stairs to give her cheeks time to cool. Was she so obvious? Not that it mattered. Whatever her feelings for Russ, he'd made it plain that he didn't share them.

If she were smart, she'd be on that wagon with Alannah and the children. She'd tie her heart back together and leave without a backward glance.

If she were smart.

CHAPTER 24

F OR THE PAST THREE days, Russ hadn't seen Emmie alone for a minute. Not one minute. Which was what he'd wanted... or so he'd thought.

Of course, he hadn't expected that old dragon to be lurking in his doorway. He'd expected to be alone with Mickey. Not that he'd seen the boy for more than it took to give him his work orders every morning. Another clear indication of the young man's intelligence was his ability to avoid Aunt Maggie at all costs.

He wished he could do the same, if for no other reason than to be spared the accolades of the good preacher. Aunt Maggie obviously wanted to impress upon Emmie all the excellent reasons why she should be considering the preacher as a potential husband. All those excellent reasons why the preacher was everything Russ would never be. Not that Aunt Maggie put it exactly that way. But close enough.

He almost looked forward to the doctor's visit today.

Emmie poked her head around the corner, keeping her feet in the kitchen where—no doubt—Aunt Maggie kept vigilant watch. "Do you need anything, Mr. Fields?"

Yes. He needed to hear her call him Russ again. Ever since that old woman had moved in, he'd been Mr. Fields.

"A glass of water?"

She nodded and stepped out of sight. He counted to twelve before Aunt Maggie showed up in the doorway. Emmie brushed past her with the glass.

"Here you go. The doctor should be here any time."

Their fingers brushed as he took the glass, her body blocking the old woman's sight. What would Emmie do if he held onto her hand for a moment? What would he see if he looked into her eyes? Did her pulse quicken at their touch the way his did?

It didn't matter. The doctor would be here today and clear him to walk with the crutch that leaned against the wall. Mickey had brought it back from town on Monday.

Emmie would move back to Aunt Maggie's and he would... what? He sighed.

"Are you concerned the doctor won't deem you mended enough to walk?"

He glanced up at the warmth in her dark eyes.

"No."

Her lips lifted a sad sort of smile. "Then I should pack my things. Perhaps the doctor can offer us a ride back to town."

"I'm sure he will," Aunt Maggie said from the doorway. "If you'll assist me up those stairs one last time, I'll pack my bags as well."

Was that sympathy, pity, or something else in Emmie's eyes before she turned away, her fingers lingering a moment on the edge of his bed? He leaned his head against the headboard.

She was leaving.

He should be relieved, but he was mostly exhausted. He'd barely allowed himself to sleep since that incident she'd witnessed. Once she was gone, he'd sleep himself out. And then...

He'd try his best to forget she'd ever been there.

Running her hand over the sturdy wood dresser in Russ's bedroom one last time, Emmie stopped by the window and gazed out at the pastoral scene before her. Mickey walked from the barn to the garden, a hoe in his hand and the puppy tugging at the cuff of his pants. The air smelled fresh and clean after last night's shower. Just enough to water the crops, not enough to muddy things up. Goblin and Song grazed beside the barn, but the sheep must have wandered over the hill. The puppy barked and darted away from Mickey, only to circle around and attack his cuff again.

She'd miss this. She already missed it. Almost as much as she missed Russ's letters. But that was over now. Gone. Once her brothers received her letter, she'd be hauled back to Pittsburgh and her gray, dreary life there.

"Emmie!" Aunt Maggie's voice cut through the calm. "The doctor has arrived."

Emmie blinked as Penny snapped her bony fingers in front of her eyes.

"Aunt Maggie done told you to quit mooning over that man." The little woman's hair fanned above her like a frizzled heavenly halo, but her frown would make people think of a hotter place.

"I'm not mooning over anyone."

How such a slight woman could produce such a large snort was something that still took Emmie by surprise.

"I'm merely preoccupied thinking about my students and planning tomorrow afternoon's lessons."

"And I'm the Easter Bunny."

Emmie rose and gathered her dignity as best she could. The rest of the boarders had left the breakfast table long ago. She pushed aside the urge to help Penny clear the table, not that the little spitfire would let her. It had only been four days, but Emmie missed the easy camaraderie that had developed between her and Alannah as they'd shared the chores at the farm.

Penny crossed her arms, her pointed stare saying more than most people could with a mouthful of words. She wanted Emmie out of her way.

"I'm going to the post office." Emmie ignored the answering snort and walked to the front door, refusing to stomp her feet. If there were anywhere else to live in this town, she'd move. Her next step faltered.

If only Russ had been who she'd thought he was from his letters, then she might be moving to the farm.

She stepped outside into the sunshine. The cleansing scent of morning dew still lingered as a wagon rumbled by. It was past time to start her day. Head high, she strolled toward the main street.

Mr. Fields might not be who she'd thought he was, but he was a man in need of help. With any luck, Helen's letter would arrive today. Then she could take it out to the farm and present Russ with some options.

Except, how would she get there? And back? The idea of renting another buggy from the livery did not bear thinking of.

The train's whistle announced its departure, and she strode along the street, lifting her skirt a few inches to avoid collecting too much dust on her hem. She stepped onto the boardwalk of the main street and strode to the post office, heart hopeful with the thought of what might be waiting for her.

"Emmie?"

Stopping so abruptly that she had to grasp a nearby post to avoid falling, she searched the sparse crowd for that familiar voice. A tall woman with curly blond hair poking from around a dainty straw hat and dressed in a navy traveling suit headed straight for her.

"Helen?"

Her friend spread her arms and smiled. "Who else?"

After a laugh and a heartfelt hug, Emmie leaned back and shook her head. "What are you doing here?"

"I received your letter after weeks of worrying myself sick about you, and I had to come. I had to see for myself that you're all right." The nurse in Helen snapped to the fore as she scanned Emmie from head to toe and back again. "You're a trifle pale, but you've not lost weight, and your eyes have their old sparkle."

"Thank you, Dr. Edwards."

"Not yet, but maybe someday." They both laughed.

"It's good to see you, truly, but I never intended—"

"I never thought you did," Helen said, "but I had to come and see for myself this man who has captured your heart."

Emmie's smile slipped, and she let her arms drop to her sides. "It's not like that."

Helen cocked her head and pursed her lips. "Are you sure?"

Was she? Yes. Sure she'd just lied to her best friend. She shrugged.

"When can I meet him?"

When? Emmie opened her mouth but couldn't find any words.

Helen looked her over again. "The man at the station recommended I lodge at a boardinghouse run by some aunt or something."

"Aunt Maggie."

"That sounds right. He's having my trunk delivered there."

"That's where I'm staying, I'll show you the way." The reality of Helen being here was beginning to sink in. "You know, I was just coming to check the mail to see if you'd responded—"

"And I did. In person. Let's get me settled, and then you can fill in the gaps about Mr. Fields and his medical condition. Maybe this afternoon we can pay him a visit."

"He lives five miles out of town."

"We'll rent a buggy at the livery."

Emmie's heart sank. "I did that once and it... it didn't end well."

Helen stopped in her tracks. "He refused to see you?"

"He saved me."

Blond eyebrows shot to Helen's hairline. "Then I simply must hear the rest of this story."

Emmie swallowed before plunging into the whole sordid tale, leaving nothing out. Helen listened in silence until they stopped in front of the boardinghouse.

Voicing none of the chastising Emmie deserved, Helen said, "Well, you're in luck."

"I am?"

"You're looking at a girl who learned to drive a rig before she was ten years old." Helen nodded toward a wagon in front of Aunt Maggie's porch, already unloading her trunk. "You can fill me in on the little details while I unpack, then we'll visit the livery and be on our way."

Helen had always been a take-charge kind of person. Her nursing abilities often relied on it. Maybe she'd be the one to get through to Russ, to convince him to seek help. Something bittersweet twisted inside her.

Maybe Helen would succeed where Emmie had failed.

Who was this flaxen-haired force of nature who'd marched into his kitchen? Russ looked between her and a very subdued Emmie.

"Mr. Fields, please, let's sit and discuss some options."

"What options? What are you talking about?" Anger rose at her demanding tone.

"I'll make coffee." Emmie scurried to the stove while the blond woman watched her with an open mouth.

"You can make coffee?" Disbelief colored her voice.

Emmie shrugged, not turning to face them. "I've learned a few things since I left Pittsburgh."

Pittsburgh, she'd said. Not home. Russ leaned against his crutch and studied her movements in his kitchen. She looked... like she belonged.

"Very well. May I be seated, Mr. Fields?" The woman still stood beside the kitchen chair across the table from him.

Heat climbed his neck. What would Ma have said about his lack of manners? "Please, have a seat."

Once she'd seated herself, he eased onto a chair, resting his crutch against the table, keeping his face angled away from his uninvited guests.

"You look confused, so let me begin again." She folded her hands on the tabletop. "I'm Helen Edwards, a friend of Emmie's from Pittsburgh. I'm also a nurse."

He stiffened.

"There's no need to keep your face averted. I guarantee you that I've seen worse. Much worse, to be sure."

No matter what she'd seen, showing his full face to such a strikingly beautiful woman didn't sit well with him.

"In fact"—she nodded toward Emmie's back—"Emmie requested my opinion on what might be done for you, because in the past few months I've been working exclusively with Dr. Timothy Lawson, who has studied under Surgeon J. Cooper McKee. You've heard of him?"

"I make it a point not to hear of—or from—doctors." He gritted his teeth at her slight nod. If she were a man, he'd toss her out the door. One couldn't do that with a woman.

"Surgeon McKee has pioneered the field of plastic surgery." She paused as if that were something significant, then frowned when he didn't respond.

Emmie moved to the table and sat beside Miss Edwards. "Plastic surgery is a fairly new procedure. It's used to minimize scarring and repair areas that have been disfigured."

He leaned back in his chair until the front legs left the floor.

"I know how much your scars distress you." Emmie laid her hand, palm down, on the table next to him. "Perhaps if you see Dr. Lawson he can—"

"No."

"Mr. Fields." Miss Edwards smiled, an action that accentuated her beauty. "I can assure you there are things the doctor can do. He can't replace your eye, of course, but he can minimize the scars and stretch some of your skin so that it doesn't pull across your cheekbone.

How did she know it did that?

"No, I can't read your mind," she said, "but I've worked with hundreds of men just like you. Men who lived in constant discomfort and shame over their appearance. Men Dr. Lawson has helped."

He rose and grabbed his crutch, then limped over to the window near the stove. The coffeepot burbled its aromas into the air.

Mickey hoed the garden while the pup tussled with an old twist of rope the boy had given her.

A chair creaked and Emmie took the coffee pot from the stove, the scent of something flowery swirling with her movements. The same scent that had accompanied her into his room while she'd nursed him for two weeks. He closed his eye and drew in a long breath, his hand gripping the crutch until his fingers burned.

"I won't mislead you," Miss Edwards said. "Dr. Lawson does good work, but he can't do miracles. You'll always carry scars, but he can lessen them to a large degree and make you more comfortable."

He rubbed his hand over the scars, then turned to face her, letting her see the full extent of the damage. She didn't recoil, didn't flinch, didn't even blink. Neither did Emmie, but she'd seen it all before.

"Emmie has also told me about your nightmares and—"

"She had no right." Anger flashed through him like a tornado through a cornfield, ripping out any budding thoughts of listening to this nurse. A nurse. Why had he listened at all?

Emmie dropped a spoon onto the table, her hand trembling as it covered her mouth, color leaching from her face. The nurse touched her arm, reassured her, while he stood glowering like the monster he was. He thumped toward the back door.

"Enjoy your coffee. I have work to do."

He didn't slam the door, but he didn't look back, either. He swung his splinted leg as fast as he could and leaned on the crutch for support. Mickey stopped working to stare at him. The pup raced across the grass and did her best to tangle in his feet. He made it to the barn and sank onto a barrel, then scooped up the pup. She washed his face, and the tension eased.

"They've no idea, pup." She squirmed, and he set her on the barn floor, where she scampered after a chicken feather.

What those women had offered him was nothing more than a feather blowing in the wind. He couldn't go into a hospital. The terrible dreams, while asleep and awake, would take over again. He needed to be here on the farm, rooted to the soil that his pa and grandpa had both worked.

Soil he'd never pass down to a son of his own.

CHAPTER 25

E MMIE TRUDGED BACK TO Aunt Maggie's after her last piano lesson for the day. She swatted at the gnats that circled her hat. It was a good thing all her students were at the basic level. After yesterday's disaster with Russ, she'd barely been able to concentrate on the scales and chords. Music had always been her refuge, but not anymore. Her heart was filled with the love of a man who refused to consider what a specialty-trained doctor could do for him. But it was more than that.

He'd refused her.

Maybe Helen was right. Maybe she should return to Pittsburgh and complete her training to be a full nurse. Archie would balk at that, of course, but Richard might support her. Having lost James—and now Russ—she wouldn't allow Archie to push her into a marriage with someone he deemed suitable. Suitable be hung. She'd live as a spinster first, making her own way. If she couldn't find a nursing position, she could always teach the piano. If she could find enough students to support herself in Jonesville, she certainly could in Pittsburgh.

Gray, smelly, crowded Pittsburgh.

She paused and raised her eyes from the street to the trees and houses that lined it. Children ran and laughed down an alley between homes. Sunlight poured between the leaves of the trees that shaded the street. A wagon rolled past—just one, not a steady stream that jostled together with drivers shouting and swearing at each other. Birdsong twittered overhead and a dog barked down the street. The deputy sheriff watched over a trio of those street boys as they painted the porch of the sheriff's office. She swatted at the gnats again. Maybe she should stay here even without Russ to love and support her.

For the moment, however, Helen awaited her. They had two more days before Helen returned to Pittsburgh, and they'd made plans to see some of the countryside that afternoon when her lessons were finished.

She continued to the boardinghouse, arriving slightly out of breath, and wiped a damp sheen from her forehead before entering the house. Helen waited for her in the foyer, wringing her hands at her waist.

"I didn't tell him, Emmie, I swear." Distress filled her friend's voice.

"You didn't tell whom?"

Archie crowded behind Helen into the foyer. "Me."

Emmie's heart dropped into her shoes. What was Archie doing *here*? It was Tuesday. If Alannah had mailed the letter yesterday, like she'd promised, there was no way he could be here already.

"Hello, Archie."

"Do you have any idea how worried I've been? As well as Caroline, Richard, and Fannie? Even the children? What were you thinking?" His voice rose with each sentence.

"Perhaps we should retire to a more private part of the house?" Helen's cool tones cut through the heated foyer.

"Yes. We should. Now." Archie's voice had settled, but his glare cut Emmie to the bone.

She removed her hat and followed them into the house. Helen led them to a small parlor on the ground floor. It was empty, and she shook her head at Penny, who'd followed, before pulling the door shut behind them.

"This is a better place to have your discussion," Helen said.

"Thank you, but this is a private matter." Archie's dismissal sailed over Helen's head as she took a seat on the settee.

"I think I'll stay."

Emmie wanted to hug her.

"Very well." Archie pivoted to Emmie. "What do you have to say for yourself?"

"I've already said hello."

He waited a moment then crossed his arms. "That's it?"

"No." She walked past him and sat next to Helen. "I owe you an apology."

"You certainly do."

"I shouldn't have left without a word. That was inexcusable. But I left you a note"

Archie thrust his arms out from his sides and leaned toward her. "That said precisely nothing."

"It told you I was safe, and that I'd taken a position." She pulled in a deep breath, then plunged on. "You shouldn't have tried to foist me off on the first man you could find who would offer me marriage." It had been a mistake to sit down. Now she was forced to look up at him.

"What I tried to do was provide for your future."

"What you tried to do was get rid of me."

He took a step back, his arms lowering to his sides. "Is that how you saw it?"

"How else could I see it?"

He sank onto an upholstered chair opposite the settee. "Emmie." He lifted one hand and let it fall to his knee, then stared out the window. "That was never my reasoning."

She stifled a snort when he turned back to her. Archie might be a lot of things, insensitive being at the top of the list, but he'd always been true to his word. "All right. Then I concede that I misunderstood your motives."

He inclined his head in acknowledgment.

"But I'm not leaving Jonesville."

Helen twisted to look at her, eyebrows raised, but said nothing.

"May I ask why?" Archie's attempt to remain calm was marred by the twitching of his cheek muscles.

"I've made a place for myself here."

"In a boardinghouse?"

"Yes." She raised her chin. "Teaching piano lessons and playing at the church."

He scowled. "Have you any idea the time and money I've spent on private investigators to find you?" All attempts to remain calm had fled the room.

So that's how he'd found her. "For which I truly do apologize. Several of my friends"—she glanced at Helen—"had advised me to write you. In fact, I did write you. The letter will probably be awaiting you when you return."

He shot to his feet. "You're coming with me."

She rose more gracefully, straightened, and lifted her chin. "I am not."

Splotches of color mottled Archie's cheeks and neck. "If I say you're coming with me—"

"I'm of age, brother, and I don't have to do what you say."

He took a step toward her. "What's the real reason that you're here?"

"To make my own—"

"No. I mean, why *here*." He jabbed a finger at the floor. "Why this backwater town on the edge of civilization?"

Jonesville was not a large city, or even close, but it certainly wasn't on the edge of civilization.

"Tell him, Emmie. He's got a right to know."

She whirled around at Helen.

"He does. He's your family. You don't have to leave with him, but he deserves to know the truth. All of it."

How could her best friend betray her like this?

"Ain't sure who's comin' up the lane, but it's a man drivin'," Mickey hollered into the barn. "Looks like he knows what he's doin', so it ain't the preacher."

Russ sat on a crate oiling Goblin's harness, one of the few jobs fit for a one-legged man on the farm. He set the leather aside and stood, fumbling with his crutch until he caught his balance. He lifted his hat and swiped his forehead with a rag. It was hot for early June, but heat made the corn grow.

The rig pulled up to the barn, and a smartly-dressed man stepped off. Mickey secured the horse while the man helped his passengers to the ground. That nurse lady and... Emmie. His heart stuttered a moment between his ribs. He hadn't expected to see her again, at least not here. Maybe at church. He hadn't wanted to see her again on his farm.

Liar.

The man turned to him, shooting him a look meant to skewer him to the barn wall. Mickey walked to his side and crossed his bony arms over his chest. The boy's loyalty was touching if a mite misguided. The fancy gent in front of them wasn't going to soil a knuckle on anyone.

"I'm Archie Mason."

Or maybe he would.

If Russ were Emmie's brother, he'd be looking for someone to punch right about now.

"Russ Fields."

"You know the ladies, of course." By the twist of his mouth, those words must have tasted sour.

"I do."

Emmie stepped around her brother. "Russ—"

"Russ? You're on intimate terms with this man?" Archie looked hotter than a cannon after an afternoon of heavy artillery shelling.

"As I explained to you yesterday," Emmie said, "we've been corresponding for many months."

"Without a word to me."

"You're my brother, not my father, and as we've also agreed... I am of age." This was the same brother who'd tried to marry her off. She barely reached the man's shoulder, but there was no sign of her backing down.

He'd better lend her a little support. "What can I do for you?"

Archie wheeled back to him. "You can explain how my sister came to be here in the middle of nowhere. She claims you didn't entice her, but I don't see how else she picked up and moved—without a word to her family—unless she had been assured of your... honorable intentions toward her."

Mickey tensed beside him.

"I didn't know that Emmie"—he ignored the man's raised brow at the use of her name—"had planned to travel here or even that she'd arrived until she'd been here for a couple of weeks."

The man's jaw muscles worked, but he didn't respond.

Russ would've done the same if he were facing down a man who he'd thought had compromised Becky in any way. But since he hadn't compromised Emmie—and never would—Archie didn't need to know about that first meeting. The meeting that had scared him half out of his mind for several reasons, the out-of-control horse being the least of them.

"When she came to call, accompanied by the preacher, there was an accident." He gestured toward his splinted leg. "Because of her nursing experience, she offered to stay and help until the doctor would let me out of bed. Mrs. McCann and her children moved in as well. It was all very respectable."

"You're obviously on your feet again, so why is she refusing to return to Pittsburgh with me... unless you accompany us?"

Emmie clenched her emerald pendant until it bit into her hand as she waited for Russ to respond. He hadn't mentioned their first encounter, or the runaway buggy, or the disastrous silent ride back to town. That alone had loosened a bit of the hope she held so tightly within her. Even if he never came to love her, she'd still do everything she could to help him. But she couldn't do anything if he didn't agree to come to Pittsburgh and see Dr. Lawson.

The puppy grabbed a mouthful of her skirt and tugged at it. Russ stepped forward and, balanced on his good leg, tried to disengage the animal's teeth from her hem.

"I'm sorry. She's hasn't learned her manners yet," he said. He lifted the puppy, but it grabbed another mouthful of fabric and pulled Emmie's skirt halfway up, showing the snowy-white petticoat beneath.

"Oh!" She reached for the puppy's mouth, her hands tangling in Russ's as they both worked to free her once again.

"For pity's sake." Archie glared at Mickey. "Take that creature and contain it."

Beet red to his ears and keeping his eyes averted from her petticoat, Mickey grabbed the pup and retreated to the barn.

Russ's fingers brushed hers one last time before he stepped back. "My apologies. If she's torn your dress, I'll pay to have it repaired."

"Nonsense. It'll be an easy mend." She might lack most of the skills needed on the farm, but she could sew. She brushed her skirt down and shook the wrinkles out, then caught a glimpse of Helen's face. Her friend was doing her best not to laugh, which made Emmie's lips twitch so that she had to look away from Archie. Her brother would never see the humor in the situation.

"Now can we get back to the issue at hand?" Archie said. "Are you agreeable to come to Pittsburgh to see this doctor—whatever his name is—and if he can repair..." Archie waved a hand toward Russ, her brother's face reddening a bit. Good. Maybe he'd realized how insufferably insensitive that comment had been.

Russ settled the crutch securely under his arm. "Mickey?"

The boy appeared—minus the puppy—in the barn doorway. "Boss?"

"I'm not going to be much good to you for another couple of weeks. You suppose you can keep the farm going while I'm gone?"

"I reckon I can do the normal stuff, but I don't know nothin' about cuttin' the hay."

"I expect I'll be back in time to show you how." Russ tilted his head toward Helen. "Wouldn't you say?"

Helen stepped next to Emmie. "You may need to make several trips back and forth for the reconstruction procedure, but in between, you can return here and keep working."

Russ turned and gazed out over his fields.

They looked just the way she'd always pictured them. The grass in the sheep pasture waving in the breeze, the corn growing tall in straight rows, and Goblin standing in his paddock, stomping at flies and swishing his tail. She could understand Russ's reluctance to leave it.

He didn't turn back to them but he said, "I'll come."

Emmie grabbed Helen's hand and squeezed, the answering pressure reassuring her that she'd heard rightly.

"Fine. We'll leave on tomorrow's eastbound train," said Archie.

"Won't be an eastbound train until Friday," Russ said.

"Then we'll catch it on Friday." Archie turned and motioned her and Helen toward the buggy. "Let's return to town and pack your things."

She glanced at Russ's back. "I'll be able to leave most of them here for when I return."

Russ whirled around, catching his balance with the crutch.

"We'll speak of that later," Archie ground out between his teeth, his eyes locked on Russ.

Oh, yes. They'd speak of it later.

But Emmie'd said she was coming back to Jonesville.

Dust lingered over the road after the buggy had dropped from sight below the hill. Russ rubbed the back of his neck.

"What was that pretty lady talkin' about, Boss?"

Russ startled at the voice on his blind side. He'd forgotten the boy was there. That's what he deserved for getting lost in his thoughts.

"She's a nurse. Says she works for a doctor who specializes in fixing scars."

"You gonna get your face fixed?"

Russ shrugged. "Doubt there's much the doctor can do, but..."

"But what?"

He gave the back of his neck one last scrub. "But it irked me that Miss Mason's brother was trying to run roughshod over her and, well, it means something to her that I go and have the doctor look at me."

"Don't you want to go and see if he can fix it?"

"No." He suppressed a shudder. "I'd as soon get run over by a run-away team of horses as face another doctor. Or walk into a hospital." And face the terrors that would surely follow.

"Ah." The boy nodded.

"Ah...what?"

"You're sweet on Miss Mason. Kinda figgered that anyway, what with her movin' in to take care of you and all."

"I'm not—"

The insolent boy actually raised an eyebrow at him. Russ ground his teeth, then turned and headed into the barn to finish oiling the harness he'd left there. He wasn't going to justify his reasons to a half-trained, half-grown farmhand.

"Don't blame you none, Boss. She ain't the looker that other lady is, but she's always been sweet to me."

She'd always been sweet to him, too. Even when he'd tried to chase her away. Even when he'd acted so surly after the accident. And even when she'd witnessed the terror of his dreams. Sweet on her? The kid had that right.

Sweet enough to face a doctor and a hospital again.

CHAPTER 26

F RIDAY'S TRAIN DIDN'T LEAVE Jonesville until after lunch, but Emmie had been up and pacing since before dawn. She'd spent yesterday avoiding Archie by visiting each of her piano students to leave them with exercises to work on until she returned. Because she would return, if for no other reason than to appease Aunt Maggie. The old woman had bemoaned the thought of listening to Mrs. Calhoun at church all during dinner last evening.

Emmie'd also spoken to Pastor Anderson who, strangely enough, hadn't seemed surprised when she revealed that Russ was traveling with them to Pittsburgh to see the doctor. He'd given her a slow smile and a nod then wished her a safe journey. She'd turned to leave and he'd said, "Bless you for what you're doing. Mr. Fields might not realize what it means yet, but he will."

She stood on the train platform between Archie and Helen, praying that Russ would show up. She'd tossed and turned half the night worrying that he'd change his mind. At the distant bellow of the train's whistle, she grasped Helen's hand.

"What if he doesn't come?"

"I think he will, but we can't force him."

"There's no need to whisper. I know what you're talking about." Archie adjusted his hat for the third time since they'd arrived at the platform. "If he's changed his mind, so be it. We're leaving."

She was trying to summon the courage to outright defy Archie on the very public platform when a familiar gray horse plodded into view.

"He's here!"

Helen squeezed her hand. "I was sure he'd come. For you."

For her? He'd made it plain enough that he wasn't attracted to her. He'd not told Archie about their first meeting, but that was likely in order to avoid any unpleasantness, not to protect her. She tried to contain her spinning emotions as Russ lowered himself from the wagon, grabbed a carpetbag from the back, and spoke to Mickey before limping toward them. The doctor had fashioned him a smaller splint, so he wore the same brown suit he'd worn to church. His hat pulled low, he'd cocked it over the damaged side of his face.

Her heart fluttered against her ribs.

The train's whistle blew again, its gray-and-white plume visible over the rooftops. He'd made it just in time.

He climbed the platform steps one at a time and stopped near Archie. "Mason. Ladies." He touched the brim of his hat but didn't remove it.

"Fields," Archie answered.

"Hello, Russ." He turned to her, taking her in from head to toe in one swift glance. Was that a hint of approval in his eye?

"Sorry I'm late. Nip got in with the sheep. We had a devil of a time getting her out."

"Nip?"

He nodded, a grin pulled at the corner of his mouth. "Mickey named the pup."

"A most suitable name." It fit the little beast who'd grabbed a mouthful of her dress.

The train chuffed and squealed into the station, rendering any other conversation impossible. They waited while a few passengers disembarked, and then joined those who formed a line to board. Archie showed his ticket, then Helen, then her, she waited while Russ presented his. The conductor glanced up, jerked back a step, then returned the ticket to Russ, a wary—or was it disgusted?—expression on his face. Russ took the ticket and joined her.

Her face must have mirrored her thoughts because he shrugged, gripped her elbow, and guided her to the open door.

"Think nothing of it."

She barely heard his words over the hissing steam of the engine, but she glared at the conductor, who unfortunately wasn't looking her way. She was sorely tempted to give him the dressing down he deserved. Russ's fingers pressed around her elbow. Could the man read her thoughts?

"You'll get used to it on this trip."

"I won't." Her words came out louder than she'd intended, and Archie turned, pinning her with his sourest big-brother look. She turned her back to him. "He was unforgivably rude. You're a war veteran and deserve respect for the part you played in keeping our country together."

"People don't see that. They see my face."

"Then they don't see the real you."

He sighed and looked away, but his quiet words still reached her. "This is the real me."

He shouldn't have come. Shouldn't have put her through this. Russ tucked his chin to his chest as he sat beside the window. People were going to notice him, no matter how hard he tried to keep to himself. Archie sat next to him, and Helen joined Emmie on the bench seat facing them. There was no way he could speak to Emmie privately. He couldn't even look at her without exposing his face to the passengers in front of them. Those seated facing the back of the train.

He settled his splinted leg as comfortably as he could and then scanned the rail car for a moment. Sure was an improvement over the boxcars he'd ridden in during the war. The padding on the bench would make the trip a lot nicer than sitting on a packing crate or lying on dirty straw that smelled of horses, mold, and mice droppings.

He gripped the cushioned seat until his fingers hit the wood beneath, and took long breaths of air tinged with coal smoke, not dirty straw. His vision clouded, so he concentrated on his knees, breathing deeply. He wasn't in a boxcar. This wasn't during the war—

"Are you all right?" Archie's voice sounded far away, but Russ clung to it.

"I will be."

"What's wrong?"

How could he explain this? "Nothing." Emmie's brother didn't need to see him dissolve into the past. He had to keep his grip on the present. He must.

A soft hand brushed over the top of his, still locked onto the seat. "Russ?"

Emmie. She was here. What was she doing here? Panic rose in his chest as sweat trickled from his temples, down his cheeks.

"We're in a passenger car, Mr. Fields." Another voice. A woman. What were women doing here? They were on their way to another battle. Smoke belched through the open window. He had to get them out of here.

"Mr. Fields, it's all right. We're not in the war." The voice was soft and low. "We're on a passenger train, going to Pittsburgh. Emmie is here."

Emmie? Why was she here?

"I'm here, Russ." He knew that voice. Something rubbed the top of his hand, something soft. A mouse? He couldn't let go, couldn't move it away.

Women's voices murmured close to him. The rough plank beneath him moved as someone stood and another sat.

"Russ? It's me, Emmie. I'm right beside you. We're going to Pittsburgh."

Pittsburgh? Had the Rebels penetrated that far north? No. They couldn't have.

A hand cupped the side of his face. It didn't feel right, but it was a hand. No, his face didn't feel right. The hand's gentle pressure moved his head until his eyes unlocked from his knees. Not eyes ... eye. He could only see out of one eye.

Emmie's face came into view. Her skin was pale, and her lips trembled. She should be afraid. There was a war going on. She should be terrified.

The train lurched into motion, metal squealing against metal beneath their feet.

"We're moving now, we're going to Pittsburgh. It's going to be all right, Russ. I won't leave your side."

Pittsburgh. Doctor. Emmie. Hospital.

I can't.

His breath came in great heaves, as if he'd run the five miles to town. Emmie sat next to him, not Archie. Miss Edwards leaned forward from the seat across from him, their knees almost touching. Archie sat ramrod straight next to her, his face a pasty color.

A conductor frowned down at him from beside Emmie. "He sick? Should we put him off now so he can find a doctor?"

Yes. Put me off now. Please. I can't do this.

"No, sir." Miss Edwards stood. "I'm a nurse, and I'll be with him the whole time. He's on his way to Pittsburgh to see a doctor there. A specialist."

The conductor gave Russ a doubtful look. "He was in the war?"

"Yes, he was," Emmie said.

"He one of them what ain't right in the head?"

Yes. I am. That's exactly who I am.

Emmie bristled like a poked porcupine, but Miss Edwards touched her hand.

"As I said, I'm a trained nurse, and I'll be with him the entire trip. You've nothing to worry about, I assure you."

The conductor gave Russ one more glance, then moved down the aisle shaking his head.

"Thank you, Helen," Emmie said. "He must have slipped back into the war for a moment, that's all."

That's all? She had no idea, and he couldn't tell her what it was like, what it meant to live that way. Now he couldn't even shield her from it.

"I'll stay here beside him," Emmie said.

Helen nodded and when Archie opened his mouth—no doubt to object—she tapped him on the arm and frowned. The man snapped his mouth shut but looked as if he'd taken a bite of something rancid.

Emmie eased Russ's fingers from the seat cushion and cradled his hand in both of hers.

"It's going to be fine. You're going to be fine."

He slumped against the seat, all rigidity leaving his muscles like water down a funnel. Even keeping his head upright became a chore. These waking dreams drained him like nothing else he'd ever known. Even more than that, Emmie'd witnessed it. He'd seen in her eyes the one thing he never wanted to see there.

Pity.

The bread and cheese Penny had packed was almost gone. Emmie pushed their remains aside in the hamper and pulled out the last jar of lemonade. She removed the top and took a sip of the tangy liquid. If only it were still cool, but nothing was.

She wiped her wrist over her brow and frowned at the gritty moisture there. Opening the window allowed in cooler air, but also cinder dust that permeated the coal smoke. How could it be this hot in early June? Sunlight slanted into the train. It must be mid-morning or close to it. They should be in Pittsburgh in a couple more hours.

Helen was wedged against the opposite window, her shawl wadded into a makeshift pillow. Archie was gone, probably standing on the back platform of the train car again, smoking a cigar. Russ slouched against their bench seat, his hat low over his face, his breath coming deep and even.

The heat was making her sleepy as well. She returned the jar to the hamper and stood, stretching her legs and back for a minute. She'd love nothing better than to join Archie, but she wouldn't leave Russ while Helen napped. The two of them had reached an unspoken understanding that one of them would be awake with him at all times. Not that there'd been a repeat of... whatever had happened. She knew about the nightmares, what Helen had called soldier's heart, but Russ had been awake when they'd boarded the train, when he'd had that... episode.

The emerald pendant pressed into her fingertips.

It must be frightening to live like that, never knowing when the horrors of war would return to you. It would make it difficult to—oh. She sank onto the seat. Russ's breathing had quieted. Was he awake? He'd exchanged very few words with her, and practically none to anyone else, since they'd boarded. Maybe his reluctance to open up to her wasn't all because of his face. Maybe these episodes were the main reason he kept to himself. If so, this trip to Pittsburgh wasn't going to solve the problem.

She hadn't admitted it, even to herself until now, but the underlying reason she'd pressed so hard for him to make this trip was so that he'd feel better about himself and how he looked. Maybe even feel able to think about her as something other than someone to correspond with via letters. Moist heat pressed against her eyes, and her throat tightened. She blinked and drew in a deep breath. If his outward appearance wasn't what was stopping him from—

"Is there any more of that lemonade?" Russ asked in a scratchy voice.

"Yes." Emmie bent over the hamper to find the jar and to hide her face. That was a switch, her hiding from him. But he didn't need to see her teary eyes. "Here." She passed it to him, then glanced toward Helen, but her friend still napped across the aisle.

Russ took several long swallows, but she didn't look at him.

"Much obliged." He passed back the near-empty jar.

"You're welcome." She replaced it in the hamper.

He shifted on the seat. She stared down the aisle. He cleared his throat. She folded her hands. He rubbed his palms down his thighs. She grasped her emerald necklace. Could things get any more awkward between them?

"We must be getting close to Pittsburgh," he said, his voice a little less gravelly.

"I expect we are."

He grunted, then shifted again, this time angling toward her. "Emmie?"

She closed her eyes for a moment. If only he'd say her name like that for another reason. With another inflection. "Yes?"

"I appreciate what you're trying to do. For me."

Opening her eyes, she faced him. The blue of his eye was clear and steady. He didn't smile, but neither did he frown. He appeared... sincere.

"I hope the doctor can repair the worst of the damage so that you can hold your head up in public and not worry about what others may say or think."

"I know you do. That's why I'm here."

He was here to please her? Or here for the help she hoped he'd find? Oh, if only it could be the former. At least he was talking to her. She smiled.

"I miss our letters." Resisting the urge to slap a hand over her traitorous mouth, she held her smile with an effort.

His face softened. "So do I."

He did? Really?

Archie appeared beside them. "Shouldn't be much over an hour now."

Why had he picked that moment to return? She loved her conventional, exacting, overbearing brother, but his timing was terrible.

Helen stood and stretched. "I can't believe I fell asleep. I'll go freshen up, unless you need to do that first, Emmie?"

Emmie shook her head. Helen walked to the back of the train car. Archie plopped into his seat. Russ went silent again.

Frustration gnawed at her middle. Why was it that every time they started to connect they were interrupted? Why couldn't Russ overcome that? Why did she care so much? She knew why, but she didn't want to admit that either. Not now. Not on this train. Not when a spark of new hope had just been lit between her and Russ.

Hadn't it?

CHAPTER 27

PITTSBURGH WAS EVERY BIT as gray and drab as Emmie's letters had painted it. Church bells tolled from multiple directions as Russ limped off the train station platform. Archie had a hackney carriage stopped and was ushering the women into it.

"We're too late for church, but there's nothing to be done," Archie said. "We'll get everyone settled, and I assume we'll all need a good long nap this afternoon. We can regroup at the house this evening."

"The house?" Emmie stopped, one foot in the carriage, one foot on the step. "Which house?"

Archie cleared his throat, rocked back on his heels, and stared somewhere over Russ's left shoulder. "Father's house—my house—where Caroline and I now reside."

"You moved in?"

"Yes, we moved in. As you knew we'd planned to do." He clipped his words as if biting them off.

"Yes. Of course." She turned to enter the carriage but swung around again. "Then where will I stay? And Russ?"

"I'll take a room at—" Russ began.

"Nothing of the sort." Emmie kept her eyes on her brother. "He'll stay where I'm staying, either with you or Richard, as you think best."

"Perhaps one of you should stay with Richard and the—"

"I think not. We'll both stay with Richard if that best suits you."

Archie made that half-growl sound Russ was getting too used to. "You'll both stay with Caroline and me. We've more than enough room."

Emmie tilted her nose up in acknowledgment and took her seat in the carriage.

Russ leaned toward Archie. "I fully expected to take a room at a hotel."

"What you or I expected doesn't matter, apparently."

"I think it would be best," Russ said.

Archie shrugged and jerked his head toward the vehicle's open door. "Even if Emmie hadn't suggested it, I'm sure Caroline would have. Let's go."

Russ got into the carriage, his splinted leg resting at an awkward angle in the narrow vehicle.

"You can rest it on the seat next to me, Mr. Fields." Helen scooted closer to Emmie on the narrow seat.

"No need." A day and a half on the train had the leg aching and stiff, but he wasn't about to put his boot on the seat, no matter how worn the fabric. He might be a country bumpkin, but he didn't intend to look or act like one in front of Emmie's brother.

The carriage rattled over cobblestones, curtain fluttering over the open window. Russ pushed it back. Gray and drab and... what was that stench?

"It'll smell better once we get past the mills," Emmie said.

He must have wrinkled his nose, but how could one avoid it?

"Is this your first trip to a large city, Mr. Fields?" Miss Edwards asked.

"No, miss. I've been to Washington." How long ago that seemed. "And Richmond."

The two women exchanged glances.

"Of course," Miss Edwards said. "You must have seen a lot of this country during the war."

Seen it ripped apart by cannon fire, fields trampled by men and horses, creeks that ran red—

"But this is your first time to visit Pittsburgh, isn't it?" Emmie asked, an anxious light in her eyes. Was she worried he'd disappear into the past again?

She should be.

He was.

He tightened his grip on the window's edge, the wood molding biting into his hand. "Yes. It looks like you described it."

"It's an industrial city. We make the steel that's taming the west." Archie pointed out the window on his side of the carriage. "My father started in that foundry and worked his way up the ladder. Pittsburgh is a place of unlimited opportunity."

"And some of the best hospitals staffed by the best doctors in the country," Miss Edwards said.

That anxious light in Emmie's eyes tugged at him. As much as he wished he were back on the farm listening to Mickey natter on about nothing interesting, he'd do almost anything to make that light in her eyes change to one of joy. If he could.

That remained to be seen.

The carriage rolled onto something much smoother than cobble-stones. The houses stood farther apart, most with some sort of garden in the front, and then fences. Tall fences of black wrought iron with fancy curls at the top. Stately trees almost hid the houses behind them. The carriage turned into a drive that curved up to such a house. The driver stopped the horses. This was the home where Emmie had grown up.

Not a home. A mansion.

At least her room was still... well, not hers, but neither of Archie's girls had claimed it. Emmie pulled a lavender evening dress from the wardrobe and held it up. Should she wear this for dinner? It was, after all, to be just a family affair. Richard and Fannie were coming with their brood of children. No doubt to meet Russ.

She lowered the dress. Richard had been the one who'd stood by her when she accepted James. Father had been skeptical—to say the least. Archie had been too busy to notice much. But Richard had. Would he stand by her again?

Not that it mattered. She was of age now, and Russ had no interest in her other than as his little sister's friend. As a correspondent.

She hung the dress back in the wardrobe and pulled out a cotton frock in dark blue. It suited her mood. Serviceable and no-nonsense. The type of garment worn by an old-maid piano teacher in small-town

Michigan. Would Aunt Maggie let her keep a cat? Didn't all old maids keep a cat? Maybe a dog—a twinge of grief caught her by surprise. Poor old Jigs. Perhaps a bird would be better. One that talked. Yes, that sounded like just the thing.

Smothering a yawn, she cast one last glance at the rumpled bed. After a long soak in the tub, she'd slept the afternoon away, but the nap had hardly made a dent in her fatigue. Worry, stress, and train travel hadn't allowed for much sleep the past few days. She slipped out of her dressing gown and into the serviceable blue. She fluffed her mostly-dried hair with her fingers before sweeping it into its normal twist and securing it with a handful of pins. If she pulled a few wisps free—but what was the point?

The point was that sometimes, when she least expected it, Russ showed signs of... *something*. On the train, right before Archie had returned, there'd been that *something*. Every fiber within her wanted it to be the beginning of a future with Russ. Just like she'd wanted a future with James.

The tintype of James still stood on her bedside table. She picked it up, her fingers tracing his smooth face. While a sadness lingered as she held the framed image, the pain was gone. Without a doubt, she knew she was ready to get on with her life. If only Russ could be part of that getting on. The biggest part.

She'd probably wind up at Aunt Maggie's with a bird.

A bell chimed downstairs. She gave one last glance in the mirror, then tweaked a couple of wisps of hair to lessen the severity of her twist, before hurrying down the stairs. It wouldn't do for Russ to arrive in the parlor before she did. She should be there before he had to face her whole family.

Richard stood as she entered the room. "Little sister, you gave us all a fright."

"I'm sorry." She walked into his embrace, then pulled away. "It was selfish of me to leave as I did, and I regret it. Truly."

"As you should." Archie stood by the window, his pocket watch in one hand.

Emmie nodded. What else could she say? Fannie embraced her and then the children crowded around, even little Ned, who was standing on his own. Had she been gone that long? Children changed so quickly at his age. She scooped him up and planted a noisy kiss on his cheek as Russ came through the door.

Setting the toddler next to Fannie, she crossed the room and took Russ by the elbow. "Let me introduce you to my family."

His Adam's apple bobbed a couple of times.

"You've already met Archie, of course, and Caroline when we arrived." She led him toward Archie's three children. "This is David, he's twenty and ready to take on the world. Belinda is seventeen, and Yvonne is nine." They exchanged polite greetings. Russ kept his chin tilted into his chest, but the children—no doubt briefed by Archie—made no outward show of surprise at his appearance. She'd never been prouder of them. She tugged Russ toward the next batch.

"This is Richard and Fannie. They have five children. Sissy is nine, Louisa is eight, Christopher is six, Adelle is four, and Ned is a year and a half now." The girls smiled shyly, Christopher stood straight and tall. Ned popped his thumb in his mouth.

"Everyone, this is Russ Fields. Some of you remember his sister, Becky, who came to stay some holidays and weekends while we attended the Ladies Seminary."

Once the extended greetings were over, Russ said, "Thank you for allowing me to stay here while I see what the doctor can do about..." He waved his hand in the direction of the scarred side of his face. The only sound for a moment was the ticking of the grandfather clock.

"Does it hurt much?" Louisa, ever the tender-hearted child, asked.

Fannie looked fit to swallow her tongue, and Richard was shaking his head at his middle daughter.

Russ simply bent down to the little girl's level. "It did, for a long time."

Louisa touched the scars. Richard's breath hissed through his teeth, but Russ stayed still, watching the child, allowing her touch.

"I'm so sorry—" Fannie said, but Russ's raised hand stopped her.

"She's only curious," he said.

Archie cleared his throat. "Dinner is on the table."

The children filed into the dining room, their parents behind them. Emmie leaned close to Russ. "Thank you."

He cocked his head.

"For not making Louisa feel uncomfortable or as if she'd done something wrong."

He smiled, but it was more sad than not. "Children are curious and honest. If only more adults were the same way."

"I try." She slipped her fingers around his elbow again.

His hand covered hers. "I know."

That *something* was there in his voice, and her heart thumped in response.

Dinner had gone surprisingly well. Neither brother had grilled Russ with questions. *He* would have, had it been Becky who'd run off to meet someone. Although, that wasn't really what had happened with Emmie. She'd come for the position at the church. Still, he'd have been asking some very pointed questions.

Someone rapped on his door. "Yes?"

The butler pushed it open but stayed in the hallway. "The carriage is out front for you, sir."

"Thank you."

The man tilted his head, then closed the door. A butler, a cook, and a housemaid. He shook his head. No wonder Emmie hadn't known how to do anything until Mrs. McCann had shown her. It made him grin to remember how they'd had to toss out two pots of coffee that had been undrinkable. She'd been a quick study, though.

He glanced at the mirror beside the door. A mirror large enough to see not only his whole face, but the length of his body. A mirror fitting of a house with servants. His scars stood out in the morning sunshine that flooded the bedroom.

The carriage would take him to see the doctor. At a hospital. A shudder worked its way up his back and across his shoulders, but he held them still. He'd rather stand here and think about Emmie's brothers and her servants... anything but what lay ahead of him.

He closed his eye and bowed his head, rubbing his palms down his sides. "Emmie wants me to do this and... and..." He ran out of words.

He looked back into the mirror and shrugged. He wanted to do it for *her*. Because she cared. Probably more than she should.

With his hat in his hands, he thumped down both staircases, his borrowed room being on the third floor. One step at a time was all his leg would allow, but he wasn't in a hurry anyway. Emmie waited by the front door, speaking with the butler.

"Thank you, Evans," she said before turning to Russ with a falsely bright smile. "Are you ready?"

No. He'd never be ready for this, and it must have shown because she plowed ahead without waiting for him to answer.

"It's a bit of a feat that Helen was able to get you in to see Dr. Lawson today. He's generally backed up several days if not weeks to see a new patient."

He nodded. "Let's not keep him waiting, then."

The hand he opened the door with trembled, but maybe Emmie didn't notice. He helped her into the carriage and climbed in after, settling his leg as comfortably as he could. The coach moved forward, its smooth action a definite difference from the starting lurch of Goblin hitched to his farm wagon.

More refined, like everything he'd seen here in Pittsburgh so far.

The ever-present odor of the steel production process hung over the city, although not as rank here as it had been at the train station. Sunlight shone on the buildings, but it didn't chase away the sooty grayness, only lightened it a bit. The carriage wheels rattled softly across the cut stones that paved the streets here. They must still be in a more upscale section of town.

Emmie twisted the drawstring of her reticule. Was she nervous? Did she worry that the doctor would be unable to make him look more acceptable? Or was she worried that he'd have another waking dream where he slipped back into the war? Both were possibilities. Only the second one plagued him. If the doctor could do nothing, then Russ would go home where he belonged. He'd wake up to the slippery tongue of Nip washing his face instead of the polite knock of a butler.

He sighed.

"Are you worried?" Emmie asked.

How could he not be? "Concerned."

"That the doctor might not be able to..."

He shrugged. "More about the other thing."

"Oh." The reticule's drawstring took more punishment. "Even if—"

"I don't—" They spoke over the top of each other. He inclined his head for her to go first.

"Even if you do have an incident of the war coming back on you, you'll be among doctors and nurses who can help."

"Maybe." Or maybe that would make it worse. It had been Emmie's voice that had pulled him out of the waking dream on the train, not Miss Edwards's. He hadn't needed a trained nurse. He refused to explore, even to himself, why Emmie was the one who could reach into that dark place and draw him out.

The carriage stopped in front of a many-storied building of gray-tinged brick. He opened the door and swung his leg out. He hopped to the ground and retrieved his crutch before assisting Emmie from the vehicle.

"Give us two hours, please," she said to the driver. "Then meet us here again."

He tipped his hat and shook the reins over the horses' backs. Russ squelched the urge to dive back into the carriage before it rolled away.

"There's Helen." Emmie waved to a woman standing next to a smaller door to the side of the main entrance.

Russ swallowed once, twice, and then followed the swish of Emmie's skirts as she hurried toward her friend. Maybe, if he concentrated on that sound, nothing else would overtake him.

Maybe.

CHAPTER 28

T HE SMELL HIT HIM first. Not the stomach-turning stench of blood, raging infection, and bodily decay that had clung to the field hospital he'd first awoken in. For that mercy, he was thankful. It was camphor and ammonia, two scents he'd been surrounded by while convalescing at the hospital in Washington. A hospital with white walls just like those before him. Walls that stretched into a never-ending tunnel.

Miss Edwards was talking, but her words made no sense. His breathing sped up, and he stopped, one hand against the wall of the tunnel. His heart raced between his ribs. It was happening again. He had to stop it. He couldn't let it take over. Not now. Not in front of Emmie. Never again in front of Emmie. But the tunnel yawned in front of him. Men's low voices grew, getting louder. They were closing in on the enemy.

Rockfish Gap, Confederates in front of them, dismounted, and sneaking through the forest. Could they make it close enough to surprise the enemy? John Henry moved at his side, and then he was gone. Where was the rest of Custer's force? Why couldn't he hear the mounted units?

Emmie's voice reached him. What was she doing here? He had to find her, had to get her away from the coming fight. How had she gotten ahead of them? He had to get her out.

Now!

Emmie stopped when Russ did, his hand pressed against the wall. "Russ?"

Helen, who'd continued on a few steps, turned and hurried back to her side. "Mr. Fields?"

Russ's chest heaved, his eye was wide and wild, his nostrils flared.

"Russ. It's Emmie."

"Why are you *here*?" His voice was gravelly, the words slurred a bit. She cast a glance at Helen.

"Mr. Fields, do you know where you are?" Helen asked.

"Rockfish Gap." He started down the hallway, each step picking up speed from the one before until he was running as fast as his splinted leg would allow. A nurse carrying a tray backed up against the opposite wall. Another came out of a room.

"What's going on here?" the first nurse asked.

"Soldier's heart," Helen said as she ran past.

Emmie hiked her skirt to keep up with Russ's uneven strides. "Russ! Stop!" She grabbed for his arm and got only a handful of sleeve. He shoved her away. She slipped on the waxed floor, went down, and skidded into the wall.

"Emmie!" Helen slowed to check on her.

Emmie waved her on. "Catch him!"

With an anguished look, her friend took off after Russ. With Helen's long legs, she reached him just before he got to the double doors at the end of the hallway. Several men had heard them and gathered there.

With a groan, Emmie climbed to her feet and hobbled behind. One of the men had Russ by the shoulders, another came around the other side.

"Emmie!" Russ called, trying to escape from the men holding him. "Emmie!"

"I'm here. Right here." Why couldn't he see her?

"Emmie!"

"She's right here, Mr. Fields. Look behind you." Helen instructed the men to turn Russ around. "See, she's right here. We're at the hospital in Pittsburgh."

Recognition flickered in his eye. His shoulders sagged, his breath still coming in deep gasps. "Emmie."

"I'm here. I'm right here. You're okay." She touched his arm, moving the other man's hand away. "We're in Pittsburgh, at the hospital. You're to see Dr. Lawson."

The first man who'd grabbed Russ by the shoulders released him and stuck out a hand. "I'm Dr. Lawson."

Russ stared at the hand for a moment, his breath evening out, then he clasped it. "Russ Fields."

"My office is just around the corner. Let's step that way, shall we?"

He'd disgraced himself in front of Emmie again. Russ fell into the chair in the doctor's office, ignoring the pain in his leg. He couldn't look at Emmie, so he stared at the edge of the desk in front of him. The doctor closed the door and took his seat on the other side of the desk. The women sat on a bench along the wall.

"How often do these episodes happen, Mr. Fields?" the doctor asked.

Russ shrugged. "Hard to say."

"Daily, weekly, twice a month?"

Russ rubbed the bridge of his nose. "In the beginning, they came frequently. Maybe daily, I don't remember. Now they don't usually happen unless something..." He fumbled for the right words.

"Sets it off," the doctor said. "Instigates it, so to speak."

"That sounds about right," Russ said.

"What set it off just now?"

He searched back in his memory. Even though it'd been only moments ago, it seemed like hours. And then it hit him. "The smell."

"What smell?"

"Ammonia and camphor."

The doctor nodded, making a note on the paper in front of him. "Smells are a common problem for men dealing with this. Can you think of anything else that you've experienced before one of these episodes happens?"

"Sounds."

"Mmm." The doctor made another note. "That's very common as well."

Common? "You know of others who have these..."

"Episodes."

"Episodes, too?" He wasn't the only one. He'd known that other men struggled with memories of the war, but not that others had experienced the same sort of waking dreams he did. Somehow, that helped. The tension inside him eased a bit.

The doctor folded his arms and leaned them on his desk. "Many men who served in the war have experienced these types of episodes. I've seen hundreds myself."

Hundreds? Russ leaned back in his chair.

"There are likely thousands, maybe tens of thousands. We have no way of knowing. Most will never come forward or seek treatment."

"There's treatment?" Hope he might be cured sparked within him.

"Not a medication. Nothing we can do physically, but bringing the issue to light, learning what instigates it and how to avoid those things, practicing techniques to help you keep from sliding into an episode—we are having some success with these approaches."

No cure. Why did the disappointment hit him so hard? He hadn't expected one, had he? Emmie bent and rubbed her ankle, the motion catching in the corner of his eye. He couldn't look at her. Especially now that he knew there was no cure for his waking dreams.

"We can talk more about that later. Let's have a look at your scars." The doctor stood and came around to kneel by Russ's chair. He pressed the skin on Russ's face. "Does this hurt?"

"No."

"Can you feel this?"

"A bit."

They went back and forth, a question and an answer to each poke and prod. He even looked in Russ's mouth. After a while, the doctor sat back on his heels.

"I can lessen the scarring on your cheek and jaw, as well as temper the scar along your neck. The bones that were broken in your cheek have healed nicely, so there's little distortion from that. You're very lucky you didn't lose any teeth."

Lucky? Russ closed his eye for a moment. That wasn't how he'd have described himself, but he'd seen men with worse disfigurements. One man had lost his entire lower jaw. Maybe he was lucky. He opened his eye and nodded. "When?"

Dr. Lawson stood and returned to his chair. He scratched a few notes on the paper. "Nurse Edwards was most insistent that I see you right away. I understand you live in Michigan and have a farm to tend."

The doctor looked up, and Russ nodded.

"Therefore, I suggest you return in the morning, let's say eight o'clock? I've reserved the surgery already."

Surgery.

His breathing sped up again, his hands clenched the arms of the chair.

"Mr. Fields." The doctor's voice came from a long distance away.

A hand clasped his. Not the doctor's. This hand was soft, smooth, cool. "Mr. Fields, hold on to me." The nurse, Emmie's friend. "Hold on, squeeze my hand."

He did.

"It's going to be all right. I'll be with you every step of the way." Her voice firmed in his ears, as if it had come into focus.

His breathing slowed. Emmie stood behind Miss Edwards, her face pinched and pale. Was she afraid that he wouldn't go through with this? For himself, he never would. But for her...

"I'll be here."

Because it was all he could offer her.

Sixteen paces down the hallway, turn, sixteen paces back. That's what Emmie had been doing all morning. Her heels clicked on the floor. Her bruised ankle from yesterday's fall throbbed in a dull ache that she ignored, just like the nurses ignored her. They must have seen dozens of people waiting outside the surgery every day. It wasn't new to them.

It wasn't frightening to them. Their lives didn't hinge on how well the surgery turned out.

Neither did hers.

This wasn't about her. It was about what she could do to help Becky's brother. About helping Russ see that he could move on, that he could let go of the past, of the war. That he could reclaim a bit of his dignity by lessening the effects of the war on his face. Maybe, if he didn't have to look at that every day, maybe the soldier's heart episodes wouldn't happen or at least happen less often.

Maybe.

So much hung on the skill of Dr. Lawson with the assistance of Helen.

Emmie stopped and rested her shoulders against the hallway wall, her fingers caressing the emerald pendant. Yesterday, when Russ's breathing had started to speed up again, Helen had grabbed his hand and talked him through it. She'd known what to do. Emmie had stood like a statue, fearing the worst.

She sighed, glanced at the clock over the nurses' desk, and then resumed her pacing.

Almost two hours. How much longer could this go on? Why hadn't she asked the doctor or Helen? The door to the surgery opened, and Helen walked through, tying a pristine white apron over her black dress.

"How is he?"

Helen took her arm and steered her toward the window down the hallway. "Russ woke up a few minutes ago. Dr. Lawson did a remarkable job. Now, we wait and make sure that no infection sets in, keeping him quiet and well hydrated for the next few hours."

Hope brought a lump to Emmie's throat. She swallowed. "Can I see him now?"

Compassion darkened the blue of her friend's eyes. "I'm sorry, but only family and clergy are allowed into the patients' wards here at the hospital."

"What?" *No!* "But what if being here does that—whatever the doctor said, and he has another episode? Russ has no family to sit with him."

Helen bit her bottom lip. "You make a good point."

"Can you speak with the doctor? Surely he can override the hospital's rules for the good of his patient." He must. The idea of Russ lying somewhere in the belly of the hospital, surrounded by things that could set off the soldier's heart... she couldn't let that happen. She wouldn't. No matter that Archie would have plenty to say about it later.

"I'll talk to him," Helen said.

"Hurry."

Helen took her hands in hers. "Russ is very groggy and will most likely sleep for several hours. Maybe you should go home and try to rest. You don't look like you slept at all last night."

She hadn't. Not after the go-around with Archie. He'd been dead-set against her coming to the hospital with Russ today. As if she would stay home while he braved this on his own. When she didn't return, Archie would no doubt come looking for her. She'd be easy to find. She'd be at Russ's side... until he didn't need her anymore.

"I'll be fine. Take me to Russ."

"First, I must get Dr. Lawson's permission." She gave Emmie's hand one last pat, then hurried back through the door to the surgery.

The nurse at the desk glanced up and gave her a wan smile as Emmie resumed her pacing. She just had to be the one to sit with Russ as he recovered. He was here on account of her. Because she wanted to help him feel good about himself again. A tiny twinge of conscience vibrated deep in her chest. She didn't mind his scars, she really didn't, but if he were to look a bit more... She crushed down that thought. Mentally thrust her heel on it and ground it away. She refused to think of his scars the way some other people did. Refused to see Russ as anything other than... Russ.

Helen reappeared. "Doctor is allowing you into the ward in lieu of any family present."

Unable to suppress the grin that probably showed every tooth including her molars, Emmie grasped Helen's arm and squeezed.

Her friend returned her smile. "I'll take you there. Remember, he's not the only patient in the ward. You'll have to be quiet and sit still." Helen raised a finger. "No pacing."

"I won't." She'd be an absolute statue if that's what was required to stay by his side. One battle down... another to go. Archie was sure to turn up before dark. But she'd worry about that later.

They walked halls at once familiar and yet strange. She'd been gone from the hospital for months now. How had she ever looked at these halls as a haven, a place she longed to be? In her mind's eye, her haven was now a farmstead nestled among rolling hills covered with sheep. If only in her dreams.

Helen stopped beside the door and pressed her finger to her lips. Emmie nodded and followed her into the ward. The long room held sixteen beds, eight to a side, with most of them occupied. Helen led her to the last bed on the left, its occupant swaddled in linen wrappings from his shoulders and across most of his head. His eye, his nose, mouth, and chin remained exposed. More than enough to identify the man she loved. There was no denying it.

She loved Russ Fields.

She sank onto the wooden chair next to his bed. His deep, even breathing never faltered. Helen's heels clicked in the distance. Emmie battled with herself for a moment, then drew Russ's hand into hers. Warm and dry, his fingers twitched at her touch, the merest of movement, and then they curled around hers as he sighed deeply, never opening his eye.

CHAPTER 29

T HE RATTLE OF A cart's wheels. A low moan of some man nearby. Metal clinking against metal. Russ drew in a deep breath when warm fingers squeezed his hand. Soft but firm, reassuring. The vague scent of flowers cut through the harsh tang of camphor.

Emmie.

Opening his eye took a monumental effort. As the blurred surroundings solidified, the sounds and smells came together in the dim light. He was in a hospital. Fear spiked through him, and he struggled to sit. A shadow covered him, hands pressed against his shoulders, holding him down.

"Russ, you must lie still."

Emmie's voice. Here? His heart galloped in his chest. He had to get her out of here.

"You're going to be fine. You just need to rest. The doctor said the surgery went very well."

His shoulders sank into the mattress again.

"Doctor?" The word burned his throat, surfacing as little more than a rasp.

"Here." Emmie's hand slid under his head, lifting it until the cool edge of a cup pressed against his lips. He gulped several mouthfuls until she moved it away. "That's enough for now. You can have more in a few minutes."

"I see he's come around."

A nurse leaned over him—Emmie's friend. What was her name? Her hand was cool and light against his cheek.

"Welcome back, Mr. Fields." The woman turned to Emmie. "Your brother is in the lobby and none too happy about it. You'd best go home and sleep. You're dead on your feet. I'll be in the ward until morning."

"Surely you need to sleep more than I."

"I did," the nurse said, "for the past several hours. Go on. I'll watch him as if he were my own brother, I promise."

Emmie looked from the nurse to him and back again. Dark circles outlined her eyes, mussed hair escaped around her face. She'd never looked better, but his eyelid drifted shut before he could take in more.

"I can't believe you told Evans not to wake me." Emmie jabbed a pin into her hat and grimaced when it grazed her scalp. "It's a good thing I woke up on my own." She glared across the parlor at Archie.

"That's a matter of opinion."

"Perhaps it is, but as he's my friend and it's my life, it's my opinion that matters." Oh, if only he weren't so infuriating. So... so... so Archie. Her fingers curled into her palms.

"While you're living under my roof, visible to all my friends and neighbors, I insist that you act with at least a modicum of propriety."

His roof? The very roof she'd spent her entire life under until—a sharp stab of grief caught her unawares. Until Father died. She pressed her hands to her middle.

"I don't wish to have a row with you, but I am going to the hospital."

"Why?"

She clenched her teeth and stared at him.

He looked away, burying his fingers into his neatly combed hair. "He's not interested in you, you know."

Heat flamed across her face. "What do you mean?"

He stepped closer to her, something akin to compassion tempering his look. "I watched him—and you—on the train. He was much more at ease with your friend Helen than with you. While you"—he lifted one shoulder in a shrug—"you are obviously smitten with him."

She wished she could deny it. She wished she were just doing what she could for Becky's brother. But smitten? Her feelings went far beyond that. Not that she'd admit as much to Archie. But she'd at last admitted it to herself, even knowing that heartbreak was her only reward.

"Regardless of what you saw and what you think you know, Becky's brother is lying in the hospital, and I'm going to sit with him."

"For how long?"

"For as long as he needs me."

The pause that followed lengthened into an uncomfortable silence.

"And then?" Archie's voice lowered to just above a whisper, all his usual bluster and arrogance gone.

Her heart trembled as she looked away. She wouldn't be less than honest.

"I don't know."

He gripped her shoulder. "This is your home too, you know."

"It used to be."

The grip tightened.

"It always will be. You scared me half to death when you ran away. Don't do that again."

Emmie leaned against her brother's side. "I won't. That was wrong of me." She tilted her head to look into his face. "But I won't be staying. My life isn't here anymore."

"Emmie, he doesn't love you."

Pain exploded around her heart and pushed heat against the back of her eyelids. "I know."

"Then why?"

"Because I found something in Jonesville that I don't have here."

"What?"

"A purpose."

"Playing piano in church? Teaching other people's children?" Incredulity seeped into his voice. "You should have a husband and children of your own. Let me find—"

"No." She shook her head. "You can't find a husband for me. It wouldn't be fair to him or me. My heart belongs to Russ, whether he wants it or not." There. She'd said it. Admitted it to Archie, of all people.

"Oh, Emmie." His arms came around her. She let herself relax into his embrace, marveling that this was Archie. Perhaps that's what kept her tears at bay. After a moment, she straightened.

"He's still Becky's brother, and for her memory, I will do everything I can for him until he's ready to return to his farm."

"And then?"

"I'll go back to my room at Aunt Maggie's and resume my new life in Jonesville. But I'll keep my distance from Russ, if that's what he wishes. I promise you that. I have no desire to be where I'm not wanted."

"You're wanted here." Archie pointed to the floor. "We'll keep your room just as it is."

She nodded, spun around, and marched out the front door. June's morning heat met her on the steps, but she walked to the hospital instead of hailing a carriage. Tears dribbled off her chin, but she didn't wipe them away. She needed the time and exercise to gather her wits.

To come to grips with her emotions.

Russ's face hurt, but it wasn't unbearable. It'd hurt far worse than this before. Miss Edwards's hands were cool and efficient as she changed the bandages.

"No sign of infection," Miss Edwards said. "Doctor will be pleased. He's a firm believer in Joseph Lister's sterile surgery techniques."

"I remember the infection, the fevers, the smell." None as bad as the pain and the fear. Fear that he wouldn't live. Fear that he would.

"You were very lucky to survive at all. Many didn't. If we'd known about carbolic acid before the war..." She sighed, a delicate furrow marring her brow. "But we did the best we could with what we had."

She'd suffered through the war too. How many patients had she watched slip away? Too many, no doubt. He took her hand and squeezed it. Her eyebrows shot up, but understanding filled the blue of her eyes. They'd both seen too much. She returned his squeeze.

Emmie appeared beside Miss Edwards, her eyes flicked between their clasped hands and his face. "How are you feeling this morning, Russ?" The words were cordial, impersonal, very nurse-like.

He slid his hand from Miss Edwards's and attempted to sit up.

"No, not yet." Her hand on his shoulder stopped him. "You need to stay down for at least another day."

"I'll stay with him." Emmie moved to the chair on the other side of the bed.

Miss Edwards covered a yawn. "Now that you're here, I'll get some sleep. Doctor Lawson should come through in another hour or so. You can ask him any questions." She rose and left the ward.

The silence was broken when another man sneezed, and then swore. A nurse rushed to his side. Emmie sat with her back straight, her fingers playing with the green pendant she always wore.

He cleared his throat.

"I've felt better, but I've felt a whole lot worse."

She startled, as if she'd forgotten the question she'd asked. "Is there anything I can get for you? Do you want your pillow adjusted?"

The nurse-talk was back.

"No."

He'd never been much of a conversationalist, and lying flat on a hospital bed didn't help matters.

She fidgeted on the chair, then leaned toward him. "Miss Edwards held your hand. Did you have another..."

He closed his eye and bit back a groan. So that was the problem. She thought he'd had another waking dream. And why wouldn't she? He was broken, both inside and out. They might be able to fix the worst of the outside—maybe—but inside? That wasn't fixable. The doctor had admitted as much.

And yet, he'd awoken to the sounds and smells of the hospital without slipping back into the war. Why?

"I'm sorry," she said. "I shouldn't have asked."

"No. I mean, that's all right. It didn't happen."

"No?" The nurse-voice was measured, controlled. Impersonal. He should send her on her way. Emmie had better things to do than sit with him and hold his hand—

Oh. Had she mistaken that gesture with Miss Edwards for something more? Maybe that was for the best. After all, he had no intention of saddling her with a man scarred both outside and in.

Not that her brother would ever allow it.

What had she expected? That Russ would wake up from surgery, see her, and then declare his undying love? Emmie snorted, then looked around to be sure nobody had heard. The walls of the music room were her only witnesses. Her fingers rested on the silent piano keys. For once, even the music failed her. With a sigh, she folded her hands in her lap.

She wasn't a child. She wasn't expecting the fairy-tale ending of happily-ever-after. At least, she hadn't thought she was.

Then why did it feel as if her heart were stripped bare, laid open in her chest?

Becky would have been happy though, to see Russ healing. He hadn't had a single incidence of soldier's heart since the surgery. Not one. She hadn't seen the scarred side of his face, of course. It was still covered with bandages. Helen said he'd need to keep it covered for a least a week, and it'd only been three days.

Three days of seeing her hopes—hopes she'd known she shouldn't hold on to—slip away.

Russ was polite, even friendly, but there was no spark between them now. No *something* like there'd been on the train and again at dinner the night before the surgery.

"Are you going to play, or just sit there?" Richard's voice in the doorway jerked Emmie from her morose thoughts.

"You startled me." She plinked one finger on a key, the note dying away quickly. "But please come in."

Richard stopped behind her, resting his hands on her shoulders. "Want to talk about it?"

"About what?"

"Whatever is making you look so forlorn. Or maybe I should say, whomever?"

She leaned against his chest and tilted her head until she could see his face. "I suppose you think me the queen of fools."

"Hardly."

"Well, I am."

"Tell me why."

Emmie closed her eyes and shook her head. "It won't change anything."

"Come here." He took her by the arm and led her to the settee. She sat, and he joined her. "Now, tell your big brother why you are the queen of fools."

She leaned against his shoulder. "Once I knew Russ had no interest in me, I should have come home."

"Why didn't you?"

"Becky."

Richard's face scrunched. "She passed away before you left, didn't she?"

"Yes, of course, but I kept thinking about her and how she'd feel with her brother the way he was, living all alone, avoiding people, refusing to go to church." She shrugged. "I'd hate it if you or Archie were ever to be like that. I knew about Helen's work with Dr. Lawson and that there was help for the scars Russ carries. If he'd accept it."

"And you felt duty-bound by your friendship with Becky to stay and urge him to seek that help?"

"Yes." The word came out in a sad squeak.

"But?"

"Oh, Richard, I was only fooling myself." She grabbed a fistful of her skirts and twisted them into a knot. "I fell in love with Russ before I ever saw him."

"Through the letters the two of you exchanged?"

"Yes."

Richard scratched his chin. "Do you think he lied to you, in the letters, because he didn't tell you about his deformities?"

"Don't call them that."

"You know I don't mean that in a belittling way."

She did, but she hated how it sounded. "No, he never lied to me. He just didn't describe himself."

"And you don't think that was dishonest?"

"No. I never described myself to him either. Our letters, they weren't... like that."

"What were they like?"

She sighed and gave a half shrug. "They were like talking to my best friend."

Richard leaned against the back of the settee and pulled her to his side. "For what it's worth, I like him."

She drew in a wavering breath. "Me too."

"I'll speak with him if you—"

"No." She shook her head. "Thank you, but no." She'd not beg for a man's affection or send her brother to beg in her stead.

She would have to be content to be Russ's friend. And only that. But could she find contentment with only that once they returned to Jonesville?

CHAPTER 30

F IVE DAYS SPENT BESIDE Russ at the hospital had reduced Emmie to a pile of doubt as she sat on her bed. Watching Helen interact with him brought thoughts and emotions to the surface that Emmie hadn't realized herself capable of. Jealousy, plain and simple, was a vulgar emotion, and one she wanted no part of. Yet every smile, every touch, every warm word that passed between the two people most dear to her outside of her family left her with its bitter taste.

One thing had become crystal clear—she could not return to Jonesville.

To see Russ when he drove to town and know that she'd never be an integral part of his life was one thing. But the thought of him finding and possibly courting another woman with her there to witness it? No. That she couldn't do to herself. Pain sliced through her at the very idea.

Whatever was happening between Russ and Helen was temporary. She wasn't foolish enough to think otherwise. She'd had enough patients attach themselves to her while she'd worked in the hospital to know. And besides, Helen's interest, by her own admission, was Dr. Lawson. Seeing her friend with the doctor on several occasions, Emmie was fairly certain that the doctor returned Helen's regard.

But someday, there would be someone for Russ. When the time was right, a woman would come along and touch his heart in the way she'd hoped to. Longed to. She couldn't be there when it happened.

Tucking those truths into her heart and closing its door, Emmie pinned her hat in place and took one last look in the mirror. Russ was leaving the hospital this morning, and she was taking him to the train station.

To say goodbye.

Damp heat gathered in the corners of her eyes, but she blinked it away and lifted her chin, pasting on a pleasant smile. This was the way it had to be. Archie would be thrilled when she told him she was staying. No doubt Russ would be relieved as well. Richard would pat her shoulder and say nothing. Helen? She had no idea how her friend would react. Not that it mattered. Emmie was only doing what must be done.

She'd miss Alannah and the children, Aunt Maggie, even Mickey, and the irascible Penny, but she couldn't dwell on what might have been. Once Russ was gone, she'd take stock of her situation and make some decisions. Staying in Pittsburgh held little appeal, but she wasn't sure she had enough gumption left—or maybe courage—to strike out on her own again.

A carriage rattled to a halt in front of the house. She slipped on her low-heeled shoes and buttoned them. After grabbing her reticule, she left her room and headed down the stairs. Caroline waited at the bottom.

"What have you decided?"

Emmie spread her arms and let them drop to her sides. "There's nothing left to decide. I'll wait with Russ at the train station, and then I'm returning... home."

Caroline blinked several times, opened her mouth, and then shut it again.

"I believe Archie will be pleased," Emmie said.

"Doubtless." Her sister-in-law looked her square in the eye. "But will you?"

"Not immediately, of course. But, with time." Just as she'd healed from the loss of James, she'd heal from the loss of Russ.

And she'd never put her heart in this situation again.

Miss Edwards had come and shown Russ how to change his bandages, which were now less bulky than the originals. He was to rub on a special oily salve and change the bandages every morning. After a week, he could stop wearing the bandages as long as he was out of the sun, but he must keep the salve treatment going for a couple of months.

He was almost afraid to admit it, even to himself, but the new skin was growing in more normal-looking than his previous scars. That scar on his neck didn't bulge out to catch on his shirt collar, the corner of his empty eye socket no longer pulled down, and the lumpy tissue in front of his ear and across his cheekbone was now flat and almost smooth. It didn't pull anymore.

The best thing of all was the doctor's report that he'd cleaned up the scars as well as could be expected with the one surgery. Russ wouldn't need to return for any more or other treatments. For that, he was very grateful.

He'd never be handsome, hadn't expected that, but at least he wouldn't be so repulsive. His face would always show the damage, but maybe, if he followed the doctor's orders to the letter, he could fit himself with a patch and hold his head up in public again without frightening anyone.

That was something. Something more than he'd had when he came to Pittsburgh. Was that why he hadn't slipped back into the war over the past week?

The click of heels on the floor stopped his thoughts and dried his mouth. When had he learned to recognize the rhythm of Emmie's footsteps? He flicked a glance at the clock. She'd said she'd come to see him to the station. That's about all she'd said yesterday. Miss Edwards had carried the conversation, and, when she'd left, Emmie had read to him from a novel about a lonely old weaver who loved money more than anything. It hadn't held his interest much, but hearing her voice made up for that.

She swept through the doorway in her usual way, walking as if on a mission. Her back was stiff, her head held high, and she wore a pleasant smile, which she turned to each man she passed. Then she was right in front of Russ.

"Good morning. Are you ready?" Her nurse's voice was back. Cheery, impersonal, and no-nonsense.

He stood and lifted the satchel with everything he'd brought to Pittsburgh in it. "I am."

"Splendid. We'll make it to the train station in plenty of time."

He motioned for her to precede him. She pivoted and strode back the way she'd come. He had to stretch his bad leg to keep up. It was healing nicely, according to the doctor, but it was still stiff. However, he couldn't maintain the pace for long.

"Emmie."

She halted and turned so fast he almost ran her over.

"I can't keep up with you." He patted his leg.

"I'm so sorry. Forgive me. I'd quite forgotten." Her brown eyes melted into puddles of chagrin.

"I know. I'd almost forgotten about it myself what with all the attention on..." He pointed to his bandages.

She smiled. The first authentic Emmie smile he'd seen in... how long?

"Come, I'll walk more like a lady."

"Well, in that case." He presented his elbow to her.

She flushed, her eyes darting around the hospital's hallway for a moment, but then she slid her fingers around his arm.

Something warm and solid settled in the base of his throat. People whisked by in the hurried fashion of nurses and orderlies. Most smiled or gave a quick nod as they passed. Nobody stopped or stared. None seemed to find it odd that this lovely lady would be on his arm. His chest swelled for a moment, and he released a long breath.

"Are you in pain?"

Did his heart count? "Just thinking."

She opened her mouth, then shut it again. Had she been about to ask what he was thinking? Did he want her to? Would he tell her if she did?

He hadn't reached any conclusions before they arrived at the hired carriage. He tossed his satchel in, then turned and assisted her into the vehicle. He joined her, taking the opposite seat.

Only his satchel sat on the floor. Perhaps she'd brought a trunk. That would be loaded on the top. He hadn't looked.

She crossed her feet, the toes of her shoes poking out from her skirts. Then she uncrossed them and fidgeted on the seat. Looking out the side window, she touched her hat as if checking that it remained in place.

He was staring, making her uncomfortable. That must be it.

He cleared his throat. "You were right to insist I come."

Her head snapped back in his direction. "I'm happy you think so. Now."

He grimaced. "I know. I was less than cordial about everything. Please accept my apologies if—"

"No." She held up her hand, palm toward him. "Please don't apologize. I can't imagine how I would have reacted had I been you."

Relaxing for the first time that morning, he nodded.

"Becky would be so pleased." Her voice wobbled on the last word.

Yes, she would have. He blinked a couple of times.

"I know if the roles had been reversed, she'd have done anything she could to have helped one of my brothers."

That sounded... final. So much for relaxing.

"When we get back to Jonesville—"

"I won't be going back."

Her words hit his midsection harder than the ram that had broken his leg, tearing his breath from his lungs. Not going back? How could she not go back?

The thought of never seeing her again left him more than breathless, more than broken, it left him...

Empty.

"I've decided to take up Richard and Fannie's offer to move in with them and help with the children." Emmie clenched a handful of her skirts in one hand and her emerald in the other.

"You have?" His voice was low and scratchy. Could he be disappointed? No. She wasn't going to look for hope that wasn't there.

"Yes. Fannie is..." She shrugged and looked out the window again. "She'll need help in the months to come."

"Oh."

Silence stretched between them, thick enough she almost thought she could see it.

"But after?"

How she wanted to believe there was a wisp of longing in his tone. But she was done with all that. She was nothing but practical now. Caring for the children, not her own but her family at least, was her new priority. There would be no time to worry about what might have been. No time to chastise herself over her rash and impetuous decision to go to Jonesville in the first place.

"They'll need help for a few years, at least. Then perhaps I'll apply to the hospital again."

"Unless Archie finds you a suitable husband."

She shook her head but kept silent. Knowing Archie, he'd do his best, but at least she had Richard on her side. There were worse things than being an old maid.

She pulled an envelope from her reticule and handed it to Russ. "Would you give this to Aunt Maggie for me? It's instructions and money to ship my belongings back... home."

"Of course." He slipped it into his inner coat pocket.

Silence returned inside the carriage, the clamor of street noises barely registering through its gloom. They might as well have been two strangers sharing the ride. With each rotation of the wheels, a tiny part of her heart broke away.

The carriage rattled to a stop on the rough cobblestones outside the station. Russ grabbed his satchel and opened the door.

"There's no need for you to wait with me until the train arrives."

But she wanted to. These might be the last moments she had to spend with him.

"I—"

"It looks like rain." He glanced at the gray sky. "If you leave now, you should be home before it starts."

The sky was almost always gray in Pittsburgh, but she didn't remind him. He didn't want her to stay. That was plain enough. She was done trying to change his mind. "Perhaps you're right."

Standing on the carriage step, he reached in and took her hand. "Thank you, my dear Emmie, for all that you've done."

My dear Emmie. Why did he have to say that? Why now? Her throat pinched off any sound she may have wanted to make. All that was left was to nod. He returned the motion and dropped to the ground, then shut the carriage door.

"Return the lady to her home," he told the driver.

Then he turned and limped away... without a backward glance.

Emmie didn't realize she was crying until the tears dripped onto her hand holding the pendant. She took in a long shuddering breath of Pittsburgh's sooty air.

Her hopes, her dreams, her choice of a future... they were all gone.

CHAPTER 31

"**N**O, MA'AM, SHE'S NOT coming back." Russ stood with his hat in his hands in Aunt Maggie's parlor.

"Cyrus Fields, what did you do?" Penny asked from across the room, the feather duster in her hand an obvious ploy for listening in on the conversation.

"Penny, that's enough." Aunt Maggie lowered her brows into a line that even Penny wouldn't cross. Then she settled the same glare in his direction. "Did you ask her to?"

Ask her? He swallowed. "No, ma'am."

A snort sounded from across the room. Aunt Maggie's glare narrowed to twin slits, and Russ suddenly thought of several errands he needed to complete before he left town. He pulled at his collar. "I best be getting on my way."

"Best? You think it best?" Aunt Maggie clearly didn't.

He dropped Emmie's envelope on the small table beside the old woman's chair. "Yes, ma'am. I guess I do." Not that he really understood her question, but he wasn't going to stay long enough to figure it out either. He beat a hasty retreat from the two women.

Several customers were waiting at the mercantile. One man tipped his hat to Russ. A fellow he recognized from the church.

Two ladies scurried by on their way out the door. One paused next to him, "Good morning, Mr. Fields." She smiled at him.

Smiled. At him.

Russ touched his hat brim. "Good morning." He couldn't remember her name, but she looked familiar. Maybe another person from the church. So many families had moved in while he was fighting the war.

Had the bandages changed him somehow?

"Russ Fields?" Pastor Anderson moved to his side. "I thought that was you." He held out his hand.

Russ gripped it. "Just got off the train."

"Looks like Miss Mason's friend got you hooked up with the doctor who specializes in that newfangled plastic surgery." Unasked questions lurked in the preacher's eyes.

"Saw the specialist." He pointed to his bandages. "Won't know how successful he was for a time yet."

"It's amazing what doctors can do these days."

"That it is."

"Is Miss Mason back at Aunt Maggie's?" Hope lightened the man's expression.

Russ cleared his throat. "No. She stayed in Pittsburgh."

"Did she say when she'd return?" He leaned closer to Russ. "Between you and me, the past two Sundays have only highlighted the church's desperate need of her musical abilities."

What could he say? "She has no plans to return."

"Oh." The man straightened, his brows lowering into a pale reflection of Aunt Maggie's scowl. Was everyone going to blame him for Emmie's decision to remain in Pennsylvania?

"Her brother and his wife need her assistance. I gathered they asked her to stay."

The preacher rubbed his chin. "Did you ask her to return?"

Why was everyone asking him that?

"No matter." The preacher flashed him a smile. "You'll be needing a ride out to your farm, I'll wager. I'd be happy to drive you and bring the rig back to town."

"The only way I'm riding with you, preacher, is if I'm driving. No offense, but I've seen you with a horse."

Pastor Anderson laughed and slapped Russ's back. "You're right about that. Maybe you can give me a few pointers along the way."

Russ agreed. The offer was kind and helpful. It would save him and Mickey having to return the rig the next day.

"Maybe I can give you a few pointers on something else." The pastor winked and turned to the clerk to pay for his few items.

Why did Russ get the feeling this wasn't going to be such a good idea after all?

The children tucked in bed, Richard and Fannie in the parlor, and Emmie was free to slouch onto the chair in front of the tiny desk in her attic room. The small window overlooked the street out front but refused to admit any breeze. She mopped her forehead with a damp handkerchief, then planted her elbow on the desk and rested her chin on her palm.

Her new home. Her new life. Was this all she had to look forward to?

She hadn't cried since leaving Russ at the station last Monday, not even when she'd said goodbye to her old room at Archie's and moved into the attic of Richard and Fannie's home. She'd stood firm against Helen's scolding that she should have returned to Jonesville, still a little confused at how her friend had switched on that issue. But now, the need to express herself in some way almost overwhelmed her. Richard and Fannie didn't own a piano, so she couldn't play. Giving way to the threatening tears would only add to the heat and humidity of the room.

If only Becky were still alive, she could pour out her frustration and loneliness on paper. She sat upright and blinked. Writing. That's what had brought her and Russ together in the first place. Would he still welcome a letter?

Did she dare?

Would he respond?

She drew a sheet of paper from the desk and picked up her fountain pen. It was empty. Maybe she shouldn't... She stared out the window at the colorless sky.

With a huff, she pushed away from the desk and hurried down the stairs to Richard's tiny study. It took only a moment to uncork his ink bottle and find the dropper. Armed with a loaded pen, she marched back upstairs.

The tip of her tongue between her lips, she touched the pen to paper.

June 25, 1867

Dear Russ,
A week has passed, and I wonder how you're doing.

That seemed a safe start. And true. Hardly an hour passed that she didn't think of him. Didn't wonder what he was doing. Didn't hope he was thinking of her. And didn't wish that things had turned out differently.

> *Did Mickey keep the farm up to your standards while you were away? I'll bet he appreciated having Nip for company. Soon, she'll be big enough to help with the sheep, I'm sure. I suppose you returned in time to start the harvest. The hay must be ready by now. I can only imagine how it smells, freshly cut and drying in the sun.*

She stopped and pressed her fingers against the bridge of her nose to suppress the longing that almost overwhelmed her. Maybe writing wasn't such a good idea. Still, she'd started, so she best go on.

> *I've moved in with Richard and Fannie. I have a room to myself far above the street. The children seem happy to have me and keep me busy. Darling little Ned especially. I know I shouldn't have a favorite, but that one captured my heart the day he was born.*

Emmie jotted a few more lines about the weather and seeing Helen at church. Then she tapped the end of the pen against her lips. How best to end this?

> *Please understand that I have no expectations of a response. I know it's your busy season on the farm. And*

*perhaps you deem it best not to respond at all. If that's
so, then let this letter serve as a final farewell, because I
wish you only the best.*

*Ever your friend,
Emmie Mason*

Russ jiggled the reins over Goblin's rump. The steady gray twitched an ear but didn't hurry along. It was hot. Steamy. Typical July weather. Mickey had stayed back at the farm. Even the kid didn't want to be out in this heat when he could be resting under a shade tree. It only made sense that Goblin preferred to poke along at a snail's pace. But that didn't get the errands done.

"Come on, boy. You got to do better than that." He gave the reins a slap on the gray hide. Nip barked on the seat next to Russ, and Goblin jerked his head before leaning into the harness and extending his trot.

Dust rose around the wagon. Sure could use a nice rain now that the hay was cut and forked into the barn. Emmie would have enjoyed... no, he couldn't let those thoughts get started. Not again. He'd spent too much time seeing the farm, the animals, even the kitchen as if through her eyes. He had to find a way to stop thinking about her.

The buildings of Jonesville came into view. He hadn't been to town to do any shopping since he'd stepped off the train two weeks ago, but the pantry needed refilling. The hay was cut, so he'd have a bit of a respite before the oats fully ripened.

"Too much time to think."

Nip nosed the back of his arm.

"I know. I got you and the kid. Ought to be enough."

But it wasn't.

The preacher's words when he'd driven Russ home wouldn't stop circling in his head. He seemed to think Russ should write to Emmie again. Seemed to think she'd come back if he asked. Seemed pretty darn sure of it. It was no secret that Aunt Maggie had done her best to throw Emmie and the pastor together, so why was the man doing his best to patch things up between Russ and Emmie? It made no sense.

And the folks at church... How many had stopped and asked him about Emmie the past two Sundays? He'd decided, again, that if he was going to be a good example to Mickey, he needed to be the kind of example his folks had been for him. And that included church. Strangely enough, people came up and spoke to him about more than just Emmie. It was so different from when he'd first come back home.

He rubbed his hand down the uncovered side of his face, remembering the unkind comments spoken either directly to him, or close enough for him to overhear. Church members who'd turned their backs on him. How many had it been? Five? Maybe six? The church held well over a hundred people on a Sunday. Had he condemned the lot of them by the actions of a handful?

He rolled into town and passed the post office. He hadn't written the letter. Not much sense in stopping there, unless maybe Cilla had written. Seemed he was about due for a letter from his big sister. For that matter, he was long overdue in sending her one. He ought to write her about going to Pittsburgh and the surgery and all. She'd never seen his scars, but she'd probably thought the worst. She'd appreciate knowing he was taking care of himself.

Four of the former street gang scrubbed on the planks of the boardwalk in front of the milliner's shop. The deputy sheriff was keeping an eye on them while leaning against the building. He tipped his hat to Russ as the wagon rolled past.

Russ rubbed at the tender new skin covered by a thin layer of bandage, just enough to keep the sun off. Seemed the sheriff was keeping those boys too busy to get into any more trouble.

Goblin stopped at the hitching rail in front of the mercantile and swung his head around to look at Russ.

"Yeah, I'm coming." He tied a length of rope to Nip's collar and secured her to the seat. She was too young to trust to stay with the wagon yet, and he didn't favor chasing around town to find her when he wanted to leave. He climbed down and tied Goblin before entering the store.

"Mr. Fields." Mrs. McCann walked toward him, little Alice on her hip. "It's good to see you again."

He dragged his hat off his head, tilting his chin out of pure habit. "Yes, ma'am. Good to be back."

"You're healing, I trust?"

"Yes, ma'am. Doctor says I can leave off the bandaging when I'm not out in the sun."

"I'm glad the surgery went well. Emmie had such hopes for it." She looked at the floor and then back at him. "I keep wishing she'll rethink her decision and come back."

He nodded. "Yes, ma'am." So did he.

"Well, I won't keep you." Alice waved her pudgy hand at him as they passed by.

A lump threatened to lodge in his throat. He coughed and fished his list from his pocket. After leaving it with the clerk, he headed for the post office.

Something akin to dread rippled through him. Which would be worse? Not checking at all? Or walking away empty-handed? The decision was made as he strode through the door.

Old Mrs. Russell was perched on her stool behind the counter.

"Hello, Mr. Fields. You're here for your mail, I suppose."

He gave her a half-grin at her usual greeting. "Yes, ma'am."

"I've missed you." Her head cocked in that bird-like way she had. "Tell me, how did the surgery go?"

"As well as could be expected, ma'am."

She leaned forward and clasped her hands on the counter. "Let me see."

Take off his bandages? He looked out at the street, then back at her. "Now?"

"Yes, of course." Expectation shone in her eyes.

He wanted to refuse, but he was going to have to remove the bandages at some point, and Mrs. Russell had never flinched at his scars. He swallowed and unwound the wrappings with fumbling fingers.

"Oh, my. Would you look at that?" She bobbed her head. "What a difference. The things they can do these days. You should leave the wrappings off."

"The doctor says not yet. Need to keep the sun off it so it doesn't dry out."

"Ah. Oh!" She swiveled on her stool and fished among the slots behind her. "I've a letter for you here. From Pittsburgh." She squinted at the writing. "I thought maybe the doctor, but it seems like the same handwriting—"

He snatched the envelope from her hand.

Emmie.

"I'll write to him later this week and ask after his recovery. Why don't you write a short note and I'll include it?" Helen asked, her blue eyes full of compassion.

Emmie looked out the window of the tiny front parlor. People, carriages, and wagons crawled along the street. Everyone busy. Everyone going someplace. Everyone but her. She hadn't told Helen about her letter to Russ. He should have received it two days ago, if he'd resumed his former schedule of going to town on Mondays.

She sighed and returned her attention to Helen. "No, I think not."

"Emmie, what can it hurt to reach out?"

Telling Helen she already had didn't appeal to her. After all, if he chose not to respond, only she would know she'd made a fool of herself.

Again.

"He left, Helen. I didn't push him away."

"I know." Her friend looked around the cramped parlor with the chatter of children drifting in around the closed door. "I just can't help but think that you don't belong here. You were so at home at the farm. Honestly, I would have said you'd never make coffee or sweep a floor, but you looked... happy... doing those things."

"I'm happy here, too." She wasn't. Not really. But she was a single woman dependent on her brother's generosity. This was her life for the foreseeable future unless—

Any possible letter was still a week away. And even hoping against hope, she didn't believe there'd be one.

CHAPTER 32

RUSS STEPPED OFF THE train, vaguely aware of the lingering ache in his leg. The city bustled around him with more vigor than he remembered from his first trip. A skinny boy with prominent ears poking from under a large cloth cap hollered above the commotion as he waved a newspaper at passersby.

"Big celebrations! Read where and when! Fireworks at sunset!"

Independence Day. He'd forgotten. That explained the extra hub-bub around him. The red, white, and blue bunting below the train station windows caught his eye. Something tugged at his chest. Pride? Why not? After all, he'd offered his services—his life—to see the country healed. He'd paid a heavy price, losing his brother, half his face, and even his mind at times, but the country was whole again.

He reached the edge of the street and waved at a cart driver waiting for passengers. The man touched his hat and moved his cart forward.

"Where to?"

That was a good question. Emmie's letter with her return address was in his pocket, but before he saw her, he should speak with her brother. He swallowed, took a firm hold on his satchel, and gave the driver Archie's address before climbing onto the cart's high seat.

Children ran down the sides of the street, dogs barked and gave chase, a lady shook her broom at a passing mongrel, a horse harnessed to the dray wagon in front of them reared, its driver peppering the air with profane language before gaining control of the beast. The stench of coal fires coated everything. No wonder Emmie had wanted to escape this place. A person couldn't hear himself think in such chaos.

All too soon, the cart stopped in front of Archie's house.

"Need me to wait, mister?"

"No. I don't think so." Unless Archie tossed him back out on his ear.

The driver named his price, and Russ handed over the coins. Then the cart pulled away, and there was nothing to do but approach the house. He pulled in a long breath, let it whoosh away, then marched to the door and banged the knocker.

The butler—what was his name?—opened the door. Recognition flickered in his otherwise stoic face. "Yes?"

"Is Mr. Mason in?"

"No, sir. He won't be back until this evening."

"Mrs. Mason?"

The butler raised an eyebrow and flicked a glance over Russ's attire. "I'll see if she is receiving anyone today. Please, come in."

The butler led him to the same parlor he'd been in on his last visit. Had it only been three and a half weeks? So much had happened—

"Mr. Fields." Caroline Mason sailed into the room, her cheeks flushed and eyes bright.

"Yes, ma'am."

"It's good to see you again. I trust things are going well?"

Her eyes lingered on the large leather patch he'd fashioned before leaving Jonesville. It covered his empty eye socket and part of his scarred cheek. He'd not been able to wear one before. The scar tissues had been too bulky and rigid. Previous attempts wearing a patch had been painful.

"Yes, ma'am. Seem to be."

Silence stretched between them for a moment.

"Would you care for some refreshment?"

"No, thank you. I..." How did he find the words so as not to sound like the idiot he was?

Her eyes twinkled in understanding. "You're looking for Emmie, of course."

He heaved a sigh and nodded. "Yes, ma'am."

"She's living with Richard and Fannie."

He shifted his feet. "Do you suppose it would be all right if I..."

A beautiful smile bowed her lips. "I do."

"I thought to speak with your husband first—"

"Leave him to me." She came to his side and took his arm, leading him back toward the door. "Richard's place is a bit of a walk, but easy to find." Before he could get out another word, she'd filled his ears with the directions and all but pushed him off the porch.

His feet seemed to have listened on their own because within half an hour, he stopped in front of the house that matched Caroline Mason's description. A narrow house three stories tall, it stood wedged between two other houses of similar build. The blue door—the only blue one in sight—sported a heavy brass knocker, the kind displayed to intimidate those pondering its use, no doubt. He cleared his throat and took hold of the massive metal guardian.

Before he could employ it, the door eased away from him, and a vaguely familiar cherubic urchin presented him with a wide, wet smile. A stream of babble followed that made no sense to Russ but clearly excited the little fellow.

"Neddy! Shut that door this instant, you little scamp." As Emmie's voice drew closer, the fine hairs on Russ's arms raised. Then she appeared in a doorway that fed into the narrow hall. Her black hair was neatly swept back into a practical bun. The gray gown did nothing to dim her loveliness. She might not be a beauty in the classical sense, but she was beautiful to him. More than beautiful. His breathing hitched, or maybe he'd forgotten to breathe at all.

She stopped, one hand against the wall while the other grabbed for her necklace. "Russ?"

He pulled the hat from his head. "Emmie."

The little boy at his feet squealed and ducked around Russ's legs, running toward the street as fast as his chubby legs would allow.

"Neddy!" Emmie yelled, but Russ was already on the move. He grasped the back of the boy's clothing and stopped his headlong rush.

"Whoa there, little fellow." He scooped the boy by the armpits and raised him to eye level. "We meet again, young Ned." The boy giggled and squirmed.

"What am I going to do with you, young man?" Emmie's stern voice wobbled a bit.

From fright over Ned's dash for freedom? From anger that Russ had just appeared on her doorstep? Or from something else? Dare he hope it was because she'd wanted to see him as much as he needed to see her?

She stepped forward and grabbed the wiggling toddler. "You'll cause me no end of gray hairs."

Was she talking to Ned... or to Russ? The boy threw his arms around Emmie, turning his head to peek at Russ. They were both looking at him. He'd thought about what to say first, thought about it almost non-stop since stepping onto the train. But he hadn't figured in a drooly toddler. Hadn't figured in how tight his throat would squeeze when he saw Emmie again.

"Won't you come inside?" She broke the silence before he'd found his tongue, so he nodded and followed.

"Richard is at work, and Fannie took the older children to buy peanuts and taffy for the fireworks tonight."

Russ was here. Here. In Richard's house. With her. Wearing an eye patch that made him look... dashing. Her heart stammered against her ribs. Perhaps she'd fallen asleep on the settee and was dreaming. Only she could smell the need to change Neddy's wrappings, and one didn't smell that sort of thing in a dream... did they?

"I'd forgotten it was Independence Day." His voice was strained.

"Yes. It is." So was hers.

She led him to the front parlor. "Please, have a seat. I need to change Ned, and then I'll be back. It won't take a moment."

He nodded, and she scurried away.

Oh, please Lord, don't let her hopes be raised for no reason. She couldn't stand that. Not now. Not when she'd just started to adjust to living here. She paused, the clean wrappings half secured around Neddy. Who was she fooling? She hadn't adjusted to anything but missing Russ. The same Russ who was two rooms down the hall. Her heart fluttered, stuttered, and flipped in her chest. She was too young to have a heart attack, wasn't she?

With Ned dry and better-smelling, she hurried back to the parlor, not taking a full breath until she entered the room.

Russ was still there.

His Emmie stood framed in the doorway with the toddler on her hip. The picture—straight out of his dreams—scrambled his brains. Russ turned the hat in his hands.

"You look beautiful." The words escaped before he'd realized it.

Pink splashed across her cheeks, but she didn't break eye contact with him. "So do you. Look handsome, I mean. And well."

He touched the patch. "I can cover the worst of it now, at least."

She took a step forward, and then another. Like a deer emerging from the cover of the forest. Wary. Uncertain.

"I received your letter."

"I wondered if you'd write in response."

He shrugged. "I couldn't find the words."

"And now?"

He blinked, opened his mouth, shut it again, then closed his eye and groaned.

That groan caused all sorts of havoc to Emmie. Her heart gave another kick—perhaps she truly did need a doctor—while the hairs on her arms prickled. Her mouth dried and her eyes moistened.

Russ opened his eye. The longing there matched hers. The need. Not a carnal need, at least not entirely. But a need of the soul.

James had never looked at her like that.

And then something warm and wonderful unfurled inside her, such as she'd never felt before.

She stood quietly, watching and waiting for Russ to find the words for what he'd come to say. She may have bullied her way into his house when he was injured and then bullied him into seeing Dr. Lawson, but this was something he needed to do on his own. She needed to hear the words.

In something other than her dreams.

"I went home and proved that I could live without you, but it's an empty life, not the one I want." Russ took a step closer to Emmie.

She lowered the toddler to the floor but stayed where she was, still half the room away from him. Too far. Much too far.

"And then your letter came."

She waited, neither smiling nor scowling. Not saying a word.

He should have written. He was much better with a pen than with his tongue.

"Emmie?"

"Yes, Russ?"

He closed the distance between them, careful not to step on the toddler, who had flopped onto his back to watch the adults, one thumb poked into his mouth. Russ tossed his hat onto a nearby chair and cupped Emmie's—his Emmie's—face between his palms. Her dark eyes glistened up at him, but it was the slight curve to her lips that was his undoing.

He leaned toward her, giving her time to pull away, hoping with every fiber of his being that she wouldn't. Her eyelids drifted shut. His heartbeat thudded against his eardrums.

His lips brushed hers once, twice, and a third time before he pulled her into a full embrace and covered her mouth with his. Her hands slid up his arms, burning a path until they fastened behind his neck. The groan that tore from him came from somewhere deeper this time. From somewhere inside of him where his Emmie lived—and always would, no matter what.

He loved her. He needed her. He wanted her.

With an effort, he raised his head. Her kiss-softened lips and heavy-lidded eyes beckoned him to continue, but there were words that needed to be said. Now. Before he lost them again.

"I love you, Emmie. I need you with me always. As my wife."

CHAPTER 33

S HE SHOULD HAVE RESPONDED immediately to Russ's declaration, but Emmie's tongue wasn't functioning. Her brain wasn't functioning. Her legs were barely keeping her upright.

Oh. They weren't. She was clinging to fistfuls of his shirt.

I love you, Emmie. I need you with me always. As my wife.

The front door opened, and Neddy squealed as he flopped over and pushed himself to his feet, toddling into the hallway and babbling at the top of his lungs.

It was a good thing nobody could understand him. After what he'd just witnessed...

Emmie pried her fingers from Russ's shirt and smoothed her hair back, standing straight and facing the door as four children streaked past, heading for the kitchen at the rear of the house. Fannie appeared in the doorway, Ned on her hip.

"Oh." She stopped, glancing between Emmie and Russ and back again. "I didn't realize you were expecting a guest, Emmie."

Emmie didn't look at Russ but sensed him stiffen beside her. "It was an unexpected pleasure. You remember Russ Fields, I'm sure."

"I do." Fanny set Ned down facing the kitchen and gave him a pat on the backside. "Go join the others. Sissy, keep an eye on Neddy for me."

"Yes, Momma," came the high-pitched answer from down the hall.

Fannie entered the parlor. "It's good to see you again, Mr. Fields."

"Thank you, ma'am. It's good to be here again." His voice was thick, husky, and threatened to turn Emmie's insides to mush.

Fannie shot another quick look between them. "I suppose you'll be wanting to speak with Archie?"

"Yes, ma'am."

Fannie's grin was so genuine and wide that Emmie let slip a sigh of relief. With Fannie this welcoming to Russ, surely Richard would be too. And he'd stood with Emmie once before with James.

"Then you're in luck. He passed us moments ago in a carriage. I expect he's almost home by now."

Emmie flicked a quick peek at Russ, his blue eye aimed straight at her soul.

"Then we best be going," he said.

"We'll meet you later this evening... if..." Emmie let her words run out, unsure what else to say.

"Go on, you two." Fannie shooed them toward the door as a crash sounded from the back of the house. "Run along while I see what the children have broken now."

She hadn't said she loved him. Hadn't said a word after he'd opened his heart. But that kiss... surely his Emmie wouldn't have kissed him like that if she wasn't in love with him. Would she?

No, of course not.

So why were her fingers cutting off his circulation at the elbow as they climbed the steps to the house? Archie. That was why. She'd defied him once, but could she—would she—again if it came down to that?

He'd do his best to make sure she didn't have to.

Emmie didn't knock. She pushed the door open and stepped in. Of course, she'd lived there almost her entire life, but it seemed odd to Russ. Perhaps because of who waited inside.

He'd been less nervous facing J.E.B. Stuart's boys from the Union's right flank at Gettysburg the day Pickett had led his charge. The day Billy Kline had died.

For a moment, he caught the scent of gunpowder in the air, heard the distant shouts of soldiers, the thunder of cannons—

"Russ?"

Emmie squeezed his fingers. When had she let go of his arm and taken his hand? He scanned the room. No soldiers. No smoke.

And no Archie.

"Are you all right?" Worry clouded her eyes. How he wanted to wipe it away, but he couldn't.

"I am now, but..."

"I know. I'm right here beside you."

Beside him. Where he wanted her to be. It felt so...right. Even after all he'd done to try to deny it. "I wish I could promise you that it won't happen again."

"Hush. I know."

"Do you?" He searched her face and found no hint of doubt or indecision. "I'd give anything to be whole now, for you, but as you already know, I'm broken. Inside and out, I'll never be completely whole again."

"You are whole, Russ."

He started to shake his head, but she laid her hand alongside his scarred cheek with its leather patch.

"You aren't the same as you used to be, I know that. But I didn't know you then. You're the only Russ I've ever known, and so to me, you are whole."

What an amazing woman. His throat tightened even as his chest expanded.

"And I want to be at your side. Always."

He drew in a quick breath. "Always?"

She nodded, a very becoming blush staining her cheeks as she dropped her hands to her waist.

Footsteps sounded on the stairs. Armed with Emmie's reassurances, Russ stepped forward as Archie descended. "Mr. Mason, I need to speak with you."

"I doubt there is anything we need to discuss." Archie's voice could have frozen the river despite it being July.

"There is. Something very important concerning someone we both love."

Aunt Maggie fussed with Emmie's veil while Penny muttered dire threats against anyone—including Aunt Maggie—who disturbed so much as a strand of the bride's perfectly coiffed hair. Emmie stared into the looking glass and did her best not to preen. But how could she not when these two ladies had turned her into such a vision on her special day?

Gone was plain and simple Emmie Mason. In her place stood a lady in a deep rose gown. The veil, which attached to the back of her hair, flowed in a cascade of creamy lace to her hips. Atop the veil sat a tiara of silver filigree that Aunt Maggie had loaned her. And at her throat hung the emerald necklace that had belonged to her mother, and her mother's mother before her.

She couldn't wait to see Russ's reaction when she entered the church.

Only one thing could have made the day more perfect. She sighed.

"We'll not be having that sort of a sigh on this day, Emmie Mason, soon to be Emmie Fields," said Aunt Maggie.

"I'm sorry. I just wish..." There was no sense hashing it over again. Archie hadn't disallowed the wedding—for which Emmie was grateful—but neither would he attend.

He and Russ had come to a prickly sort of understanding. In Archie's world of business and connections, she'd failed to climb the social ladder alongside him. His refusal to come to the wedding was no more than stiff-necked pride. Russ had adamantly denied accepting any form of a dowry. He'd refused to be seen as a man who married for financial gain. That was its own form of manly pride.

The two men had parted with a handshake, and Emmie had to be satisfied with that.

Richard and Fannie had planned to come, but Fannie was having some difficulties with her pregnancy, and the doctor had advised her against travel. Richard, understandably, didn't wish to leave her side. Emmie stroked the front of her gown, a gift from Richard and Fannie. Her brother's way of showing her that he was still on her side.

"If you was askin' me, I'd say your brother is just bein' mean and ornery." Penny's head bobbed as if to put a period on that sentence.

Penny was probably right, but a part of Emmie had held out hope that Archie would change his mind. She stifled another sigh as someone knocked on the door. Alannah opened it and slipped into the small room at the back of the church.

"We're ready," she said.

"Russ and Mickey are in place?" Emmie asked.

"And Robbie's at the piano, looking pale enough to pass out if you don't hurry along."

The boy had learned "Blest Be the Tie that Binds" in the month since Emmie had returned to Jonesville. For all his reluctance to learn, it turned out that Robbie was gifted in music. Emmie harbored a glimmer of hope that he might go on and study music at college. But that, of course, was still years down the road. For today, it was enough that he'd lend his talent for her wedding.

As if on cue, the piano's notes reached them.

Alannah took her hands, giving them a firm squeeze. "I've not seen a more beautiful bride."

"Thanks to Aunt Maggie and Penny."

"Never think it, dear," Aunt Maggie said. "It's love that makes a bride shine."

Emmie gave the old woman a quick hug. "Thank you for changing your mind about Russ."

"I told her the preacher wasn't the man for you," Penny said, her face screwed into a frown. "Took her a while to listen to me is all."

"I do want to see Pastor Anderson settled," said Aunt Maggie with a nod. "A married man is always much happier than an unmarried one."

Alannah took Emmie's arm. "Let's just worry about getting Russ married off at the moment, ladies." She led Emmie outside and around the church to the front where Mr. Keen stood with another man whose back was to them.

Mr. Keen took the pipe from his mouth and pointed at Emmie.

The man beside him turned around.

Emmie gasped, then lifted her skirts and ran into her brother's open arms.

"Can you forgive me, little sister?"

She pulled away from him and searched his face. He smiled at her. Not the confident type of smile Archie usually showed to the world, but a hesitant, even a humble one.

"Oh, yes. I can."

"Then you won't be needing me, I suppose." Mr. Keen held his arm out for Aunt Maggie, who giggled at him. Giggled! Aunt Maggie. Then he held his other arm for Penny, who grabbed it with a snort. Flanked by the two women, he made his way into the church.

"Robbie's gone through the whole song once," Alannah said. "Russ is probably sweating buckets at the front of the church by now."

Archie took Emmie's hand and laid it on his arm, giving it a final pat. "Then let's put the poor man out of his misery, shall we?"

"Yes." It was the only word Emmie could work loose from her throat. *Now* her wedding day would be perfect.

Russ couldn't quit staring at his bride. His Emmie. When she'd first appeared in the doorway on Archie's arm, Russ'd thought her an angel escaped from heaven above. And maybe she was, but now she was his angel.

His wife.

The church had emptied, the crowd waiting outside to cheer them after the legalities were finished.

Archie stuck out his hand. "Welcome to the family, Russ. I'm sorry it took me so long to say that. It does me no credit, as Richard and my wife have both pointed out... very effectively." But there was no resentment on the man's face, so Russ gripped the offered hand.

"I know I'm not the type of husband you imagined for Emmie, but I will take good care of her."

"I trust you will. I should have trusted Emmie's judgment on this from the start."

"Yes, brother, you should have." Emmie raised her chin and gave her brother a gracious nod that did nothing to hide the pleasure his words had brought her.

Russ couldn't have asked for anything more.

Pastor Anderson rubbed his hands together and smiled at the two of them. "All that's left is the paperwork." He waved Alannah and Archie toward the oak table set off to the side at the front of the church. "I'll need you witnesses to sign the official document. But first, let me write in the names of the happy couple." He picked up a quill pen and dipped it into an ancient ink well. "Russ, your full name?"

"Cyrus Alvin Fields," he said never taking his eye off Emmie.

The scratch of the pastor's pen sealed Russ's fate on the paper. A fate he welcomed until by death they were parted. And may that be a long time coming.

"Emmie, your full name? That is, your full *maiden* name." The pastor grinned at her.

"Emerald Sally Mason."

"Emerald?" Russ blinked. "Your name is Emerald?"

"It is." Her brown eyes sparkled as her hand closed around the pendant at her throat.

The emerald pendant she always wore.

"But that means your name is now..."

"Emerald Fields."

Could there be a better name for a farmer's wife?

He pulled her close. Ignoring the pastor and their witnesses, he lowered his head and claimed the lips of his gem of a bride.

Reviews are Golden

Reviews are the lifeblood of authors. Leaving a review on **Amazon**, **Goodreads**, and/or **BookBub** means that more readers will find our books! Reviews can be long or short - your honest opinion of the book. Shout-outs on any social media platforms also help!

ABOUT PEGG THOMAS

Pegg Thomas lives in Michigan's Upper Peninsula with Michael, her husband of *mumble* years. She creates American stories with real history and fictional characters inspired by her ancestors who immigrated here in the early 1600s.

Pegg won the 2019 FHL Readers' Choice Award for novellas, was a double-finalist for the 2019 ACFW Carol Award for novellas, and a finalist for the 2019 ACFW Editor of the Year. She was a finalist in the 2021 FHL Readers' Choice Award for novellas. Pegg won the 2022 Selah Award for historical romance and placed 2nd with her second entry. She was a finalist for the 2023 FHL Selah Award, placed 2nd in the 2024 Selah Award, and won the 2024 Will Rogers Silver AND Bronze Medallion Awards. Pegg spent 3 ½ years as the managing editor of Smitten Historical Romance.

PeggThomas.com
Facebook
Goodreads
BookBub
Amazon
Newsletter signup

www.ingramcontent.com/pod-product-compliance
Lightning Source LLC
Chambersburg PA
CBHW052031240626
47153CB00006B/2039